This book is dedicated to my late brother Bobby who believed in ghosts, and also in the magic of 'Abracadabra' to remotely open the boot of my car.

Evelyne Morris

SPURIOUS CONVERSATIONS WITH GHOSTS

AUSTIN MACAULEY PUBLISHERS™

LONDON • CAMBRIDGE • NEW YORK • SHARJAH

A CIP catalogue record for this title is available from the British Library.

ISBN 9781035803521 (Paperback)
ISBN 9781035803538 (ePub e-book)

www.austinmacauley.co.uk

First Published 2024
Austin Macauley Publishers Ltd®
1 Canada Square
Canary Wharf
London
E14 5AA

Table of Contents

January 2000, Eastbourne   7

February 2018, Hever Castle   21

March 2022, Brighton   55

April 2014, Beachy Head   67

May 2015, Leicester Cathedral   79

June 2020, Hastings Old Town   97

July 2022, M 40 Motorway, Oxfordshire   107

August 2018, Hever Castle   117

September 1996, Bodiam Castle   127

October 2016, Battle Abbey   138

November 2002, Caldwell Manor   146

December 2018, Ightham Mote   172

2084, Survival City No. 22, England   180

January 2000, Eastbourne

I woke up on the morning of my 50th birthday and I felt bemused. Something was odd. My bedroom was the same. My dog, Ella, sleeping on my toes at the foot of my bed, was the same. Yesterday's clothes, which I had left untidily piled up on the top of my blanket box, were the same. The few winter sunbeams struggling to get through the gap in my curtains were the same. The waves that I could hear splashing on the shore, on the beachfront outside were the same. But something was wrong. Something was different.

I couldn't puzzle it out. So, I closed my eyes again and thought about myself. This was a very special birthday for me. Half a century. For the fifty years that I had lived, I had never known the mother who had given birth to me. I had never known her, but somehow, I still missed her. She was an empty blank in my life. My father, whose name was Ronnie, had never talked about her. And there had never been any photographs of her in our home.

I asked myself the usual question – was it my fault? Why was I always sad on my birthday? New Year's Day. Every year. The same pain. The same feelings of unease and unhappiness. Did I really kill my mother? Was it my fault? Was this the reason that my father had not loved me like he loved my older brother, Vincent?

On my third and sixth birthdays, why did he take my brother, Vincent, who everyone called Vinny, all the way to New Orleans, America, to visit my mother's grave, and not take me? My father took him twice. And I was left at home with my stepmother, Elizabeth, who we all called Mummy Lizzy. My birthdays. Always sad. Always without nice presents and parties like my friends at school.

This is all the family history that I knew of: My father had met Elizabeth, who was an airhostess, on his journey back to England, after my mother had died in America. She was very sympathetic and caring, and she could see that a tragedy had happened. She was kind to him and to my little brother, who was only two and a half years old. Vinny couldn't stop crying, and asking 'where is my mummy?' Once back home in England, Elizabeth visited my father at his home in Acton and helped to find a nanny for Vinny. When that failed she, who was already in love with my father, moved in with him. Such a scandalous thing to do in 1950!

The following October she returned with him to New Orleans to collect me. She told me years later that I didn't stop crying for 'mummy Lisa' for six months. I remember that Vinny always called me a crybaby when we were both young. Mummy Lizzy and father were married in the local Registry office a few months later. I never knew the date.

I tried to recall everything my father had told me about my mother. So very little. He was American. She was English. She had been a pianist and singer in his Jazz Band. The Real Dixielanders. They had been quite famous in England for four years before I was born. I have three of the Real Dixielander's ten-inch LPs. So, I have her voice, eight of her songs altogether, and on the album sleeves, small pictures of her. That's all.

Fifty years ago the Real Dixielanders had been in America on a short tour for Christmas and New Year. I was born unexpectedly. Five weeks early. Two days before they were due to fly home to England. That penultimate performance was at a New Year's Eve party, and the venue was out in in the sticks. Fifty miles from New Orleans. No hospital, no doctors in the backwoods. Especially for blacks. Or their white wives. Not in 1949/1950. My mother, Jenny her name was, had been young and healthy. Only twenty-five years old. But by the time she had been taken the clinic in the city she had haemorrhaged to death.

They managed to save me. Only four and a half pounds in weight. Placed in an incubator for six weeks. Left with father's cousin, Alicia (who everyone called Lisa). Collected by father when I was ten months old. I don't know how or why I know, but I must have been told that Alicia had loved me and wanted to adopt me, but father took me back to England. That was all. Just the basic things that I had been told about my birth and early months of life.

My father continued with his band doing tours all around the UK until I was about twelve. My brother Vinny and I stayed home with our stepmother, Mummy Lizzy. Then the popularity of Trad Jazz, as it was called, faded away. It was the turn of the boy bands. First it was The Beatles. Then they were followed by the Rolling Stones and all the Mersey beat bands. All this fabulously new style of music, which pushed Traditional Jazz right off the popular music scene. However my father's band kept on playing in smaller and smaller venues until he died in 1983. He was sixty-three when he died of lung cancer. All those cigarettes he smoked.

I felt a quivering in the air, and I looked up. I rubbed my eyes. I was still in bed, so, had I gone back to sleep? Was I dreaming? What was happening? This was her! Surely, this was my mother standing at the foot of my bed? As far as I could see she was looking just like the slightly out of focus images of her on the LP sleeves. Ella growled. A light growl at the back of her throat. "Hello, Martha," she said. "Do you know who I am?"

"M…Mother?" I stuttered. "Is that you? Can it really be you?"

"Yes. It is really me," she said, with a broad smile lighting up her face. "Hello, baby," she said quietly. Almost a whisper.

"You…You're a ghost!" I stuttered.

"Yes. I am a ghost," she said, "and I think that it is time that you had some of the answers to all those questions you have stored up in the last fifty years."

I started to cry. Silently, with great blobs of tears rolling down my face. "My father hardly ever talked about you." I sobbed. "In fact, he hardly ever talked about himself, either. Especially about the early years that he spent in England, and how he met you. Why didn't you come to me sooner?"

"Well, my darling," she said softly. "Time is different in the spirit world. You call it Heaven. I couldn't just come back immediately. I would have been lost in America, and I wouldn't have been able to greet my own mother, your father, and yes, your step-mother, Lizzy, who loved you and cherished both you and your brother, when they all passed over."

"Yes, my mummy Lizzy," I said with a lump in my throat. I felt a bit guilty saying this to my new ghost mother, "I loved her, and I miss her now that she is gone. She was always there for us, wherever we were, whatever we did. Whenever we made father angry, she tried her best to protect us from his anger."

"Yes. Up in that half-way Heaven, I was always grateful that Lizzy was there to love and shelter you and your brother," said my mother. "Your father was an angry man sometimes. Life had not always been good or fair to him. But, I loved him, and until I died I was the happiest woman to be with the man I loved.

Let me tell you our story.

As you know, your Dad was American, a black American born on Independence Day, the fourth of July, 1920, in New Orleans. There was not much 'independence' at that time for black men, or 'niggers' as they were called.

It was a time of strict segregation in the USA, especially in the Southern States. Even if a black person did well and earned a living equal or better than the whites in those cities and states, they were envied, shunned, and treated by the white population not much better than they had treated the black people when their fathers and grandfathers were slaves.

New Orleans was a city of Black music – Jazz and Blues, and your father, Ethron, who was later called Ronnie…"

"Ethron!" I interjected. "I've never heard him called that! Ethron! What sort of name is that?" I was completely taken aback.

She laughed. She was so pretty when she laughed. "That's just the reaction I had when I first heard his name." She giggled again. "His parents didn't want their baby called by a white boy's name," explained the ghost of my mother, "so, they made up a name for him. His mother's name was Ethel and his father's name was Ronald, Ethel and Ronald Roberts, so you see it was a mixture of both their names."

"Ethron. Ethron." I tried it on my lips. "Strange!"

My beautiful ghost carried on. "Later, when he became well known, everyone ended up calling him Ronnie. As a child, he liked his unusual name because it made him stand out. He grew up listening to street music all the time. Always New Orleans Jazz and black-man's Blues. He started work as a shoe-shiner when he was just six-years-old, and with what he was able to keep for himself, after he had paid off his shoe-shine kit and put in his contribution to the family income, he bought himself a second-hand trumpet.

He was self-taught, copying his hero, New Orleans born Louis Armstrong. He would listen to Louis's records, and practice on his trumpet for hour after hour. As a growing boy, he played on the streets of New Orleans, especially his favourite Bourbon Street, busking they called it, and soon, he was picking up so much in nickels and dimes that he became the main breadwinner for his large family of three brothers and four sisters. His father had died when Ethron was only thirteen. Killed in a brawl with local, vigilante rednecks.

Did you ever know that you have a whole family of aunts, uncles and cousins in America?"

"No. Apart from father's cousin, Alicia, Lisa we called her, I suppose." I whispered. "I hardly ever think of myself as half American, and I did sometimes wonder about family there, but father never talked about his life before he came to England."

"Well," said my mother. "By the time he was a young man, he was well-known in the black community of the City of New Orleans as a brilliant trumpet player, but because he was black, he was never able to get a permanent booking at a hotel or a jazz club, or any well-paid work by the white bosses. Except, sometimes he got occasional work in the bands that entertained in the Bourbon Street bars, and on the paddle-steamer river boats that took tourists up and down the Mississippi between New Orleans and Natchez.

Being black, he couldn't get to play in a white orchestra or band, even though he played better than anyone else. When he did get small jobs in hotels or on a paddle-steamer, like all blacks he had to use a separate entrance, a separate bathroom at the back of the building, and a separate room for breaks and eating. Everything separate. Of course, he could never date a white girl. He couldn't even talk to a white girl, even if it was she who wanted to talk to him.

Once, he became recognised as the fabulous trumpet player that he was, he used his growing fame to become one of the earliest Civil Rights protesters in the Southern States. He became rebellious and often refused to obey the segregation laws. For example, if he got a job at a hotel, he would use the 'whites only' entrance, and the 'whites only' bathrooms. Of course, he was often in trouble with the law, and the red-neck white boys. Occasionally, he was beaten up by them. He often broke the local laws by being seen talking with a white girl."

"But, you are white. And you were married to him," I protested.

"Yes." She laughed. "But I met and married him here in England."

"So, how did that come about?" I asked.

"When the USA joined in the Second World War in December 1941, Ronnie was twenty-one years old, and when he was twenty-three, he volunteered to join the Army. He wanted to get away from all the racial prejudice and trouble he had made for himself in New Orleans. What he really wanted was to join a unit which had entertainers for US troops abroad, especially the separate black platoons, but no such unit existed at that time. However, early in 1944 just as he was about to be sent on a troop carrier to Europe, Captain Glenn Miller, have you heard of him, Martha?"

Immediately, I could hear 'Little Brown Jug' playing in my head. "Of course, I have. Father used to play his records all the time."

"Yes," continued my mother. "Well, Glenn Miller formed an Army, Airforce Marching Band. He was recruiting band members from all branches of the forces, and he had heard of Ronnie's skill with the trumpet. And although, Ronnie was black and had been in trouble with the law, he was invited to join the band. He was so happy. At last, he felt that he had got the recognition that he deserved. He was twenty-four when the Glenn Miller Marching Band was sent to England in the summer of 1944, and he and his band were a huge success. Then, it was planned that he and the band would play in France…"

"Yes." I burst in. "And Glenn Miller's plane went missing, thought to have crashed into the English Channel, when he flew to join his band in Paris in December, 1944…"

"Ah Ha! Yes! Despite the tragedy his band carried on without his leadership, and they were very successful. His style of writing music and improvisation of the work of other music writers, was so good and detailed that the players in the Airforce/Army band were able to follow the music exactly as if he had been there to conduct…"

I was impatient. I burst in again. "I know that my father stayed in England after the war in Europe ended in May, 1945. But, it's the story of you and him that is missing in my life. Can you tell me all about how you met and married? But maybe you can tell me about yourself first. I did know bits and pieces about my father's life, but he never talked to me about you. You have been the blank spot in my life that I have never been able to fill, to feel myself complete. I have missed you so!"

I started to cry again, and the ghost of my mother came nearer and sat near me on my bed. Ella jumped off and carried on with her light growling in the corner of the room. It was so strange. Here was the mother that I had always longed for. But I couldn't touch her or even hold her hand. She was so beautiful. A mass of gently curling blonde hair, a pretty face and a long, elegant neck. Her body was so slim that I couldn't imagine that she had had two babies. Yet, here was I. Her baby. Fifty, and all grown up as she could never be.

I remembered that she was only twenty-five when she had died giving birth to me. And thinking back to myself at twenty-five, I could see that I was so very like her in looks. Yes, we had different hair, hers being blonde and mine, black, and of course, my honey-coloured skin was a lot darker than her 'English rose' complexion, but in facial features, we were almost identical. I was stunned. I had never noticed this in the small, somewhat fuzzy pictures on the LP covers. My father had never said when I was growing up that I looked so much like my mother. Why? I know how much he had loved her, but he never wanted to talk about her. All my questions were ignored by him until I asked no more.

She sighed. "There's not a lot to tell about me," she said, so modestly. "I was born in Walthamstow, North London on the sixth of May, 1925. My name was Jennifer Walters. I was the only child of my parents, John and Winifred Walters, who owned a piano shop. Mainly they sold pianos, but they sold all sorts of other musical instruments too. I started playing the piano as soon as I could reach the keyboard, and I was trained as a classical pianist from an early age. I also loved the new jazz music that was becoming popular. But, my parents didn't like what they called 'that awful music'. I used to listen to jazz on the radio, and in my bedroom, I had my own wind-up record player and I used to buy the new records that were coming out from America. My favourites were Jelly Roll Morton and Scott Joplin.

When I was eighteen, in 1943, I got a job working as a receptionist at the BBC. I loved that job. I met all sorts of interesting people, especially from the world of music. And sometimes, in the evenings and at weekends I would play, and sing a little, in the Studio Jazz Club in Soho, in central London. My parents were horrified, but they didn't forbid me from doing it. After all, it was only an occasional thing."

"Good Heavens!" I exclaimed. "What a naughty girl you must have been! I'm not surprised that your parents were horrified. Soho was synonymous with sex and prostitutes, especially in the 1940s."

"I know," laughed my ghost mother. "I didn't go there often. And if the BBC had known about it, I would have been fired." She paused as if she were remembering the past, and a dreamy little smile crept across her face. "It was there at the BBC in May, 1945, just after the end of the war in Europe, that I first met Ethron. Yes, at first, I couldn't get his name around my tongue. He had come for a radio interview for a jazz programme, and when he announced his name at my reception desk, I'm ashamed to say that I lost all my professional cool, and I giggled! Then, fortunately, we laughed together, and he said, "Just call me Ronnie – everyone else does."

Anyway, after his interview, he returned to my desk and we started chatting. I told him that I was an amateur jazz player and singer, and that I would be performing at the Studio Jazz Club in Soho the following Saturday. "I'll come and see you," he said, as he was leaving. I didn't really think that he would, and I forgot all about it…"

"…and there he was!" I jumped in again.

"Yes. There he was. I was playing Scott Joplin's 'The Entertainer' when he walked in, bringing his trumpet with him." She laughed again. She had a lovely laugh and the sweetest of smiles. "What an evening we had! He was invited by the band to 'jam' with them, and all of us and the audience couldn't have enough. We played long after the usual closing time, and I think that I fell in love with him there and then. It was very late when I got home, and my father was furious with me. He wanted to forbid me from ever going back to the club.

I sort of half agreed. And it turned out that I didn't go back to the Studio Jazz Club because I had already made plans with Ronnie to go and see him and his Real Dixielanders who were due to play at the Savoy Hotel the following Saturday."

I was excited. I wanted to get on with the story. I jumped in, again. I wanted the romance. "So! There you were at the Savoy Hotel. He fell in love with you, and you joined his band…"

"Not so fast, my girl!" My mother laughed at my outbursts. "I did have a wonderful evening, and I did join in singing and playing a couple of numbers with the band. And I got home early enough not to anger my father again. Then, Ronnie and I met up again the next day for Sunday lunch at the Savoy. We talked, and talked, and talked. And one of the things he talked about was his application for a visa for permanent residence in this country. He asked if I could help him fill in the application form. And on reading it I realised that if he had an English wife his application would be accepted without any problems. But, for the moment, I said nothing.

Then, out of the blue he told me that he loved my jazz piano playing and singing, and that after consulting with his Dixielanders, he offered me a trial position in his band.

This was a huge surprise, and a big decision for me. If I accepted, it would mean giving up my fabulous job with the BBC, which I loved and had had for more than two years, to travel around the country with him and the Dixilanders. I have already told you that I was already in love with him. And I was sure that he was beginning to feel the same way about me.

I wanted to say 'yes' at once, but I knew that my parents would be against it. Especially staying away from home with a group of six men who I didn't really know. And who my parents hadn't met. I had told them about the jazz band, but I hadn't said anything about the players, especially that the front man was a black

American! Colour prejudice in the UK was nothing like the vile thing it was in the USA, but it was, nevertheless, still there."

"Well. I'm sure that I know the answer to his invitation since I am here!" I giggled. "And I know that your parents did not agree, since I have never seen them. They were never in our lives, even after you died and my brother and I were virtually orphaned." Emotion swept over me once more. How I had missed not only my mother, but all connection with her family too. Tears rolled down my cheeks. And mother gestured towards me as if she wanted to give me a hug. If only that could have happened.

"My parents certainly did not agree." My ghost mother took what looked like a deep breath. Although, I suppose that being a ghost, she actually took no intakes of breath at all. "They virtually threw me out. Well, it was my father mostly. He told me that if I joined the Real Dixielanders that I would lose my reputation entirely, and he and my mother would be so ashamed of me that they would no longer want me to live with them.

I went to bed in tears, and I tossed and turned all night, hardly sleeping a wink. At three o'clock in the morning, I made up my mind. Although, I hardly knew Ronnie, I knew that I loved him, and that my love was real. I decided to follow my heart. When I heard my mother moving around in the kitchen in the early morning, I quietly went down to talk to her.

She knew me so well. She knew that I wanted to go off with Ronnie and the band, and she took me in her arms and said, "My darling Jenny, I know what you want to do. Your father will never agree to it, but I just want you to be happy in your life." We sobbed in each other's arms. And as we parted, she whispered to me, "Just you make sure that he marries you!"

After I left home the next morning, I only ever saw my mother once again. She and my father were invited to our small wedding at St John's Chapel in Acton, west London, just a month after I left home. But they didn't come. The last time that I saw her was just after Vincent was born on June thirteenth, 1947. We were still living in Acton, and my mother, without my father's knowledge, crossed town to see me." Another pair of ghostly tears fell from her eyes. "But, I did so love your father, and I'm sure that I would have been able to bring my family around eventually. But, of course, that could never have happened." The tears dried up and she looked at me with a sad smile.

"I know," I said heavily, with my anguished guilt deeply crowding my whole being. "It was my fault that you died. I always knew that it was my fault."

"You must never think that," said my mother sharply. "It was not your fault. It was *not* your fault!"

She reached out to me, wanting to hold me. To reassure me and to try to stop the flow of tears that I didn't even know were falling down from my eyes. "I had an easy pregnancy and delivery with Vinny, and with you I had no problems at all with this, my second pregnancy," she said very quietly. "Everything was going on straightforwardly, and I was expecting you to be delivered sometime towards the end of February, 1950.

Your father and the Real Dixielanders had been invited to celebrate Christmas and New Year 1949-50 with a month-long tour of New Orleans and some of the surrounding small towns. We discussed between us whether, in view of my pregnancy, we should accept the offer. He was longing to go back to visit friends and family in New Orleans, and to proudly show off his English wife and his son. We consulted our doctor at home in London, who was also an American from the New York State, an ex-service friend of your father, and he declared me fit and well enough to travel.

We flew to New York, and took an overnight train to New Orleans, where Ronnie and I were forced to sleep in different compartments. That was my first experience of racial segregation in the USA. And, although, there were many a disapproving looks from a lot of white people, there was also a huge loving and welcoming reception for all of us from the New Orleans Jazz community.

It was a brilliantly successful and very happy time. I had never experienced a Christmas such as we had with his family. There were twenty-one people who sat down for that Christmas dinner. After years of food rationing at home, I was amazed at the amount of food of all sorts on that table. I had never eaten a turkey before! Delicious! It was the best Christmas that I had ever had in my life, full of food, fun and laughter. And overwhelming love.

My problems started when we reached Oakville, which was about fifty miles north of New Orleans. We were invited to celebrate New Year's Eve with a party, headed by the Mayor of Oakville, in the Town Hall. He was, very unusually for the 1950s, a large black mayor, beaming with confidence and goodwill. Our final grand show was due to take place on New Year's Day in the City Hall, in New Orleans, which, of course, was the following night.

When we arrived at Oakville the rednecks and 'nigger' haters, and all those who were in opposition to having a black man elected as their mayor, had already congregated outside the Town Hall. They were intimidating, but because it was the mayor's 'do', Ronnie thought that they would just continue to make their protests outside.

We had just set up and were into our first number, Chimes Blues, when a mob burst into the hall shouting insults and throwing at us whatever they had to hand, including the foldaway chairs. There was pandemonium in the hall and your father tried to get me away, and out of the back entrance. He succeeded in getting me out, but I slipped down the wooden stairs of the back porch. It was that that brought on my early labour. An ambulance was called, but it arrived too late. You were born in the ambulance, five weeks early. I was barely conscious enough to hold you for my first and only time. But I bled out, and they were unable to save me."

"Oh, Mum!" I cried. I couldn't say anything more.

"So, it was never your fault, my baby. Never your fault." My ghostly mum was crying too. "If anything, it was the fault of your father, and of mine too. He was so wanting to see his home town that he didn't consider enough the strength of hatred that there still existed firstly for *uppity niggers that done well for themselves,* and for those who dared to touch white women. Let alone have sex and children with them!"

I thought about how coldly my father had treated me as a growing child. I said, more to myself than to my ghost mother, "perhaps he did blame himself for your loss. On looking at me and being with me, he always reminded himself that he had made that fatal decision to return to America." I smiled at my ghost mother, as I felt the weight of a lifetime's sadness lift off my soul. "He wanted me enough to take me back from his cousin, although, he knew how much she loved me and wanted to adopt me. But, he couldn't quite force himself to show his love for me."

"There, you see!" Smiled my mother. "He did have love for you, but it was so difficult for him to show it. I know that in his last few months on this earth, when you were nursing him, he was as loving towards you as he ever was with me."

I was wholly alert once more. "Have you met up with him in the spirit world?"

"Oh, yes! We did have a wonderful reunion after he passed from your world to the spirit world." She shone with such a glow of love that I thought that she was about to disappear back to where she had come from.

I started trembling. "Is he with you now? Can I talk to him too?"

"No, my darling." She was shimmering, and getting fainter. "I met him only in the cross-over spirit world. And I will be going back to stay with him in the spirit world, which you call Heaven. I have returned to you only briefly in this ghostly form, and I hope that I have stayed this way just long enough to answer your questions and to reassure you of both my love and his. He always loved you. Always. Always…"

And she melted away in a soft glow of light. Her last word 'Always…' lingering in the air.

"Mother…" I called. But, she was gone.

What did I feel? I don't really know. There was loss, but there was also such a glow of comfort in my soul. I felt cleansed of all bitterness. I had such a feeling of joy and of being loved that I had never experienced in all of those fifty years of my life. I didn't know what to do immediately, so I did nothing. I relaxed in the remaining glow of her form, and the soft reassurance of the love I had, and would continue to have, from both my parents. Ella jumped back onto the bed. She snuggled up to me as I wrapped myself up in my covers and fell into a soft, healing sleep.

February 2018, Hever Castle

Tommy's face was chalky white when he came to his sister's side and whispered into her ear, "I've just seen a ghost, a real ghost!"

"Don't be silly," she said. "There are no such things as ghosts! You wuss!"

"Oh, yes there are," Tommy insisted. "I saw one upstairs on the top floor, and it scared me."

"What were you doing upstairs?" demanded his sister. "Mum said to stay in this room when she was looking at a book in that glass case."

Tommy and his sister Joanna both turned to look for their mother. She had moved away from the glass case with the highly decorated Book of Hours, and she was in the corner of the room talking with the guide.

"I got bored, and I just went upstairs and found this long, skinny room," said Tommy, who was now getting a bit of colour back in his cheeks. "And that's where I saw the ghost. It was a lady, and she was sitting on a chair in the sunshine."

"Now I know that you're making it up," said Joanna. "Just you look through that window. Look. The sky is grey and it's foggy out there. There's no sunshine at all."

Tommy was a bit sulky now. He pouted out his lower lip and mumbled, "Well, there was sunshine upstairs," he insisted.

An hour or so earlier thirteen year old Joanna and her twelve-year-old brother, Tommy, were sitting in the back seat of their mother's car, both looking very grumpy. "I don't want to go to see anymore Nashnal Trust houses," said Tommy. "They're boring! Ever since you got one of those visiting cards for your birthday last year, you keep on dragging us around to see all those horrible boring houses. I don't want to go!"

"Stop complaining," said their mother. "This is not just an ordinary National Trust house I'm taking you to see. In fact, it's not a National Trust house at all."

Tommy's face lifted a little. "What is it then? Where are we going?"

"I'm taking you to visit a castle. It's called Hever Castle. And it has a proper drawbridge, a portcullis and a moat which goes all around it."

That cheered the kids up a little. Tommy pictured in his mind the castles that were in his Great Castles X-box game. He, even, smiled at the thought that they were being taken to one of those castles for real, where there would be knights in shining armour, and dungeons and torture rooms at the bottom. He began to doze off a little bit and his imagination got going. Like in his game, there might even be a model of rack where prisoners were stretched using pulleys and ropes until their arms and legs were pulled out of their sockets. Perhaps, there were little slits for windows in the dungeons which could be just above the level of the moat, so that all the prisoners could see would be just a glimpse of water. And when there was rain, and a high wind whipped up the moat, the water would come in through those windows and…and…and… He woke up with a start when they arrived at the castle car park, and he looked around expecting to see a huge castle looming over them. Yet he could see nothing but a few trees. Mum bought the entry tickets and they walked through some grey, winter-time gardens until they reached the castle. Oh! What a disappointment. The castle was tiny, nothing like his X-box castle at all. It looked like every other National Trust house that they had visited before, except that it did have a moat and a sort of drawbridge.

Immediately Tommy was bored again. Boring! Boring! Boring! They all crossed the bridge into the castle courtyard and through a great oak door, then he followed his mother and his sister into a hall. Nothing grabbed his attention until he saw a tiny suit of armour which must have been made for a child. But it was roped off and he couldn't even touch it, or find out how the helmet and visor worked.

He dawdled behind his mother and sister, walking quietly from room to room in the castle until he had had enough, and then he went off on his own to explore. And now, when at last, he had found something exciting to tell his sister, she didn't believe him.

"Come on," he said. "If you don't believe me, you just come up to that weird room and find the ghost, too." He was getting braver now that he was downstairs again, and with his sister to back him up.

"Oh! All right," said Joanna, with a sigh. She was getting somewhat bored too, so anything that was a bit different might make the castle more interesting. "But I told you, I don't believe in ghosts."

Their mother was still talking to one of the castle guides, so the two of them slipped out of the room unnoticed and went upstairs. The entrance to the *long skinny* room where Tommy said he had seen the ghost, was roped off. For some reason, visitors were not allowed to go in there. Tommy ducked under the rope, and Joanna, who was about to say that they shouldn't go in there, just shrugged her shoulders, ducked under the rope too, and followed her brother.

It was, indeed, a long, *skinny* room, just as her brother had described. Along one side hung a line of pictures, all portraits of the six wives of King Henry VIII, with a larger portrait of the King himself in the centre, painted when he was old and fat, but dressed in magnificent robes. On the other side of the room were a few Madame Tussaud-like groups of people who might have lived in the castle a long time ago. There was only one glass case which had inside what looked like a long petticoat or a nightdress. It appeared to be made of very fine cotton, and it had very pretty, tiny pearl buttons all the way down the back of the bodice.

"Here we are," said Tommy. "See, it *is* sunny up here. And look, there's the lady ghost. She's sitting on that padded bench in the sunshine over there."

"It is peculiar," agreed Joanna, "the sun is shining outside, but I know that really it is cold and grey. Strange." She looked at the bench, "But I can't see anyone up here. There's certainly no ghost!"

"Yes, there is," insisted Tommy. He went up to the lady on the bench. "Look, Joanna," he said. "Look at this lady, and look at that picture on the wall. She's just the same! Same dress, same hat thing on her head, same necklace with a letter B on it." He wasn't so afraid now that he had his big sister by his side. He looked at his ghost. "You are a ghost, aren't you? Can you see me? I am Tommy and this is my sister, Joanna. And why can I see you, but she can't?"

The figure on the bench looked at Tommy. "Yes, I am now a ghost. My name is Anne Boleyn, and I used to be the Queen of England a long time ago," she said. "And you are right, that is a picture of me on the wall. I used to live here in this castle when I was a girl. And this room, which we called the long gallery, is where my brother and sister and I used to chase each other, and play games when we were children, especially when it was cold or wet outside. Your sister may not be able to see me, but perhaps she can hear my voice?"

The ghost turned to Joanna who had heard a lady's voice, and she was astonished. "How did you do that?" she asked Tommy, thinking that he had spoken in a different voice, to trick her. She still couldn't believe that there was a ghost talking to her. She sat down on the bench, almost sitting on Anne Boleyn's lap!

"Whoops!" said the Lady, who stood up, leaving room for the two young people to sit.

Joanna got out her mobile phone to find out more about Anne Boleyn. They had *done* King Henry VIII and his six wives in her history lessons at school, so she thought that she knew all about her, and the King's other wives, too. She had written an essay at school, and her teacher had said that it needed something extra to make it more real. So, if Anne Boleyn really was here talking to Tommy, then perhaps, she could ask her some questions too, and add something extra to her essay.

Tommy, feeling quite brave now, started with questions of his own. "What's that hat thing you are wearing on your hair?"

"Well," said the astonished ghost. "I can see that you are not embarrassed to ask me some quite personal questions. I suppose, that I was quite like you when I was a girl. I was always asking questions. And this thing, as you call it, on my head is my hood. It's not like the hoods you wear today. I see that you are wearing a hoody jumper. Everything we all wear is the fashion of the day.

Well, my hood is made of stiff silk with pearls on it to make it look pretty, and suitable for a Queen to wear. It was the fashion of my time that every adult woman wore some sort of covering for her hair. Only girls and young unmarried women had their hair uncovered."

Then, the phantom of Anne Boleyn, looking so real, so life-like, standing next to Tommy on the bench, took off her hood and shook her hair to free of all restraints.

"Cool!" said Tommy. "Did you see that, Joanna, she just took her hat thing off? Can you still hear the lady talking?" He reached out to touch the ghost, but his hand, it went right through her arm. "Cool!" he repeated. "You really are a ghost, aren't you? Can you see me? Can you hear me?"

She smiled at him and nodded. And this time, Joanna jumped in. "It says here on my phone that you were born in 1501, so, if you were alive now you would be over 520-years-old!"

"Hello, Joanna," said the Lady, with a smile which lit up her face, a smile that only Tommy could see. "Yes, I, really, am the ghost of Anne Boleyn, and I have a story to which you might want to listen."

Tommy and Joanna were struck dumb! And hoping that she would tell of all the juicy bits of her life with fat old King Henry VIII, they nodded and waited for her to start.

"Well, children, the thing is!" Joanna resented being addressed as a child, but she said nothing, and waited for Anne Boleyn to start talking. "Should I start at the beginning?" asked the ghost. "No. Perhaps I should start with my ending." She paused, then, to make her decision.

Joanna knew that she had been beheaded, "she had her head chopped off," she whispered to Tommy. He shivered, and they were both hoping to hear the gory details. And Joanna, who couldn't see the ghost, and still didn't quite believe that there was a ghost there, had to strain her ears to hear her. They held their breath, as the ghost continued, more to herself than to the expectant children.

"I really believed that he would stop my beheading. That's why in my last spoken words, I described Henry as a most gentle Prince. This was when I was on the scaffold awaiting a slash of a French swordsman's blade. A gentle Prince! A merciful Prince! Ha! In reality he was a murderer, a vile, raging murderer."

She stopped short and, although he didn't understand, Tommy could see that the ghost was struggling with her emotions. "Do you know, Joanna and Tommy, that during his reign, he was responsible for over 50,000 – possibly 60,000 deaths? And as he grew older, he became a madman with all his killings."

Tommy's eyes opened wide with a shivery thrill. "That's quite cool. Did he kill all those people himself?" he asked, with a trembling voice.

"No! Of course not. He always had executioners to do the dirty deeds for him." said Anne, the ghost. "I'll tell you both about some of his killings in a moment." She paused to take a deep breath. "Anyway, in saying what a gentle and loving Prince he was, I was hoping that he would be in the crowd that had come to watch me being beheaded, disguised as an old woman or a beggar or something. He could have stopped it happening at any time, right up to the swishing of the sword. Did you know that was the sort of thing he liked to do because he thought that it was funny? He liked to dress in disguise and suddenly take off a mask to reveal himself saying, *I am the King! Kneel and obey me!*

It was never really funny, because most of the people around weren't fooled by his disguises. Anyway, I was hoping that he would stop my execution. But, it was hope without hope. He wasn't there. And now I am dead. And, as you said Joanna, I've been dead for nearly five hundred years!"

It was Joanna who spoke up this time. Now, she had accepted that although she couldn't see the dead Queen, she did believe that she was talking to a ghost. She shivered. Was it with cold or excitement? She didn't know. "So, after all this time do you remember the day that you died? And, by the way, what do we call you? Your Majesty?"

"Just plain Anne will do." Now, it was her turn to shiver. "You mean the day I was murdered? Of course, I do. I remember every moment."

"OK, then!" said Tommy, who was beginning to feel a little bit left out. "So, what happened. Was there lots of blood?"

Joanna was shocked. "Tommy," she said. "We are talking about this lady's blood. Don't be so rude!"

Anne increased her shivering, but she said, "Don't worry Joanna. It was a long time ago, and I have got over it. But yes, I was shaking in fear, but I tried to look brave." She paused for a moment. And started again with her story.

"It was early morning and, although it was in the middle of May, it was very cold, and I was wearing a simple shift, just like that one in the glass case over there, under my fur-lined cloak. I had to walk from my state rooms in the Tower to the scaffold where I was to be killed. Please note that I say, *be killed* rather than *die*. I was being killed, dying against my will. I call it murder because I knew that I was innocent of all the charges made against me. I did not betray the King by having sex with my friends, or the horrible charge that I had sex with my own brother."

"Gross," said Tommy looking at his sister. "Did she really do that?"

Anne continued talking. "I had to force myself to walk and to look brave and strong while doing so. I don't know how I managed to climb those stairs without screaming or my legs buckling beneath me.

Once, my maids had removed my cloak I was shivering with both fear and cold. It took a great deal of effort for me to talk without showing my fear and to talk loud enough for the crowd to hear. *Good Christian people*, I said, almost in a whisper. Then, I gathered my courage and strength and continued in a more powerful voice, that at least some people in the crowd could hear. I just went on to say that I was found guilty incest and adultery by the law, and I accepted that I would die. Hoping that the King would save me, I lied and said what a gentle and loving King he was. Then, they killed me."

Tommy was transfixed, but he wanted more detail. All the gory details. "How did they kill you?" he asked.

"Henry got, as a favour for me, Ha! A very skilled swordsman from France who could cut my head off with one swish of his sharp sword. He would do the job quickly and with as little pain for me as possible," said Anne.

"But, how did he do it?" insisted Tommy.

"Well," said Anne. "I didn't have to lie down and put my neck on a chopping block like they did when they killed people by chopping off their heads with an axe."

Tommy shivered with expectation, and Anne carried on. "They got me to kneel on the scaffold, and they tied a scarf around my eyes so that I could not see. I knew that the swordsman was standing next to me, and I gave him a gold coin."

"A gold coin! Why ever did you do that?" asked Joanna.

"It was the usual thing that the one to be executed paid the executioner. It was done to encourage him to do a good job with as little pain as possible to the one being killed.

I was very afraid. I don't know how I managed to stay kneeling, and not jump up and try to run away. Of course, if I had done that I would not have got far, and they would have killed me more roughly and with a lot more pain.

Anyway, how it happened was that someone on the other side of me made a loud noise and, because I couldn't see anything around me, I was startled for a moment, and in that very moment the swordsman lifted his mighty sword and sliced my head off. Swish! And I was dead."

"Wow!" said Joanna and "Cool" said Tommy, both at the same time.

"Did it hurt? And was there a lot of blood?" asked Tommy, for whom there had not been enough gore.

Anne got a bit fractious. "Of course, it hurt. But it was over in a second. I was dead and beyond pain."

"Did you become a ghost immediately? Did you see all your blood flowing all around and splashing everyone?" Asked Tommy. He was really getting into the story now.

"I'm not sure how soon I became a ghost," said Anne. "But I was able to see from above the scramble to clear up after me! There was blood dripping everywhere, onto everyone and everything.

My ladies-in-waiting were very insistent that they should be the ones to deal with my dead body, and not some rough-handed guard. Would you believe it, the Constable of the Tower of London didn't even have a coffin waiting for my body? After all, I was, or had been, the Queen of England! Where was the respect that was due to me?" She paused for a moment, remembering the honour and dignity she had been used to as Queen. "My ladies picked me up gently and looked around for a coffin. But, the only thing they could put my dripping body, and my dripping head into, was a chest which had held arrows, that the Constable had taken from the armoury."

Joanna was stunned for a moment, but Tommy wanted to hear more about beheadings and such. "If you were killed by a swordsman because it was quicker and kinder, and you were the Queen of England, then how were others killed?"

"Do you really want to know?" asked Anne. "England was not a very nice place to live in in the 1500s, especially if you had done something bad."

"I do want to know," said Tommy. "And my sister is already looking for the answer on her mobile!"

"All right," said Anne. "But, I warn you that it will not be nice to hear." She paused. "Commoners, that is ordinary people who were not special in any way, if they were found guilty of a crime, were mostly sentenced to death. The crime could be something very simple like a poor man stealing a loaf of bread to feed his children, or killing a rabbit in the King's private hunting grounds. They were usually hanged on a gibbet with a noose around their necks, or even hanged alive in chains and left to starve to death. With birds pecking out their eyes before they were dead. Some were tied to a stake at the centre of a special bonfire that was set fire and the victim was burned alive, while most of their friends and neighbours stood around to watch them die. Then, there was hanging, drawing and quartering, which was done to men who were traitors… "

While, Tommy shivered with the thrill of such gruesome things happening, Joanna cried out "Stop it! It's horrible. I don't want to hear any more." She jumped up from the bench and ran towards the doorway. As she started to go back downstairs, she turned around to say something to the ghost, when she could hardly believe her eyes – she could see Anne Boleyn. Not clearly, but the Lady was definitely emerging out of a ghostly shimmer.

"Cool!" she exclaimed. "I can't believe it! I can see you! You are Anne Boleyn!" And then she returned to her seat.

"Wicked!" said her brother. "Now you can see that I wasn't telling lies. Ghosts do exist." He turned to Anne's ghost again and asked, "Are there any more ghosts here?" And pointing to the other portraits on the wall, he asked,

"What about all those other ladies? Did any of those ladies become ghosts when they died?"

"Oh! No!" She replied. "All of Henry's other wives are safely in heaven. Just imagine what it would have been like if we had been able to talk to each other over the last five hundred years! We all hated each other. Especially me. I, especially, hated the Spanish Katherine and Jane Seymour! What catfights there would have been! If I could, I would tear their pictures off the wall and destroy them. After all this is my house. They don't belong here." And she laughed so loudly that Joanna was sure the sound echoed all along the long gallery.

Joanna knew who she was talking about. At school, they had taken almost a whole term to learn about Henry VIII and his six wives. And she had just been checking it out on her phone.

"Why did you hate them so much?" she asked.

"It was Spanish Katherine who I hated the most." There was still some hatred in her reply, still after five hundred years.

"Why?" Joanna asked simply.

"Because she just would not let go." She almost spat at the two children. "She would not stop resisting the inevitable. If she had agreed to divorce Henry, he would have given her so much in gold, lands and property, that she could have lived the rest of her life in warmth and comfort. That's what he did for his fourth wife, Anne of Cleeves. If Spanish Katherine had agreed to divorce, Henry and I would have married years sooner." She sighed. "Perhaps, we would not have had such an argumentative marriage. And with both of us being much younger, and less stressed, I might have given the King the son he so longed for."

"Why, do you think," asked Joanna, "that Queen Katherine would not agree to a divorce if, as you say, she would have been able to live in comfort for the rest of her life?"

"She had been married to Henry for twenty years, and she still loved him," said Anne, wistfully. "But, the most important thing for her was their daughter, Mary. She insisted that Mary was his heir and would be Queen of England in her own right after Henry died. If, however, she was divorced, Mary would be declared illegitimate and would lose her claim to the throne. Especially if Henry remarried and had a son."

"And Jane?" Again, a simple question from Joanna.

"Well, that's obvious." She almost laughed. "She stole my Henry away from me."

"How?" Joanna was being very gentle with her questions.

"I don't really know how. She was just the milk-sop that I called her. She had no guts. No looks. No personality. No vibrancy." Anne almost preened herself. "She was just a *yes, sir no, sir* creature."

Joanna dared to almost criticise her. "Perhaps," she ventured, "perhaps after all the arguments with you, and no boy child to justify his marriage to you, and all the upset with his break from Rome, he just wanted peace and quiet in his domestic life."

"Ha!" Anne snorted. Then she turned to Tommy, who was getting a little fed up that his sister was taking over *his* ghost. "There is one other ghost here at Hever. You would know nothing about that."

"That's wicked! Will we be able to see and talk to her, too?" he asked.

"It's not a *her,* it's a *him.*" And now, it was Anne who was getting quite animated. She walked up and down for a bit, looked out of the window, and then back to the bench where an expectant Tommy and Joanna were still sitting. Was she going to call him? Tommy hoped so.

Joanna was a bit disappointed. She had been hoping that Anne was talking about her older sister, Mary. That she was a ghost, too.

"Who is it?" Tommy asked. "Is he famous too?"

"No," she replied, "he is a small boy of about nine years who my sister Mary rescued while I was still at the French court."

Now, that was exciting! The new ghost was younger than Tommy, and it would be easier to talk to a boy than it was to a Queen. "Is he here now?" Tommy asked. "Can we talk to him as well?"

"No. He won't show himself. He is very shy, and he is not able to talk much. I'll tell you briefly about him and then you will understand just what a monster Henry was." Anne sighed, and continued. "The boy is called Jules Woollerton, and he was the son of James Woollerton who was a wealthy wool merchant who lived nearby in the village of Edenbridge. He, and sometimes his wife, Alice, went often overseas to the Low Countries where they met up with other merchants who bought their wool. And there, in religious meetings, they also encountered people who wanted to be able to read the Holy Bible in their own languages.

"The Holy Bible everywhere, in all the countries of Europe, was written in Latin, which only educated people and churchmen understood. A hundred years before Henry, an Englishman called John Wycliff had written a translation of the

Latin Bible into English, so that everyone, from King to commoner, could read or listen to the Holy Book being read in church. And now, new translations were being written. But, any translation from Latin was proclaimed as heresy by the Pope, who insisted that only prayers and Bible readings in Latin were acceptable to God.

"My Henry, at that time, was a true Catholic, and he followed the Pope's ruling making the possession of a copy of Wycliff's Holy Bible forbidden to everyone in England. An offence punishable by death. He, even, wrote a book against the new Protestants in Europe, and because of this he was awarded the title *Defender of the Faith* by the Pope. And, it is a title that has been used by the Kings and Queens of England ever since, even though most of them were not Catholic."

Most of these comments had gone over Tommy's head, but Joanna was following everything that Anne said. She asked, "Did James Woollerton bring one of those forbidden Bibles back to England?"

"Yes," Anne replied. "Yes, he did. And both he and his wife encouraged their household of servants to join in when they held their prayers at night, and read passages of scripture from their Holy Bible, in English."

Tommy didn't quite understand what Anne was telling them, but Joanna anticipated disaster coming to the Woollerton family. "Did someone in their household tell on them?" she asked, quietly.

"Yes, you have guessed it," said Anne in a low voice. "James and Alice were arrested, tried and found guilty of heresy. And, they were burned alive at the stake in the centre of Edenbridge. The remainder of their household were all branded with an H on their right cheeks."

"What!" cried Tommy, who suddenly took notice of what was being said. "Did they put these people on a bonfire in the middle of the town? Was everyone watching? That's gross!"

"They were made to watch," said Anne. "They were being shown what would happen to them if they, too, had copies of the English Bible in their own homes."

"How long did it take those people die?" asked a shocked Tommy.

"It was an awful death for them. They set fire to the bonfire under their feet, and all the while their legs and bodies were burning, they were still alive," said Anne, with a shudder. "It wasn't until the flames reached their hair and head that they finally died. And sometimes, the people in charge made sure that the fire burned slowly so that it took a long time for the condemned people to die."

Joanna and Tommy were stunned at the thought of burning to death. Tommy said, in a whisper, "I remember how awful the pain was when a cup of scalding hot tea was spilled over my foot. Mum tripped over the cat as she was handing the cup to me. Mum had to take me to a hospital to have it treated, and it was wrapped in a special bandage for burns. I couldn't walk properly for weeks." He paused for a moment, while he was remembering the pain of his burnt foot. Then, he went on to ask, "What is branding? You said that everyone else in the house was branded with an H on their cheeks?"

"They put an iron bar with an H on the end of it into a burning coal fire, and when it was red hot they put the end with the H on it onto the right cheek of the people, and it burned deeply into their cheeks," said Anne.

"No, shit!" exclaimed Joanna. "Why did they do that?"

"Well," sighed Anne. "Firstly, it was a very painful punishment, and secondly, it was a warning to everyone that saw the H scar on their cheeks that heresy was a crime, and the punishment for heresy was death at worst, and even innocent people who were close to the criminals would be branded."

"What happened to the boy?" Joanna hardly dared to ask.

"Yes, the boy. Jules." If a ghost can cry, then that's what Anne did. Joanna had, by then, accepted that she was seeing, and talking to a ghost, and it seemed to her that two fat ghostly tears ran down her beautiful face.

After a couple of moments to collect herself, Anne continued. "The boy was sent for trial after his parents were killed and it was found that Jules Woollerton was also infected with heresy."

"What *is* heresy?" Asked Joanna.

"In those days, if someone believed in a different way of worshiping God to the way that the Pope and the King did, it was called heresy, and if they were caught, they were killed. But, because of Jules's age, they could not burn him or brand him, so instead, they took a knife and cut off half of his tongue."

"That's disgusting!" cried Joanna. "Why did they do that?

And Tommy asked, "How did they make him stick out his tongue, so that they could cut it?"

"I suppose that they must have threatened to kill him," said Joanna. "So, the poor little dude was made to suffer the cutting of his tongue, so that he couldn't talk and spread heresy."

"Yes, you are right," said Anne. "He couldn't talk properly, only mumble, making horrible noises, and because he didn't have a tongue that worked, he couldn't eat properly either." She still had tears floating in her beautiful eyes, making them quite luminous. But she controlled the tears and continued in a somewhat choked voice. "And worse still, the people of Edenbridge including his neighbours and the so-called friends of his parents, afraid that they might also be accused of heresy, thought to protect themselves by forcing him out of his home and village. My sister Mary found him starving and begging at the drawbridge here at Hever.

She took him in and helped the servants to nurse him. But, because he couldn't eat properly, he soon died. Even, the loving kindness she gave him could not save him from dying." She paused for a while, and the two children were lost for words and said nothing. Then she spat out, "So, you see just how horrible Henry's England was!"

Anne had been watching Joanna looking for information on her phone, and it was her turn to ask questions. "I have seen modern people with those things in their hands, and I know that you can find out all sort of things on them, so can you tell me what do most people say today in your modern times, when they are asked what they know about Anne Boleyn?"

Joanna answered that question, immediately. "I think that they would say that she was one of the wives of Henry VIII; that she was the cause of the religious split between the King and the Pope; the Catholics and the Protestants, and that she had her head chopped off. I also think that many people believe that King Henry VIII killed most of his wives, although, he only killed two. It's not a great deal to be remembered for, but probably much more than any other wife of a King. So," Joanna asked, "what do *you* think that your Henry is mostly remembered for?"

Anne laughed, Joanna could see how attractive she looked with her big brown eyes and her beautiful hair. She remembered pictures she had seen of King Henry VIII at school. This ghost of Anne Boleyn was such a contrast to King Henry's very English pale, freckled skin and flaming red hair. How forward and fascinating she must have been to the King with her flashing dark eyes, and her long dark hair. "Like you," she said, "I think that he is remembered mostly for having six wives, and for setting up the Church of England. But, there was much more to him than that.

"People remember him as being old and fat, just like that portrait of him over there. But, when he was a young King, and he was only eighteen when he became King, he preferred playing sports, jousting, hunting, archery and wrestling, to the management of the affairs of state."

Tommy pricked up his ears again. This was an interesting bit. "Did he do that fighting on horseback, holding a long pole, and wearing shining armour? And with two men from opposite sides charging at each other?" he asked. "That's real cool!"

"Oh! Yes!" said Anne. "That is just what I was saying. That sort of fighting is called jousting. And Henry loved it. It wasn't the sort of fight you have against an enemy. The pole is called a lance, and if you could split your opponent's lance, or you knocked your opponent off his horse, then you were the winner. It was play fighting with your friends, to see who was the most skilled."

"Did those dudes hurt each other?" asked Tommy.

"As I just said, when one man managed to knock the other off his horse, he became the winner, the champion. But, sometimes, they really did hurt each other. Often, the defeated one had nothing but big bruises, but if a split lance shattered, it could send pieces of wood, flying like small arrows, which could pierce armour, or even get through the slits of a helmet and blind the jouster. The challengers could be seriously hurt, especially if the horse also fell. Sometimes, a competitor would be trapped under his horse, which would also be wearing heavy armour…"

"Would that kill him?" Tommy couldn't wait to hear what happened next.

And Joanna was also impatient to hear what happened to the horses. "Were any of the horses killed in those pretend battles? I love horses. It was cruel to them, wasn't it?"

"Sometimes, they did die," said Anne. "But, the horses of those days were much bigger and stronger than horses are today, and they often survived with very little harm done to them, even when their rider might have died."

"O.M.G!" exclaimed Joanna. "So, the King of England risked death when he was playing games with his friends. Who allowed that?"

"That's it. He was the King," said Anne, "And no-one dared speak out to try and stop him doing anything that he wanted to do.

"He was also very rich, thanks to his mean father, King Henry VII, who, with his officials had screwed out from his poor, long suffering subjects, every single penny that they could. Henry VIII, my Henry, was happy to spend all that money, mostly on himself and on his close friends.

When he was a young man, all my Henry wanted to do was to have fun, leaving the day-to-day running of the country to the powerful men he always had about him. He used these very clever men to produce what he wanted and then, sometimes, if he had no further use for them, he would listen to malign tale telling by their enemies, have them charged with treason and execute them!

They were all reliable men like my uncle, the Duke of Norfolk, a horrible man, but a very skilful soldier, who always agreed with the King, so he kept his head on his shoulders. Another was Sir Thomas More, the Chancellor who looked after the money. Although, he had been Henry's best friend since they were both boys, he was eventually killed because he was a Catholic who did not agree with the King's divorce.

Then there was Cardinal Wolsey. He was very lowly born, the son of a butcher, but came to power because he was an extremely skilled and diplomatic churchman. He amassed a fortune, and he became the envy of Henry's courtiers who eventually had him charged with treason, but he died before they could kill him. Another was Thomas Cromwell, who was also lowly born, being the son of a blacksmith. He became a very clever and devious lawyer, but he was executed when he made the mistake of recommending a new German queen, Anne of Cleeves, for Henry after Jane died."

Tommy always wanted more details of what was done to people when they were executed. "How were they executed?" he asked. "Was it always bloody? Did they all have their heads chopped off?"

"You really are a gruesome little boy, aren't you?" said Anne with a grim smile on her face. "OK. Tommy. You seem to be most interested in the worst things that happened in the 1500s. So here goes, and Joanna you can put your hands over your ears, if you like!"

Joanna did just that, but after a moment or two she couldn't resist hearing the real details of what was done to people in those days. Her school history lessons had always stopped at saying that some people were executed.

Anne continued. "Some men had the worst form of execution by being hanged, drawn and quartered. (Or drawn, hanged and quartered, as it should be called.) These unfortunate men were drawn through the crowds to their place of execution on a low hurdle, which was similar to a wooden rack without wheels. Their bodies would scrape along the ground, and if they were unpopular, they were often pelted with rotten vegetables or even stones by the crowd baying for their blood.

They were then taken to the waiting gibbet on a high platform, and hanged by a noose until they were not quite dead, cut down and then their bodies were cut open and their guts pulled out, and sometimes burned, in front of their living eyes. Then, their arms and legs were cut off or pulled off one by one until, finally, their hearts were cut out of their still-living body. The executioners took their time to do this work, keeping the poor suffering man alive and in agony as long as they possibly could."

"Gross!" Even Tommy found this hard to listen to. But Anne had not, yet, finished.

"But, the aristocrats and gentry, like my brother and his friends, were mostly beheaded. And some, who had information which they withheld from their questioners, were tortured, too. These unfortunate ones had all sorts of excruciating tortures done to them including; being burned with hot pokers, bones crushed, or put on the rack and their limbs were stretched until their arms and legs came out of their sockets. Those who did not die under torture often had to go to their execution carried in a chair.

Their beheadings were just like mine, except it was done with an axe, and not a sword. This was carried out in the grounds of the Tower of London, or on Tower Hill. Having paid the executioner with a gold coin, they forced themselves to kneel or lie down with their necks on a chopping block. If they were lucky, the axeman was skilled and chopped their heads off in one blow. But, sometimes, they missed the target and chopped two or three times until the head was off."

"O.M.G!" exclaimed Joanna again, "that must have been awful!"

"Yes, "said Anne. "And worst beheading that I know of was that of my Henry's cousin. She was the Countess of Salisbury. She lived at court with the King and his first wife, the Spanish Katherine, and she had been the Godmother and governess to their daughter, Mary, when she was young. But, she was a strong Catholic and believed that only the Pope could grant a divorce between married couples. And as a strong-minded Catholic, she would not agree that a divorce between Queen Katherine and my Henry could be legal.

Henry and I had been together for seven years before we could marry. I was expecting a baby, and he urgently needed that divorce so that he could marry me before the baby showed. In the end, he made himself head of the Church, and he got his new bishops and lawyers to give him the divorce from Kathrine that he had wanted for years.

Henry was getting impatient with obstinate Catholics, and the Countess of Salisbury was sent to the Tower and locked up to silence her. Eventually, many years after I was dead, Henry split with the Catholic church, and formed the Church of England, and because the Countess still said that the Pope was right and Henry could not make himself the head of the Church, Henry ordered her execution. It was done in private at the Tower, and there were no crowds to cheer or even to try to stop what was going on.

By then, she was an old lady of sixty-seven, which was very old in those days when most people didn't live beyond their fifties. Well, she didn't agree that she deserved to die, and she resisted all the way to the scaffold. Then, she refused to put her head on the block, so she was held down by two strong men. But, she still twisted and turned so much that the executioner could not get a clear aim at her neck. And this is the worst part, the executioner took eleven, yes eleven swings of his axe to kill her. He chopped her all across her back and shoulders until eventually her head was chopped off!"

Joanna was shocked. "That's awful!" she exclaimed. "Disgusting and shameful. Poor old woman. No wonder you said that Henry turned into a monster as he grew older."

Tommy said nothing for a moment. He loved to hear about blood and gore, but this was just too much for him to take in. "I thought that they didn't kill women like that," he said eventually.

"Well, Tommy," said Anne. "Many women who had done wrong, or were said to be traitors were executed, but they were not subjected to torture on the rack, but many were tortured in other ways, and suffered terrible deaths, usually by being tied to a stake and burned alive, especially, those who were named as witches." She stopped talking for a moment.

Joanna was thinking of witches. *Were they really evil? Did they even exist?* She didn't want to change the conversation so she remained silent.

"Yes," Anne continued. "But there was one more punishment that Henry devised. It was kept in reserve for people who were found guilty of poisoning. Henry was terrified that someone might poison him, consequently, he had a special servant whose job it was to taste all the food and drink that was to be served to the king. Should any poisoner be caught, his punishment was to be boiled alive!"

"Boiled alive!" repeated Tommy. Even he was both awed and disgusted at that. "How did they do that? Did they just stick the person in a pot full of water and put a fire underneath?"

"Just that," said Anne. "Sometimes, it was water, but they could also use oil, lead, or hot wax."

Joanna was too horrified to say much, but she managed to ask "how often did that happen?"

"Fortunately, it didn't happen very often. It was such an awful death that it did put people off using poison to kill their enemies." Anne was thinking of one particular palace servant who had tried to poison one of the courtiers. Everyone, servants and courtiers, had been forced to watch the man's horrible death. Even after all those years, she was unable to describe what she had seen, especially to these two young people.

"Now, you see that my once-loving Henry did become a tyrant. And it was these cruel killings, that he seemed to want to do more and more, as he got older and more useless in his own body. I watched him from above, and I was almost glad that I did not have to be with him as he grew old and fat, smelling and suffering from that dreadful wound in his leg that never healed."

"So," asked Joanna with caution. She didn't want to anger the ghost of Anne, but she did have a very uncomfortable question. She spoke hesitantly. "I have a question which I would like to ask you."

Anne nodded. "Go ahead," she said.

"Ok, here goes," asked Joanna. "What do you feel about those people, mostly men, who were killed because they did not agree with the legality of your marriage to King Henry, and those who were killed because they would not sign the Act of Succession? They were amongst the thousands of killings that were put down to your Henry. Including Thomas More."

Anne stopped and stood quietly for a moment or two. Then, all she said was, "They all threatened my Elizabeth. Her life or her succession. I gave up my own life for that."

Joanna accepted that without any deeper questions. She hesitated and asked one more comment and question. "So, perhaps it was better for you that you died quickly, and while King Henry was young. But why did you choose not to go onto the spirit world, and to stay here as a ghost?"

"Yes, I'm still here. And yes, it was my choice to remain here in this nether world after I was murdered by Henry, and I suppose that my death by a single stroke of a sword, was less cruel than beheading with an axe, when often the axeman was not skilled enough to do the job with one blow!" She laughed once more. "That was the only mercy that Henry offered me. Mercy, they called it! A skilled French swordsman who wielded his highly sharpened sword with precision and skill to do the job in one blow, instead of a clumsy axeman!

The main reason he had me killed was because I had failed to produce a male child. And then, he wanted that whey-faced milksop, Jane Seymour. And how unfair it was that that milksop did produce a boy child, although it did cost her, her life. That baby boy Edward did eventually become King when he was only nine years old. Even younger than you, Tommy. Can you imagine yourself as King of England?"

Tommy started strutting about pretending to be a King, as Anne continued. "But Edward had always been a sickly child, a milksop like his mother. He died when he was fifteen years old after being King for only seven years.

I did not go to paradise as I deserved. Instead, I chose to be bound to the Earth to make sure that my daughter Elizabeth, who was only three years old when I was murdered, was not murdered, too.

There were many who wanted her killed or locked up in the Tower of London and left to rot! That is what her half-sister Mary wanted, but she did not dare to do it. Instead, she made my poor, motherless Elizabeth's life very cruelly unhappy. For the most part, the new Queen Mary had Elizabeth held in palaces and country houses far away from court. She was never free to be a child and a young woman to grow up naturally with love and care. Instead, she was continually watched and spied upon in case, wittingly or unwittingly, she raised a revolt against Mary.

It made me weep to see my beloved child so horridly treated, and I had to protect her as best as I could. I had to make sure that she eventually became Queen. Of course, the milksop's child came after Henry and then after him, Mary became Queen. That is after she had Queen Jane Gray beheaded! I won't digress by talking about the 'Nine Day Queen'. I really used all my power and influence to protect Elizabeth while she was growing up and in danger from Mary and other religious factions that were deadly dangerous. It was a time when murders and killings were done everywhere in the name of God. Catholics against Protestants. Protestants against Catholics. And the people of England were choosing who they wanted as Queen. Mary was Catholic and my Elizabeth was Protestant."

Tommy was beginning to get bored again, but Joanna was still interested in what the ghost had to say, and what a ghost could do in the real world. "What power and influence do you, or did you have as ghost to change what happened amongst mortals?" she asked Anne.

"Not a great deal," she said, "but one thing I can do really well is to change my ghostly breathing into a forceful draft or gust of wind."

"Cool. Can you do that?" Joanna asked. "Did it work?"

"I saved my daughter's life when Queen Mary was about to marry Catholic King Phillip of Spain."

"No shit! How did that happen? What did you do?" Joanna was amazed. Was this going to be a true story? Something never recorded in the history books! Something very different to add to her school essay. Her teacher would be amazed and ask her where she got the story from. Would she believe in ghosts?

Unaware of Joanna's thoughts, Anne continued. "There had been much talk by diplomats about my Elizabeth being contracted to her cousin, Prince Phillip of Spain when she was a girl. She was six years younger than Phillip, and Mary was eleven years older than him. So, you see, Elizabeth was a much better match for him," said Anne. She pulled a face and went on, "But the people of England, that is the English Parliament, did not want their possible future Queen married to a Catholic. So those plans were abandoned.

Then, years later, Queen Mary was about to marry him. She was thirty-eight and he was twenty-seven. She was well beyond the age to sustain a successful pregnancy in those times. But they both needed children. She, because she needed a successor and he, because he wanted to have a firm hold on England. He didn't want Mary. He wanted to be the King of England, and to make sure that the country returned to Catholicism."

"So, what happened between Mary and your Elizabeth?" Joanna asked.

"Mary was always jealous of her sister's youth and beauty, and she knew that Prince Phillip had been attracted to Elizabeth when he had asked to marry her some years before. But, she thought that she would get one over on Elizabeth when Prince Phillip then made his new proposal for Mary, which she accepted.

In Winchester Great Hall, Mary met and greeted him only two days before her wedding, and it was enough for Mary to see Phillip's eyes on Elizabeth to recognise that he still felt an attraction for her sister."

"What does that mean?" asked Tommy, who was stifling a yawn.

Joanna scowled at her brother. "He fancied her, silly! Phillip was going to marry Mary, but he still fancied Elizabeth!" She turned to Anne, "so, what happened? What did Mary do?" she asked.

"Mary turned her back to the Great Hall and rushed to her private chamber," said Anne. "Once there, away from all the watching courtiers, Mary screamed and threw a fit with so much jealousy that it poisoned her mind. She called her private secretary, and between them, they drew up a warrant to send Elizabeth to the Tower on a false charge of treason. The warrant said that my Elizabeth had plotted, with others, to assassinate Mary. And then, they drew up a second warrant for her execution."

Tommy was interested, again. "What's assassinate mean?" he asked Joanna.

"It means to kill someone," said an exasperated Joanna. "Mary was making up a story that Elizabeth was planning to kill her. So, what happened next?" she asked Anne.

"Mary calmed herself down and became unsure, again. She left the warrants on her desk and returned to the Great Hall." Anne must have been reliving that evening, and she gave a great sigh.

"So, how did you prevent the warrants being used?" Joanna asked.

Anne was proud of herself. "I was hoping that when Mary returned to her private rooms that she would think again about arresting and killing her sister, but I didn't dare risk it. So, I helped by breathing a forceful draft under her door and from behind the tapestry covering her wall. My breath of air was forceful enough to send the warrants flying from the desk directly into the fireplace where a roaring fire was burning. And they were gone!"

"That's way cool!" said Tommy and Joanna together. "Can you still do that?" Tommy asked.

But Anne only half heard. She wanted to finish her story. "When Mary saw that the warrants were no longer on her desk, she panicked. She thought that her secretary had taken the warrants and had had Elizabeth arrested. When she questioned him, he said that he had last seen them on the desk. Then, they both looked into the fireplace and saw fragments of the last singed pages that weren't quite destroyed. Mary thought that it was God's will and sighed a sigh of relief."

"Did Elizabeth ever know how close to death she had been on that day?" asked Joanna.

"No!" said Anne. "But, she did know that Mary wanted her gone and out of the way. Only when Mary was sure that she was pregnant, she felt safe. Safe enough for Elizabeth to be recalled to court. Then, it was that disaster struck. The pregnancy turned out to be a phantom pregnancy. Shortly after Phillip then left for Spain, never to return to his wife. Mary was distraught with misery, yet she did realise that Elizabeth was her only heir and that it was best to keep her safe!"

"So, your Elizabeth did eventually become Queen, and became the best and most successful sovereign of all the Tudors!" Joanna exclaimed.

But Tommy was still struggling with what had been said. "What does phantom pregnancy mean?" he asked his sister.

"It means that a lady can sometimes have a big swollen stomach, and think that she is having a baby, but she is mistaken. And Anne was saying that because Mary didn't have a baby, Elizabeth then became Queen after Mary died."

"Yes! Indeed," said Anne, with a good look of satisfaction on her face. "And with the same method, I even saved her Queenship in 1588 when Phillip and the traitorous Spaniards sent their Armada of one hundred and thirty deadly warships against her. My breath was more powerful then. Strong winds were already blowing and when I added my powerful force, the winds developed into a wild storm at sea. I even managed to get those winds to change direction and blow their ships away from Calais and northwards towards destruction."

Tommy was getting fidgety. He got up and walked to the window. Outside, the sun was still shining, and although the trees were bare, it still didn't look like February. It just seemed strange. He turned towards his sister. "Joanna," he said. "Don't you think that we should go and find mum? She might be getting worried about us."

"OK," she said. "In a minute. I just want to ask Anne about living here in this house when she was a girl." She turned to Anne, who nodded at her. What had started as an adventure for Tommy, his very own discovery of a real ghost, had been taken over by Joanna, and he was quite cross about it. But Joanna, who had always liked her school history lessons, was now getting drawn into the story telling.

"Do you think that you could start from the beginning," she asked. "You have talked about your middle life and your death, and I think that there is a lot more to your story than I have read in history books, and I would love to hear it."

"Of course, I will!" exclaimed the ghost. "I have been waiting hundreds of years to tell the real story of Anne Boleyn!" Anne sat next to Joanna on the bench, and if a ghost can make herself more comfortable, then that's what she did.

She gazed upwards as if she were searching her old memory banks; and started quite hesitantly. "I first met Henry when I was a mature girl of ten. I was two years younger than you are now, Tommy, but centuries ago children were very different to what they are today."

Tommy was interested again, and he sat on the floor in front of the bench. "How?" he asked.

"Well," said Anne. "For a start, most children didn't go to school."

"That's so cool!" shouted Tommy. "I wish that I didn't have to go to school!

Anne looked down at Tommy and smiled. "The lucky ones got learn to read a little, but for the most part they were treated like little adults, and they were expected to work, helping their parents mostly, at whatever their parents did. In the countryside, they helped to look after animals or work in the fields. In the towns the boys learned their father's trade, and the girls helped at home. Quite often there were lots of children and babies, and the girls were needed to help with cooking and cleaning, but especially they looked after the babies."

"Well," said Joanna, "I'm glad that I wasn't born five hundred years ago. So, in a poor family the children were set to work almost as soon as they could walk. I read in one of my history books that in a rich family the girls had to marry the man that their father chose for them. Gross!"

"That's right," said Anne. "It was better for my sort of family. We didn't do the work of a servant. The boys, and sometimes the girls, more often were taught to read and write at home with a tutor. And when schoolwork was done for the day, the boys learned archery, to ride horses and how to fight, while the girls would sit with their mothers and learn to stitch and sew.

Don't forget that there were no shops for people to just go and buy their clothes like you do nowadays. Every item of clothing that anyone wore, rich or poor, had to be handmade. The richer homes would have a seamstress, as she was called, to make the family clothes. And in the poorer homes the mother had to do the sewing as well as all the other chores.

So, when I was ten, I was considered by my parents to be a young woman. This was in an age when it was not unusual for a girl to be married at twelve years old, two years younger than you, Joanna."

"That's sick!" said Joanna. "I can't even imagine me having, or even wanting a boyfriend, let alone being married."

"In my time girls didn't choose a husband, they nearly always had to marry the man chosen for them by their fathers," said Anne. "And the choices were often made for business or political reasons."

"What happened if you didn't like the man chosen for you?" asked Joanna.

"It didn't matter." Anne shrugged her shoulders. "A girl had no option. She had to marry the man chosen for her by her father, even if the man was as old, or even older than her father!"

"That sucks!" Joanna was trembling at the thought. "How could a girl be forced into an arranged marriage?"

"She could be forced in all sorts of ways. She could be locked up at home, she could be starved, she could be beaten," said Anne. "The only way that she could get out of the contract made by her father and her husband to be, would be that she was sent to a convent to become a nun."

Joanna was shaken. All she could say was, "Wow!" Then, after a moment of reflection, she added, "I'm certainly glad that I wasn't born then!"

"Well, I will tell you what happened to me, if you are interested," said Anne.

Tommy was about to say 'no', but Joanna jumped in. "Oh, yes please. Were you forced to marry King Henry?"

"As I said before, I first met Henry when I was ten years old, and he was twenty," said Anne. "My uncle, the Duke of Norfolk took me to stay at the Duke of Buckingham's country lodge at Penshurst in Kent, which was only a few miles from my family home here at Hever Castle. That was long before Henry had the Duke of Buckingham executed for treason and took Penshurst for himself."

"Ha!" said Tommy. "Another of the King's friends who had his head chopped off. Was it just because King Henry wanted his house?"

"I'm not sure, Tommy," said Anne. "I was in France when he was killed, and I don't know what treason he was accused of. But I liked the Duke. He was a friend of my father too, and he often came to dine here to Hever when I was young."

"It sounds to me," said Joanna, "as if it was never a good thing to be a friend of King Henry VIII. If I had lived then, I would have kept as far away from him as possible."

"Indeed," said Anne. "You may well be right. But Henry was like a magnet and everyone who was anyone wanted to be invited to come to court, to entertain him in their own homes, even though, it would cost them a small fortune. Everyone wanted to be in his circle of friends.

But, as a ten year old, I not only met Henry at Penshurst, but I also fell deeply in love with him, as deeply in the love that any lovesick burgeoning young woman can have for a fascinating adult. He was tall, blond, with beautiful darting green-blue eyes that took in everything that was going on around him, and he had cheeks that crinkled prettily whenever he smiled. Forget about the old fat Henry. When he was young, he was very, very handsome. And he was full of fun and magic. But although he played games with me, and we rough-tumbled together, he never took advantage of me as an available female. He was deeply in love with his Spanish wife.

He had been married to her for two years, and he was still very happy with her although she had not yet shown any signs of producing a boy child. A male heir that Henry would soon be desperate to have. While she was not with him, he played with me and sang to me. He was so clever at making up beautiful songs, just like the professional court musicians. Do you know the song 'Greensleeves?' That was one of his and it is still remembered and sung in your England of today."

"Hey! That's so cool! I do know that song. We sang it at school in our music lessons." And Joanna started humming the tune, while Anne carried on talking.

"But best of all," she said, "he helped me to overcome my fear of horses and riding. He gave me a docile and responsive young grey mare called Damsel, and we would chase each other all over the hunting fields of Kent.

I had been at Penshurst for just six days when his Katherine came to join him, and he instantly forgot all about me. I returned to Hever with Damsel, and I didn't see him again for years. That was because when I was twelve, my father sent me to the court of Margaret of Austria to train as a lady-in-waiting. I was very fortunate to be accepted by her when I was so young. Then, a couple of years later, due to a shift in European politics, I was sent to France to become one of the new Queen's ladies-in-waiting."

This was all news to Joanna, and she was full of questions. "I suppose that, after what you were telling us about girls and their choices, you were sent there by your father without him asking you whether you wanted to go or not," said Joanna. "Was that to the court of the new King of France?"

"No," she corrected me. "I was sent originally to be a lady-in-waiting to Henry's sister Mary who, for political reasons, had been forced to marry the old French King Louis XII. He was thirty years older than her, and he had been married twice before. Poor Mary, at the time she was deeply in love with her

45

brother's best friend Charles Brandon, but she had to do as her brother, Henry the King, ordered her to do. But fortunately, the poor girl didn't have to suffer long because Louis died within three months of their marriage."

"What a drag! I bet that three months felt like three years," said Joanna.

"Yes, I expect that every day felt like a year for the poor girl, but she was still full of excited anticipation," said Anne, with cheeky smile.

"Why?" asked Joanna.

And Tommy asked, "Did that Mary poison him, or something? That would be cool."

"No, nothing like that," said Anne. "Mary told me later that when Henry had forced her to marry the old French King, she had got him to promise her that when the King died she could choose her next husband for herself."

"Awesome!" said Joanna. "That could have been a good reason to kill him off. I know that I would want to do it if it were me married to an old man!"

"Yes. Yes. Yes." Anne was eager to tell them the rest of the story. "So, when old Louis did die, Mary felt herself free to choose Charles Brandon for her next husband. She married him secretly whilst they were still in France. When she and Brandon returned to England, Henry was absolutely furious. At first he wanted to have Brandon executed, but he relented. He claimed that he had not promised his sister that she could choose her next husband. It was two years before he could be persuaded to forgive them, and after paying a huge fine, they were finally allowed back to court.

Louis, in spite of having had three wives, had no son to inherit the throne so his cousin, Francois, became the next French King. I was ordered, by my father, to remain in France to serve as the lady-in-waiting to Francois's wife, the new Queen Claude, and I stayed there for seven more years." She paused.

"I was the new young lady at court, and was thought to be very different from the other ladies-in-waiting because of my Englishness. I was not quite fourteen when I arrived at the French court. I learnt French very quickly and I tried my best to fit in and behave in the French manner. I was delighted to be treated as a grown up there."

"That's funny," said Joanna. "Because you are remembered in our history books as being a strange delight, even a little exotic, in the English court because of your Frenchness!" She paused. "But back to the French King Francois, I remember reading that he had lots of girlfriends, in spite of being married. Did he ever try it on with you?"

If a ghost could be said to blush, she blushed! "I was at the French court for all my years of growing up from childhood to womanhood, and yes, he persisted and persisted, and I did eventually give in to him. Oh! What a wonderful lover he was! I was his mistress for about ten months. That was when I was sixteen, and he was twenty-three! I'm not quite sure why it ended. Probably another new girlfriend, even younger than me! I know that I was very unhappy, but I had to hide my tears and carry on as if nothing had happened between me and King Francois.

Francois, who was three years younger than Henry, was also handsome and very attractive, in the French fashion. He was tall, with dark, curly hair, which he allowed to hang down to his shoulders, and he had dark, piercing-black eyes. And like Henry, he was very athletic and a very talented sportsman. The two Kings met quite often, usually in France, and they became fierce rivals for everything, including all their sports of wrestling, archery, jousting and hunting. They also counted up who had the most female conquests in their courts. Each one wanted what the other one had, and to go one better!"

"So, they were both real fit!" exclaimed Joanna. "And you never told Henry about your adventures with Francois! You were supposed to be a virgin," Joanna blushed when she used the word *virgin*. To her, it was a bit of a naughty word! "When you married Henry! He had spent seven years chasing after you, and I read in my history books that you told him that he could only have your virginity if he married you." She blushed, again, when she repeated that word.

Tommy, who was definitely getting bored by then, and ready to go back downstairs again, pricked up his ears. He knew when his sister was getting embarrassed, and it was usually easy to wind her up. "What's virginity?" he asked, in a very innocent voice.

His ghost didn't know what to say, and Joanna went bright red. "Er!" she coughed. "Er, it's when a girl chooses not to go to bed with her boyfriend."

Actually, although Tommy was only twelve, he and his mates had already taught each other lots of words which were used when two people had sex together, and he knew perfectly well what it meant for a girl, or a boy even, to be a virgin.

Anne ignored him. She flicked a loose strand of air out of her eyes and she, too, blushed again. "Did I say that? Did I say that I was a virgin when I came home from France?" she asked with an equally innocent look on her face. "It was such a long time ago! I do remember that when we all met up six years later when

Henry, with me on his arm, returned to France, Francois acknowledged me as Henry's future Queen. And because of that I gave in at last to Henry.

You should have seen Francois giggle and wink his eye at me behind Henry's back. I was very fortunate that he never told Henry about us, but he did laugh secretly to know that I had pulled the wool over Henry's eyes by telling him that I was still a virgin, and that he had bedded the Queen of England before Henry."

She looked straight at Joanna. "Did you read in your history books that when Henry started chasing after me that I had promised myself to Henry Percy, who was the son of the Earl of Northumberland?"

"Yes. I did read about that." Joanna had a quick think. "Henry Percy was your boyfriend, and I bet that he was real fit too! And wasn't it the Archbishop who stopped that relationship? How serious was it?"

"It was Cardinal Wolsey who stopped us getting married. The country was still Catholic at the time, and we didn't have Archbishops until Henry had created the Church of England. I truly hated Wolsey because of what he had done, and I did not know until sometime afterwards that he did it because he had been ordered to do so by Henry."

Was there now another hint of a tear in the ghostly eye? "Percy and I were really in love. And we had promised ourselves to each other, which in those times was as sacred and unbreakable as marriage vows said in front of a priest." She sighed, and then continued. "Before Henry decided that he wanted me, Henry Percy and I spent many hours together. And, of course, we made love whenever possible!"

"No shit! You naughty Lady!" Joanna exclaimed. "So, you had both King Francois of France and Harry Percival as lovers before you met King Henry again as an adult. Did anyone else know that you were no longer a virgin?"

Anne scowled at Joanna. "When I first refused King Henry, I was sent back here to Hever by Wolsey. My father was furious with me, and I was locked in my bedroom for days. He knew that if the King had what he wanted, then he could benefit, too. He desperately wanted more wealth and titles for himself. He felt that he had missed out on being given the highest rewards when my sister Mary had been the King's mistress, and he wanted to make sure that he didn't miss out this time. He knew nothing about King Francois, and I told him nothing. He made me swear on our household Holy Bible that I was still a virgin and that my promise to Henry Percy was no more than a childish fancy."

Anne twisted her hands in memory of those unhappy times. "Did you know that to swear on the Holy Bible was a really serious thing in those days? I didn't do it lightly. And for months, I prayed to Jesus every night for him to forgive me for my lies. But I really did love Percy, and I was heartbroken when he was sent back to Northumberland." She looked at me directly again. "Do you know that he betrayed me. Not only by denying my love and marrying immediately the bride that his father chose for him, but also, at my end, he was on the panel of judges that condemned me to death?"

"It's funny," mused Joanna, "That you were condemned to death because you were found guilty of sleeping with other men, friends of both you and Henry. You say that you were innocent. But, before you married Henry you had sex with both King Francois of France and Harry Percy of Northumberland. And you told him that you were a virgin! It seems to me that everything about your relationship with Henry was back to front. Perhaps, it was right that in the end you were found guilty."

"That's very harsh," protested Anne. "Although, I was heartbroken when Harry Percy deserted me, in the end I did love Henry, and I would never have betrayed him."

"Did you really love each other?" Joanna asked.

"I think that maybe our loving *was* back to front, as you said." Anne sat down and put her head in her hands. "He loved me for seven long years before we were finally allowed to marry. For many of those years, I clung onto the hate that I had for him for taking Percy away from me. But during that time, my feelings gradually changed. I saw Percy for the weakling that he was, and I could feel the love that I was getting from Henry.

By the time we were married I did truly love Henry, and for a short while, we were both very so happy together, especially when I found out that I was having a baby. But it all started to go wrong when Elizabeth was born. Whilst I was disappointed that she was a girl, and not the boy child that we both wanted so much, I adored my baby. Henry, on the other hand, was angry. So very angry. He would hardly even look at Elizabeth. He needed a son and heir. He often shouted at me that I was as useless as Queen Katherine. And he hardly ever came to my bed at night.

We snapped at each other for three years, and during that time Henry started to look around at the other unmarried women at court, and for some reason, he seemed to find attraction in my milksop lady-in-waiting, Jane Seymour.

Away from public eyes, he became an angry bully with me. Yet, when on show in open court, he could be very charming and loving, especially when he was into a new affair. With my ability to watch him from the afterlife, I did see him with others. He was gentle with the milk-sop, but he felt no attraction for his next wife, the German woman, chosen by Thomas Cromwell, who he married after Jane, and she felt none for him. With so very little English, she was unable to flatter or coax him in bed as his other wives had done, and would do so in the future.

After me the only one of his wives he really loved was young Katy Howard, my cousin, whom he adored. He was so much older than her and by then he had grown old and fat. And he was suffering with that awful leg wound that was extremely painful and beginning to suppurate."

"What does suppurate mean?" asked Tommy.

"It means a deep wound which does not heal, and becomes full of pus," said Anne.

"Yes. Young Katy was very caring and gentle with him, almost more of a nurse than a wife. And, in turn, he treated her as if she were so fragile in body, like a small child, that even his touchings would harm her. Yet, she was the most experienced one of all. I don't know how many lovers she had before Henry chose her to be his fifth wife. And he was truly heartbroken when he found out the truth about her."

"But that didn't stop him from killing her," Joanna said, bluntly.

"He was a brute!" was all Anne said.

Joanna looked at her watch then, and she noticed that it was behaving most oddly. She thought that she and Tommy had been up there in the long gallery for at least half an hour, but her watch showed that only five minutes had passed. Perhaps, time goes more slowly when you are talking to a ghost, she mused!

"Come on," said Tommy, tugging at his sister's arm. "We ought to be going. Mum must have noticed that we have left that room downstairs."

Joanna looked at Anne. She turned into a polite schoolgirl and said, "It's been so nice to meet you. Perhaps, if Mum brings us here, again, might we see you again?"

"Oh! Yes," said Anne. "If you are interested in what went on during Tudor England, I have so much more I can tell you. And look there on the bench, there is a little pearl button that used to be mine. Just put it in your pocket to remember our little conversations."

Joanna turned to the bench, and sure enough there was a tiny pearl button on the padded seat. *Funny,* thought Joanna. *I'm sure that it wasn't there when I was sitting. I'm sure that I would have noticed it if it had been there, before.* She picked it up quickly and slipped it into her pocket.

"Thank you," she said.

Anne's body was fading even as Tommy and Joanna started back downstairs, and before reaching the top step Joanna turned back into the room just in time to see a shadowy Anne take a little boy by the hand. A child who must have been the shy Gilles Woollerton, and they both disappeared through the door at the other end of the long gallery. They had gone from the room and Anne Boleyn was back in her portrait hanging, with all the others, on the wall.

Tommy and Joanna ducked under the rope barrier and skipped down the stairs, preparing to be told off by their mother for wandering off and being gone so long. But, they were surprised to find their mother still talking to the guide.

"Mum," interrupted Tommy, "we have just been speaking to a ghost. She wasn't at all scary. We talked to her for ages. It must have been at least half an hour. She really was there!"

Their mother laughed, and the guide did too. "There are no such things as ghosts. And, anyway you have only been gone for a couple of minutes, otherwise I would have started hunting for you both myself," she said.

The guide laughed too. "Sorry," she said. "No ghosts here, I'm afraid. Though, they do say that the ghost of Anne Boleyn walks at night through the Tower of London!"

"But, Mum," Tommy insisted. "She was here. She was upstairs in the room with all the paintings!"

The guide looked concerned. "Did you go under the rope barrier?" she asked.

Both Tommy and Joanna nodded their heads and looked very guilty. "Sorry," they mumbled together.

"Well," said the guide, "I hope that you didn't touch anything." She turned to their mother. "A very weird thing happened yesterday, during the night. The portraits of Katherine of Aragon and Jane Seymour fell off the wall and smashed. We don't know how it happened because no one stays in this part of the castle overnight.

And it looked as though it had been done in anger. The portraits, especially of Katherine of Aragon, looked as though they had been stamped on. Also up there, there is a glass case which has one of Anne Boleyn's actual shifts. It is exactly the same as the one she wore on the morning that she was beheaded. It's made of fine lawn cotton with tiny pearl buttons at the back to do it up. Last night that was also pushed over and smashed. There were tiny slivers of glass everywhere, so that is why the room is roped off. We will have to do a deep clean-up there, and the shift has been taken away to check that it has not been damaged."

"Oh!" said Joanna guiltily, while she was feeling for the tiny button which was still in her pocket. "We didn't see anything like that. The pictures were all on the wall, and the glass case was just there in the corner. Could the ghost have done it?" she asked. "Maybe she blew it over?"

"Well, I don't know what you two have been up to, and what stories you have been making up!" laughed their mother. "We had better be making our way home now."

"I think that might be a very good idea," said the guide with a wry smile.

March 2022, Brighton

The Covid virus had made me so fragile that when I passed over from this world to the next that I didn't even realise that I was dead. There was a great shining light, and suddenly, I found myself at the gates of Heaven, where St Peter was sitting on his golden throne, ready and waiting to judge me.

He looked at me with a determined look in his eye, and I knew that I would have trouble passing through those golden gates.

"You have led quite an ordinary and dutiful life," stated St Peter. "For the most part you have been considerate and kind, but some of your behaviour in your youth makes me question your eligibility to pass through these gates. So, I'm going to give you forty-eight more hours in the world that you have just left, to try correct some of your past errors, or if correction is no longer possible, at least make real and heartfelt apologies."

"How do you mean?" I asked. "Are you telling me that I will be a ghost?"

"Yes," he said. "That's exactly what you will be. And as a ghost you will be able to make contact with some of those people that you hurt in your lifetime on earth."

"Just forty-eight hours?" I asked. "Will there be an absolute deadline?"

"Those forty-eight hours will be flexible enough while you are staying in one place and talking to one person," said St Peter. "I will be overseeing you and if I think that you are doing well, your last hours on earth may be paused, or even extended, so that you can visit other people. That's if you need too." St Peter stood up, and pointing in the opposite direction, away from the queue of Covid victims that was beginning to form, he said in a rather gruff and slightly threatening voice; "Now off you go to Heaven's waiting room, and have a good think about your past and how it may be possible for you to correct some of those errors and choices that you made."

I felt like a naughty schoolboy who had just been told off by my headmaster. It was like I was walking back to my classroom with my tail between my legs, having been told to go away and think about all the bad things I had done. *You have let the school down. You have let your parents down. And, most importantly, you have let yourself down…* was echoing in my head from my schooldays.

As I sat down, I suddenly realised that's all the aches and pains of my seventy-eight years old body had all gone. I could move without walking. I could breathe without battling for breath, and I had no need for food or drink. Especially of alcohol that I had so abused in the past. But it was the Covid that had got me in the end!

I didn't need to think for long. My mind was flooded all at once with pictures of the girl who I had hurt so much when I was twenty years old, and she was just seventeen. To tell the truth I had often wondered what had happened to her over the years. She would now be about seventy-four. I didn't know, whether she was still on earth or whether she had passed through the gates of Heaven before me.

Suddenly, I was no longer in God's waiting room but sitting beside an elderly, but youthful looking lady who was enjoying the spring sunshine and the birds and flowers in her garden. How did I get there? Did St Peter know who I needed to see, and where I could find her?

"Eva," I asked, quietly. "Is that you? Are you my lost love Eva?"

She looked up at me and I could see that she still had those beautiful blue eyes that could look at you directly and see straight through you at the same time.

"Pierre?" she queried. "Can that possibly be you? I was just sitting here in the sun, gently thinking of my past life. Am I now dreaming? I must be…"

"Yes. It is me," I said, a bit shame-faced. "You're not dreaming. And don't be afraid. I have just passed away and before I move on to the spirit world, I have one last chance to try to correct some of the mistakes I made when I was a young man. So, I have come to see you for a while. I want, if I can, to make amends for what I did to you when we were both young. I know how much I hurt you. And, I am so sorry."

"Are you telling me that you are a ghost?" She was still thinking that she must be asleep. Must be dreaming. "A ghost? A real ghost?"

"Yes," I said. "I really am a ghost, and I've come to you to tell you that I am sorry that I hurt you when we were young. I knew that you were hurting when I left you for that other Eva. And the other things that…"

"I don't believe that you could ever be sorry!" She jumped in. And she looked at me with those big blue eyes which were now icy. "You knew how much I loved you, and just because I wouldn't give in to your demands to make love, which I so wanted to do by the way, you left me and found another girl who let you have everything you wanted. The tart!

You must remember that we girls all lived together in that boarding school in London. And you boys lived in bed-and-breakfast accommodation, spending the days with the girls in that secretarial cum language college. So, after you dumped me, I saw you walking arm-in-arm with her every day. Or cuddling up with her daily in the classrooms, the dining hall, or in some corner of the day room. And to make things worse, she also had the same name as me. Eva. Since then, I have tried to have a happy life, but I have never been able to forget that hurt, and what it led to."

"And she wasn't half as nice as you," I admitted. "But she was so available, so good at sex." I said with a grin. Then, I realised what she had just said. "What do you mean by saying, 'what it led to?' What did it lead to?"

"You bastard!" was all she said.

I was bemused. "I can't believe that I was so cruel to you. I saw you so often crying in the corner, or out in the school gardens," I said. "I wanted to comfort you and tell you that I was sorry, but I just couldn't tear myself away from the other Eva. I shouldn't make excuses, but my teenage hormones were dominating my sense of what was right and wrong."

She softened. "Oh Pierre!" she sighed. "I did so love you. And I so wanted to marry you. Do you remember what you did on the night of our final college dance?"

My ghostly face suddenly turned red with guilt and embarrassment. "I...I...I don't know how I could have done it to you," I stammered.

She continued as though she hadn't heard me. "Well, I remember that evening as clearly as if it all happened yesterday." She stopped talking for a moment, and a dreamy look came over her face. "You took me in your arms and told me how much you loved me, and how wrong you had been to go off with the other Eva. And oh! How sorry you were that you had hurt me.

I just melted with love and forgiveness. And for the next half hour, we danced so closely that our bodies were touching from our shoulders to our knees, and I could feel that you were aroused, as I was too. I didn't see any danger in the ballroom, where the end-of-year college dance was being held. We were surrounded by all the teachers and students, so nothing untoward could happen there.

I should have let you go then and return to my room in the college. But instead, I let you lead me through a door at the back of the ballroom, which led to a dark storeroom lit only by the moonlight that was coming in through the curtainless window. The room was filled with tables and chairs. And in the corner, there was a long leather couch. You must have sussed it out earlier in the evening.

It wasn't quite rape, but there was a lot of coercion on your side, and we did make love. I remember the long passionate kisses and the erotic touching. You roused me to a point where I no longer had any fears. I remember you undressing me. It was just an undoing of the zip at the back of my dress, and I was all but naked. I should have continued to resist, but I couldn't. I so loved you, and all my resistance melted away. And yes, I so wanted you."

I wanted to tell her that it had been real for me. That I had loved her too. That I hadn't meant to force her. But, I suppose, I knew that I was to blame. I did coax her. I did force myself upon her.

I let her continue with her story.

"It was the first time for me, but you were very experienced. You were so gentle with me, and you knew everything that you needed to do to get me to climax. After we had finished making love, you assured me of your love, and you told me that once you were back in France you would speak to your parents and make arrangements for us to be married. Three days later, you left London. You kissed me goodbye; and I never saw you again!

It was nearly two months later, when I realised that I was pregnant. I couldn't quite believe it. I tried to ignore what was happening to my body, and I did everything I could to avoid showing my expanding waistline."

I gasped. "You mean we had a child? Oh! My darling. I never knew." I doubled in pain. It was if I had been hit by a moving vehicle. "Oh! My darling…" I whispered. "My darling…" I wanted to hold her to me, but of course, I couldn't. I had forgotten that I was a ghost. I had no substance. I couldn't hold anyone or anything anymore.

Eva ignored me. I was as if she were so wrapped in the remembrance of her story that she didn't even see me, or feel my presence. "Eventually, when I could hide it no longer, I told my mother that I was going to have a baby. I told her the whole story of our love and of your desertion. She was horrified. She knew how strict my father was and that his frequent threats to turn me out of the house if I ever got pregnant before I was married were real. Remember this was the mid-

1960s and in spite of 'flower power' etc. going on, it was still thought to be wicked for a girl to have a baby outside of marriage. And, of course, it was always the girl's fault. She was the slut. She was the whore. It was never the man's fault.

I wrote, and I wrote, and I wrote to you. I don't know how many letters I sent to you in France. I wanted to tell you what was happening. And I never got a reply. Eventually, my letters were all returned marked *gone away, address unknown.*"

"What!" I cried. "I never got any letters from you." I had a quick think. "My parents must have taken them and sent them back. I had told them all about you and they were absolutely against the idea of me marrying so young. They didn't forbid it, but told me that I had to wait for at least a year. I wrote to you to tell you what they had said. And I asked you to be patient and wait for me. I wrote to you several times, and I waited anxiously for you to reply."

"Oh! No!" she cried. "I never received any letters from you. I thought that you had denied me, abandoned me."

All of a sudden, I realised what must have happened. "My mother! I put my letters to you in the office mail box, and she must have seen them and removed them. So, all our letters to each other were taken by my parents to stop us seeing each other again.

I don't know if you remember, but my father owned a small business in the French Alps, near the border of Switzerland, where we made small and very delicate wrist watches for ladies. They were exquisitely beautiful, and we were beginning to make profitable sales in America. I was my father's only son, and it was down to me to take over the business when he wanted to retire. That's why I had been sent to London in the first place. To learn good commercial English so that I could communicate with clients both in England and America.

After a while, when I heard nothing from you, my darling. I started having second thoughts about getting married when I was only twenty. And, yes, I was already looking at the pretty young French girls in our town." I hung my head in shame. "If only I had known about the baby, I'm sure that I would have returned to England. Which was, of course, what my parents feared the most."

I waited for her reaction. Nothing. It was as if she had heard nothing of what I had just said. "Please tell me about the baby." I begged.

"When I was six months pregnant, I was still small, but getting bigger every day," she said calmly. Seemingly without any emotion at all. "My mother told my father that she was taking me to Brighton for a little holiday with my aunt. My mother's sister, Lucy. We came to this house which my aunt left to me when she passed away, nineteen years ago. My mother stayed with us for a week while my aunt Lucy was making arrangements for me to have my baby in a nursing home.

She also arranged for an adoption agency to find a good home with loving parents who would adopt my baby when it was born. Perhaps, she had always felt guilty about the arrangements that she and my mother were making for me without my consent. Perhaps that's why, many years later she left me this house. I was a widow by then, and I had had enough of London. And I was glad to come here, to live by the sea."

Eva started to cry. Tears were rolling down her face as she was remembering the most terrible time in her life. "My child, a little boy. He was born on April the fourth, 1964. I'll never forget that date. 04.04.64. And I remembered that your birthday was also April fourth. Such a coincidence! Father and son born on the same date. He was such a beautiful baby. I loved him immediately. And I wanted to keep him. But that wasn't allowed, and I only had him with me for one week before he was taken away.

But, by then, I had formed a complete bond with him. A lifelong bond. I named him Pierre for you, and it broke my heart when they took him away from me. The milk in my breasts was overflowing, and I cried without stopping for days and days. Our little boy was called Pierre Westwood, but on his birth certificate instead of Pierre Girardet, it was written *father: unknown.*

My mother had already gone back home well before little Pierre was born, and I stayed with aunt Lucy another two months to try and get my body and my emotions back to normal. But, of course, my emotions were never back to normal from that time on. How I missed my baby! I cried for him every day for months. And I mourned his loss for years. Funnily enough, unbelievably, I also missed you. I loved you, and I hated you at the same time. I felt utterly unloved and utterly rejected. I thought I would never forgive you when I realised that I would never see my baby boy again."

I could hold my own floods of my tears no longer. "Oh! My darling," I said. "I am so, so sorry. I promise you that I never knew about your pregnancy and I never received those letters that you sent me."

"But you never tried to find me either." sobbed Eva. "You just got on with your life. I expect you made a happy marriage, and in due course, you took over your father's watch-making firm. No more thoughts about *poor little Eva crying in the corner*!" She looked at me accusingly. The love for me seemed to drain out of her.

"Well!" I said. "Some of that happened, but I never forgot you. In 1972, I married a girl called Michelle. She was my father's secretary, and my parents were all for the marriage. We were wholly unsuitable for each other, and it lasted only nine years. We didn't have any children." I was crying now. "So, you see that the only child I have ever had was your little Pierre. What a happy life together we missed because of my cowardice!"

"But I did eventually marry," Eva said. "That was in 1974, when Pierre would have been ten years old. I had a happy marriage, and I had two baby girls, who are now grown women. But, I never lost the ache in my heart for my missing son. 04.04.64 is etched on my heart forever."

I suddenly had a flash of memory. "Wow!" I said. "Listen to this," I said. "After my father passed away, I decided to sell the watch business. I never really cared for it. And I moved to England. To Brighton. And I have lived here ever since. With the proceeds from my father's business I opened a little school to teach English to summer students from all over Europe.

Well. This is the thing. On the morning of my sixty-fourth birthday in 2008, I was walking the hills of Seaford Head with my little dog, Alfie. I sat on a bench overlooking the Seven Sisters, the most famous view on the South Downs, when a middle-aged man came and sat next to me. He petted Alfie and said what a lovely dog he was. There was something familiar about him. I couldn't decide what it was, and we started chatting. I told him that it was my birthday. That I was sixty-four just like the Beatles song, and I started singing. Then, he jumped up. 'It's my birthday, too,' he cried. 'I am forty-four years old today!' We laughed at the coincidence, and we sang the Beatles song together! He was 44 on 04.04, and I was 64 on 04.04."

"What!" Eva almost shouted. "It can't be. But it must be."

"He was our son!" We both exclaimed together.

"Did you have any more contact with him?" Eva was desperate. "That was fourteen years ago. He will be fifty-eight now. Can we find him?"

"My darling," I said. "Remember that I am a ghost. And St Peter has given me only forty-eight hours to try to right some of my wrongs of the past. But, he may extend my time. I will do whatever I can to help you find him."

"Did you ask him his name?"

I thought hard. "I don't think that he mentioned his name, but he did say that he worked for the Brighton Council." I dug deeper into my memory banks. "Yes!" I exclaimed. "He said that he had started a new campaign for re-election to the Borough Council the next month. He also said that he was aiming to challenge the sitting MP for his seat in the House of Commons at the next General Election. That would have been in 2010."

"Oh my goodness, I think that I am going to faint!" Eva was so excited. "All we have to do is go to the Brighton Main Library and look up the list of candidates for the Local Elections for May 2008. I'm sure that we will find his name there. If not, he may listed in the candidates for the 2010 General Election."

"Oh! I am excited too!" I cried. "I think that there is still time for us to get there before it closes this afternoon."

"Will you be able to get in without being seen as a ghost?" Eva asked.

"I think so. I'm sure that I am visible only to you. I will be there at you side as your silent support."

So, we, rather Eva, caught the bus to the city centre, with me hitching a ride for free! The Public Library was still open. We had fifty minutes to see what we could discover. The librarian was very helpful, and we were able to look at discs which held those details. We both held our breaths, although I'm not sure if a ghost can do that. And there he was at the end of the list of candidates: Peter Wilson. Date of Birth 04.04.64.

Eva could hardly breathe. She was just able to whisper, "It's him. It must be him. Same date of birth, only Peter instead of Pierre. I suppose that his adoptive parents were called Wilson, and they anglicised his name. Wow! I can't believe it. All these years, I've been wondering where my boy was. What he was doing. How he was faring. And there he was, all the time, sitting on my very own doorstep. Fifty-eight years and he was here all the time." Two great blobs of tears came rolling down her cheeks. She didn't wipe them away and they just got soaked up in her roll-neck jumper.

"Let's go back to your home and google him on the Brighton Council website," I said. And that's exactly what we did.

And there he was. He hadn't become an MP. He was still employed by the Brighton Council. He was head of the Planning Department.

"Look!" exclaimed Eva. "They are holding a public meeting for a planning issue tomorrow evening. He's going to be there in the Council Office meeting room. 7.30 pm. We've got to go. We've got to meet him. What shall I say? Will you still be here? You've got to meet him too!"

"Whoa! Slow down!" I said. "We've got time tomorrow to talk this through. I have still got twenty-four hours on this earth, which St Peter might extend. I only wish that he could make me visible to others too. Oh! I'm just so happy for you!"

I so wanted to hold her and kiss her. I wanted so much to make amends for all the hurt in her life that I had given her. If she could make contact with Peter Wilson and tell him her story, then the extra time on earth for me would have not been wasted.

"Good night, my dear," said my lovely Eva. "I haven't been so happy for years. And I am sure that we will have success tomorrow. If only you were real and not a ghost!"

"If only!" I replied, with a saddened heart.

The next day, with my last few hours on earth coming to an end, we sat calmly chatting about our pasts, and what she would say if she did make real contact with the man we thought to be our son that coming evening. We were both so excited, but I could feel my power waning, and I wanted to conserve my spirituality for the coming event.

We arrived on time for the meeting, which was quite a boisterous affair, with both sides giving passionate arguments for and against planning permission for eighty-two houses to be built on a derelict small holding on the edge of the city. There was no definite result, and no votes held. Peter Wilson stood his ground and seemed very knowledgeable and sympathetic to both sides of the argument. A new date was set for the next meeting.

It was as everyone was leaving the meeting that Eva stepped up to the platform. "Please, Mr Wilson, could I have a quiet word with you?"

He looked very tired. "This evening's meeting is concluded now," he said wearily. "You will have another opportunity to voice your concerns about planning for Foxlands Down at the next meeting."

"Please," said Eva again. "It's a private thing that I want to talk to you about. Not houses for Foxlands." She looked at him with soft loving eyes.

He was about to say "No" when he felt a tingle inside. He looked at Eva carefully and he didn't understand why, but he felt a connection. He came down from his seat on the platform and sat beside her on the front row of the chairs in the meeting room. "Whatever is it?" he asked.

I gave Eva a loving, and encouraging look, and she plunged in at the deep end. "It may seem strange and very personal, the question I am going to ask you." She took a deep breath. "But. Were you adopted as a baby?"

Peter Wilson's eyes opened wide with surprise, and before he could think of a suitable reply he just said "Yes." He didn't know what to add.

Eva reached out and took his hand, and before he could withdraw it she said quietly, almost tremulously, "I believe that I am your birth mother. When I was just seventeen I gave birth to a baby boy on the fourth of April, in 1964. I was unmarried and I named him Pierre after his father, his French father." She gave a small sob, and continued. "He was taken away from me after only a few days, and he was given to an adoption agency who placed him with, I hope, a loving married couple. I believe that you are my long lost child, Pierre."

"O.M.G!" He exclaimed. "Can this be true? Are you really my mother? I was told by my parents that I was adopted. And I was told that my father was French. Wow! I've got to think about this."

He put his head in his hands and lent forward, looking at the floor. "My mother! Is this true?" He lifted his head and looked at her, closely. "Shall we both take a DNA test to confirm it, although I already feel it in my bones that you are right." He paused for a moment. "And my father, what happened to him?" he asked.

"That's a long story for another time," said Eva. "But I do believe that you met him by chance several years ago. Do you remember your forty-fourth birthday?"

"Yes. I remember meeting a chap on the South Downs. It was his birthday, too. And he was singing the Beatles song *When I'm sixty-four*. Was that him? I knew that there was something strange in that meeting. But, we separated and went on our own ways. We didn't swap any details, and after I was home and thinking about the morning, and I remember that I wished that we arranged to meet up for a beer or something. But it was too late. Wow!" he said again. "My dad!"

"Did you have a happy childhood with your parents?" Eva asked, timidly.

"Oh, yes!" He smiled. "They were loving and fun to be with when I was a boy. Unfortunately, they divorced when I was fifteen. But I still see them both."

"I'm so glad," said Eva.

"You didn't say any more about my father, but I do feel a presence. Are you together now? Is he waiting outside?" Peter looked around the room, looking for someone to step out maybe?

"What would you say? Would you laugh at me if I were to say that your father died recently, and he is now a ghost?"

"A ghost!" He laughed. Then, he looked strangely at Eva. "Is he really a ghost? Is he here with you?" He looked all around again. And then, St Peter gave me the gift of revealing myself. It shortened my time on Earth, but it was so worthwhile. "Wow!" he said, again. "I think that I can see him."

I showed my visible self for a few seconds, and then I was shimmering, getting ready to depart from this world. I could feel my power fading rapidly. "Eva," I said, with all the strength I had left. "Eva. I love you. And I am so happy that I have been able to unite you with our son. Goodbye, Pierre. Goodbye, my Darling."

And I was gone, leaving an astounded mother and son vowing to meet up the very next day and talk about *everything*.

I returned to St Peter who was waiting at Heaven's Golden Gates. "Thank you so much for giving me this last chance to make things right." I said as he was waving me through. "Well done!" was all he said. And then. "You have earned your place in Heaven now."

April 2014, Beachy Head

My name is Arlita Robson. I was forty-eight years old and a very wealthy widow, when I first met Jim Foster.

He was so dazzlingly different from my lovely John, who had been an executive in the oil business. He had been very loving, very quiet, and very unadventurous except for the fabulous holidays we had had together all around the world. We were married for thirty years, and we had a beautiful home in South Kensington, London, and another on the South Downs, near Alfriston. When we were at home in London, we very rarely went out. John only liked classical music for entertainment. He hated social evenings with colleagues, neighbours and the few friends that we had, and during the thirty years of our marriage I had got used to our semi-secluded way of life. I was always quite content.

Some months after John had passed away, I met Jim. I was having a rare night out with my friend Chris, in Rules Restaurant in Covent Garden. Chris and I had been friends since our schooldays in Roedean College, near Brighton. We had grown up together in that school. And what fun we had had as naughty teenagers when we slipped away from college to visit nightclubs and the like in Brighton. How many times had we been put in detention together? We knew each other inside out. All our best points and all our foibles. She had been one of the few people who had been welcomed into our London home.

And now she had been the one who had stood by me during all those months of my John's illness and death. How I valued all the care and love she had given which had helped me so much while I was grieving. It was she who had gently brought me back to life.

So, there we were having our quiet night out in Rules, and Jim was also there. He was part of a noisy group who were, I think, celebrating someone's birthday. Chris and I asked him very nicely if they would turn the volume down. He just shrugged his shoulders and mouthed "sorry!" It was an evening completely spoiled by the brash and selfish behaviour of strangers.

Two weeks later, I met Jim again, quite by chance, in Harrods. I was in the Food Hall buying some of their delicious chicken roulade, when someone whispered in my ear "good choice." I spun around and there he was. Cheerful, smiling and apologising for the noise he and his group had been making in the restaurant.

"Sorry about your spoilt evening," he said, with a grin. An unapologetic grin. "It was Verity's birthday, you know," as if I knew who Verity was.

"And why should I be interested in Verity's birthday? I don't even know who she is." I asked. Very straight faced.

"Coo! What sort of world do you live in, if you don't know Verity?" he put on the look of someone who is completely taken aback. "She is only the front singer of the rock band *The Red Cherries*. Surely, you have heard of them?"

I shook my head. "Can't say that I have!"

"Well! That's hard to believe. Verity and the Red Cherries are world famous. Just like The Rolling Stones. Maybe, you have heard of them?" He asked sarcastically. "Anyway, The Cherries are doing a show in the Dome next week." He said, with another big grin on his face. "Would you like to come as my guest? By the way, my name is Jim Foster."

Something was making me break down the icy barrier that I had instantly put up on seeing him again. I was very hesitant. "Well, my name is Arlita Robson. And I'm not sure that I like rock bands," I told him.

"Arlita! What a lovely name," he said. "Then go on. Give it a go."

He could see that I was weakening. He became very insistent, and I began to feel an awakening in my soul. I hadn't been out to see a modern show of any sort for years. Apart from a few special visits to The Royal Opera House, John and I didn't go to theatres at all. And a pop show! Never! Not even with Chris when we were young. Although, we did join the girls in the Common Room to listen to The Rolling Stones records, and were duly told off for doing so!

I looked at Jim Foster. I was tempted, but I was still hesitant. "OK," I agreed. "If you take me there." Now, why did I say that?

"Of course!" he exclaimed. "I'll pick you up, and you'll have the best seat in the house."

Unfortunately, the *best* seat in the house, was also the noisiest seat in the house! I wouldn't say that I hated the show, but I certainly wasn't keen to see another. But, Jim was so enthusiastic about his show that he did awaken in me the pleasure of the fun days of my youth. Jim Foster was totally different to anyone or anything I had known my life. To begin with I didn't like him very much. He was flashy, bossy and was never at a loss for words.

I couldn't understand why I didn't just cut him off! As the manager of what was, indeed, a famous pop group, The Red Cherries, he had all sorts of contacts in the world of show business. I was dazzled, even excited. From the first date, he took me everywhere. Shows, parties in places like The Shard, weekend parties in fabulous country houses. My head was spinning. As well as stars of the pop world, I was also meeting stars of stage and screen. I grew to like this new life that I had, sort of, been drawn into, and I grew to like Jim.

I told Chris all about him, including the pop world and parties that I had been to. She met him several times when she joined us for lunch. Always somewhere glitzy, somewhere slightly trashy. And she didn't like him. She didn't like him at all. She warned me off. "He is so insincere. I don't know what you see in him." She said after the fourth time that she had met him. "He's brash. He's a bit crazy. And what does he want with you?"

"What?" I jumped at her. "Do you think that he only wants me for my money?" I was quite angry. "So, you think that I am too old for him. That I have lost my sense of fun and youthfulness?"

"Don't get cross with me, darling," she said in a soothing voice. "He *is* ten years younger than you, and I just don't want to see you hurt!"

Her voice didn't soothe me. Nor her opinions. Just the opposite. "You're jealous." I lashed out at her. "You're just jealous." I repeated. "You're a dried up old prune!!" I was sorry as soon as the words had come out of my mouth. I stopped as she started to gather up her coat and handbag. "I'm so sorry," I said. "I didn't mean…"

But the apology was not being accepted. Chris just glared at me and left without saying another word.

I so regretted upsetting my best friend. I was ashamed of myself, and I phoned her several times trying so hard to persuade her that I was indeed so sorry for what I had said to her. She was unforgiving.

But now, I was ready to love again. And, I thought, I was in heaven when Jim asked me to marry him. I said "yes" without any hesitation at all. I persuaded him to not make it the big, grand affair that I knew he wanted. No film stars, or rock stars in attendance. But even given an invitation to a simple Registry Office wedding, my dearest friend Chris made excuses, and stayed away. But I was still happy. As happy as I had been in the first years of my marriage with John.

Although, she had not come to my wedding, a few weeks later I did make it up with Chris, and I was delighted to have her back in my everyday life. In fact, when I made my new will, as I was advised to do by my solicitor, Chris was a big part of it. I did, of course, leave the bulk of my estate to Jim, but to Christine Angelina Montacute (Chris's full name) I left my lovely house on the South Downs, near Alfriston. I left it to her with all the contents. And, I also specified a gift to her of two small paintings by Picasso, which had been given to my father by the artist himself, in the 1930s.

But, my happiness didn't last long. I didn't want to go out to all Jim's rock gigs. I went to some of them, particularly the overseas ones to America and Canada. And I was getting used to the loudness of the music. And, yes, I even grew to like some of the songs. So different from my previous life with the music of Mozart, Beethoven and Verdi etc. for our exclusive entertainment.

After a few months I began to feel unwell. I seemed to have continuous digestive problems. I fell sick for a week or two, and then I would get better again. Back to normal. In all my forty-eight years, I had never been a sickly one. I had always been so fortunate with my health. I had always had a superb constitution. After being sick, I was completely well again. Then, all of a sudden, the sickness came back. Again. My doctor was puzzled. The specialists at the private hospital were puzzled. I was tested for gastroenteritis, gastric ulcers, bowel cancer and even leukaemia. Nothing.

Then I was well again, and this pattern started to repeat. I was well and happy for a couple of months, and then the sickness would return. The periods of sickness got longer, and the times of full health and happiness got shorter.

Chris, who had eventually forgiven me for my outrageous outburst, came to see me regularly. "I'm sure that it has something to do with Jim," she kept saying. "You're never as ill as this when he is away with the Cherries."

"Oh! Don't keep blaming him," I said. I was no longer cross with her, just a little exasperated.

"I'm not saying that he is deliberately making you ill," she insisted. "But, since all the doctors can't find anything, there must be some sort of stress in your relationship that causes you to be unwell."

"I don't know, Chris," I said. "I'm just too tired to think or to worry about it. I love Jim, and I don't want us to divorce."

"You don't have to divorce, but you could try living apart for a while," insisted Chris. "You could give him this house and go to stay in your country house on the Downs, in Sussex. The one near the sea. I could even come and stay with you for a while. See that you are settled in. It's not far from Roedean. We could pretend that we are back at school again," she said with a chuckle.

"Thanks, darling," I said, wearily. "I'll think about it." That was all the response that I could summon up.

We didn't have a chance to discuss the idea further, because three weeks later I was dead! No evidence of maltreatment. No post-mortem. Just a simple service and cremation! And I was gone!

But, I wasn't. I found that I had not departed this world. I had become a ghost. No haunting! No wailing! Not even a spook covered in a white sheet! Just me hanging around our London home, not saying *boo* to a goose.

I asked myself why I was still in this world. What was I doing? What did the spirits ethereal expect me to find? So, after my cremation I followed Jim back to my house in South Kensington. In fact, I actually sat on his lap in the funeral car on the way home! And I giggled to myself. I planned to stay undiscovered in the house. I didn't want to reveal myself to Jim. I wanted to watch what he did.

The first thing he did was really strange. He started to wash and then break all the dishes and plates that he had served me with when I was too sick to cook meals. Too sick to get out of bed. He broke all my glasses. I cried about that because some of them had been given to me and John as wedding presents all those years ago. I was sure that they had been valuable antiques. Then, even more strange, Jim gathered up all the pots and pans that he had used to cook food or soup for me, and he took them, a few at a time, to the various charity shops that had sprung up recently in the South Ken area.

Why was he doing that? I asked myself. Had he been giving me food that was bad or off? No! Could it be? Had he been poisoning me? Did he find a substance that could imitate the symptoms of all the stomach upsets that I had been having for the last year of my life?

Had he murdered me?

My suspicion was confirmed when six weeks later Verity moved in!

"You did it!" she exclaimed. "This is all ours now."

"Not so much of the *ours* young lady," said Jim. "It was all left to me, thank you very much!"

"Except, of course, for the house down in Sussex," giggled the Verity. "And how come you didn't get Arlita to leave you those two Picasso's? They must be worth at least a million pounds."

"And the rest!" said Jim, who had been my darling husband, with pouting lips and scowling face. "But at least there was enough cash in savings and investments to save the Cherries. Arlita never knew how near we were to bankruptcy. I didn't want to tell her. To worry her. We've now got enough to push and promote this new song that was written by Goldsmith and Evans. Let's get you back on the top spot."

"Yea," laughed Verity. "'I Could Kill For You.' Very appropriate." She started to hum the song.

I was staggered. Chris had been right after all. He *had* married me for my fortune. And killed me so he could promote a bloody pop song! Outrageous!

"So, tell me," she asked. "How did you do it?"

"I was super careful," said Jim, almost in a whisper. Did he think that anyone could possibly overhear him? He didn't know that his darling wife, in her new ghostly self, could hear every word he said! "I used the old-fashioned poison – arsenic. Real Agatha Christie stuff!"

"Wow!" Verity exclaimed. "Where on earth did you get that from? And how did you do it?"

"I started by giving her miniscule amounts." He did his usual fatuous grin, which now looked like a horror mask to me. "Just to give her a tiny tummy upset. Then, I would stop for a week or two, giving her time to recover. And, bit by bit, I increased the amounts of arsenic. Mostly by tiny drops in her home-made soup." He laughed. "She simply adored my home-made soup, and the sicker she got the more she asked me to make some for her."

Verity stared at him, as if she were expecting him try it on with her, too. "I can't believe it. I don't believe it. I thought that you were joking. And I'm sure that those doctors that she consulted would have been able to detect poison in her blood samples."

Jim laughed out loud. "Ha! Ha! Got you," he cried. "Of course, I didn't kill her. I have no idea what was making her sick." He gave an empty sort of chuckle.

Verity looked at him as though she couldn't quite believe him, and said no more. I was now convinced that he had murdered me. And I was surprised that Verity had nothing to do with it. I always knew that she had fancied Jim, and thought that he was disgusting to have married such an old woman. I had, even, heard her jokingly describe his lovemaking with the 'old bag', as she called me. "Was it a one or two paper bag job?" She asked.

But, how could I make Jim pay for his crime? I couldn't go to the police. Not exactly in the powers of a ghost. But, I suspected that although they were unable to see me or feel my presence, I thought that I could influence their thoughts and ideas. I hoped that I merely had to suggest something directly to one of them, or both of them, and then they would think that it was their own idea.

I tried it out. "How about I make us a nice cup of tea," I said pointedly at Verity.

Immediately, she responded. "How about I make us a nice cup of tea," she said to Jim.

"Tea? Tea?" He looked at Verity as though she had gone mad. "Whatever are you talking about? It's eight o'clock in the evening. You know that I only ever drink tea at breakfast. If you want to make a drink for me, then I'll have a gin and tonic, thank you!"

It was Verity's turn to look dazed. "Did I really say tea? Why ever would I suggest that. You know that I hate tea!"

Then, I looked directly at Jim. "I don't think that I want to go to bed with you tonight. Why don't you just go home?"

And, he immediately repeated the same words to Verity. I don't even think he knew that he was saying it. She reacted immediately.

"What do you mean 'go home'?" she said, angrily. "You know that I have given up my flat. I live here now, don't I? And if you're going to be nasty, I don't want to go to bed with you, either." She got up from the couch, and flounced out of the room, slamming the door behind her.

"Verity! Verity!" Jim called after her. "Come back, darling. I don't know what got into me. I didn't mean anything that I have just said." There was puzzlement all over his face, as Verity opened the door a crack and poked her face through.

"Well, I don't know what's going on," said Jim, all his grinning expression banished. He looked pale and shocked. "First you say something silly about tea. Then, I said something totally unreal about not wanting you." He leaned forward and put his head in his hands, as Verity came to sit next to him, and put her arms about his shoulders.

Then, he tried to laugh it off in his usual way. "OK!" He sat up, grabbed hold of Verity, kissed her and said with the old grin back on his face. "OK! Joke over.

Perhaps, the old witch is haunting us. Whooooo!" he laughed, making ghost noises while waving his arms about.

Verity, though, she laughed too, still looked somewhat shaken and worried. Their evening eventually returned to normal as they started discussing the new song which they both hoped would put The Red Cherries back on the top of the charts.

I decided that I had had such a success with my giving them thoughts and ideas, that I would hold back until such a time as it would be advantageous to bring Jim down. So, much against my will, I stood by to watch their conversation and interaction. I was also quite tearful as I saw Jim using the same words and loving gestures with Verity as he had used with me. Even though I was a ghost, it still hurt.

The following day, the members of the Cherries arrived to discuss the planned recording and release of 'I Could Kill For You.' "I think that we should make a video of the song and release it on YouTube," said William, the lead guitar player.

"Yes," agreed Jim. "I have been thinking about that, too. Now, where should we set it?"

"A murder scene somewhere," says Alan, the drummer.

"In a dark room," suggests William.

I looked hard at Jim. "Why not on the top of Beachy Head? Verity could push someone off!"

Jim looked at all the members of The Cherries. "I know," he said. "Why not on the top of Beachy Head. Verity could push someone off."

"Wow! That sounds like a winner to me," said Alan. "We could get all our kit up there, no problem. But I think that we had better not actually chuck someone over the edge!" And everyone laughed.

"Seriously, I think that it's a great idea," said Jim. "But I don't think that we can just turn up and film there, so I'll look into getting all the permits needed from the local authorities."

Jim had to work quickly so that they didn't lose the impetus of the new song. After two weeks of repeated recordings and some messing about at the recording studio, he finally had the version of 'I Could Kill For You' that he thought would be a winner. And the following week there they all were, assembled at the top of Beachy Head cliff near Eastbourne. They looked at the memorial stone recording some of the suicides who had jumped off in recent times, along with the telephone number of the Samaritans. In the hope that some lives might be saved with a sympathetic phone call.

I had hitched a ride in the back of Jim's car, and I was carefully watching the proceedings. The filming was going well. Verity and the Cherries were doing a splendid mime to the song. Then, I looked directly at Jim, and said, "Don't you think that we would have an even better effect if I stand at the very edge, and Verity acts as if push me over the cliff."

Then Jim, who had been doing the directing, looked at the cameraman and said, "Don't you think that we would have an even better effect if I stand at the very edge, and Verity acts as if to tip me over. Then, we could push a dummy dressed like me over the cliff."

"Wow, that's a good idea," said Jonathan the cameraman, "but we don't have time to go about getting a dummy made up to look like you."

"Well, it was just an idea," said Jim. He was a bit disappointed. "I know," he said, "let's give it a dummy run, as it were." And he gave a huge belly laugh at his own joke.

I watched as the rest of them joined in. They were playing around, and Verity said, "Do you mean like this?" She acted a huge push. She didn't touch Jim at all, and film shown at the coroner's court showed exactly that. However, a sudden gust of wind came from nowhere. Well, just a little puff from me! And he was gone!

I met him at the shoreline. I could see him, and, at last, he could see me. "Are we quits now?" I asked, with a smug look on my face.

He was shocked. "Arlita! What's happened here? Why can I see you? It can't be you." I pointed to the cliff behind him. He looked around and saw his crumpled body on the rocks at the bottom of the cliff. He had fallen five hundred and thirty feet to his death.

"I don't understand," he said. "I can't be dead. And what do you mean by saying that we are quits? Are we both ghosts?"

"Yes, we are," I said. "And you killed me, so now I have killed you!"

"What do you mean when you say that I killed you?" He sounded astonished.

"I heard you," I said. "I heard you tell Verity that you fed me with arsenic. I saw you get rid of all my table china, my beautiful wine glasses, and all my pots and pans."

"Oh! You silly thing." He was shaken. "Of course, I didn't kill you. How could you even think that I wanted you dead? I loved you, and I would never have got away with giving you arsenic. All those tests that were taken would have found arsenic immediately if there had been anything of that nature in your blood. Besides, the doctors told me after you had died that they were about to test you for pancreatic cancer. That's what you died of. Not arsenic poisoning!"

"Oh my God. Why didn't anyone tell me? And why did you tell Verity that you had poisoned me?" It was now my turn to be astonished. "I so loved you, and you were both mocking me. Calling me an old bag."

"You silly goose," said Jim. He seemed to have accepted that he was dead. Or, maybe he was still just stunned. "I really did love you. And I was fed up telling them all, especially Verity, that I loved you. She always believed that I had married you for your money."

"Didn't you?" I asked, sharply. "Then why *did* you get rid of all my chinaware, my crystal glasses, and the saucepans?"

"No! I didn't kill you. And I got rid of your china and stuff in a fit of anger. I was so angry that I had lost you. All that stuff reminded me of your illness and death." He sighed. "I loved you, truly. I loved your seriousness. And I loved bringing you out of your shell," he said, with true sincerity. "Under all that prim and proper façade, you were bursting out to be young and have fun."

"Oh!" I gasped. "Whatever have I done?"

"Whatever you've done, it's too late to undo, my girl." I didn't understand why he seemed to have his usual grin on his face.

"Why aren't you angry with me? You don't want to be a ghost like me, do you?" I asked. "I was too revengeful, and that's why the spirit world wouldn't accept me." I sighed. "They wouldn't let me through Heaven's Gate." I started to cry.

"Darling. You see why it is that I loved you," he said. He wanted to put his arms around me. But, of course, he couldn't. "You were so down to earth. So practical. And I thought that you were funny. I was truly saddened when all that sickness stuff started. And no one could fix it. All your money couldn't fix it. And now it's my turn to have something that can't be fixed."

"Why? What? What are you talking about?" I asked. I stopped crying. If a ghost can be in a daze, then I was in a real daze.

"I've got, or rather I had, cancer," said my dear boy. "I had it in my lungs. Caused by all those years of smoking, I suppose. The doctors said that I had only six months to live."

"Darling! How horrible!" I exclaimed.

"So, you did me a favour really." His charming grin was back on his face. "I don't think that I would have had the courage to throw myself off when all the pain kicked in. But, I guess, you did it for me. How did you do it?"

"I am ashamed to say that my ghostly powers were strong enough to suggest to you that you came here to make that video film," I admitted. "As for the rest, I was able to draw up enough puff to blow you over." I was devastated with shame.

"Don't worry, my love," he said. "I really did mean it that I am glad that I died quickly, and relatively painless..."

"Sorry..." I butted in. "I'm so sorry."

"...death." He looked down at his ghostly self, and laughed. "And, by the way, I didn't leave all your fortune to Verity. Most of it will be going to the Music for All Charity, and UNICEF." He gave me one of his biggest, goofiest smiles. "Don't be sorry, my darling Arlita. I'm here with you now." And he came to me in the best way that ghosts can hug. We just merged into each other.

May 2015, Leicester Cathedral

Last May, I was in Enfield, London, visiting my younger brother, Alan and his wife, Jane. Alan is six years younger than me, so I think of Alan as the baby of the family. Alan is young and quite lively, and he is happily employed as the manager of a DIY store in Enfield. Jane is a school teacher who is always in a rush with her long blond hair flying behind her, tied back in a ponytail. They live in a lovely, modernised end of terrace Victorian house with a surprisingly large and very pretty garden. When Jane has any free time, she spends it mostly doing up her garden, keeping herself very fit with daily snipping here and there at her plants and shrubs, and looking after a large natural pond. At that time, in May, it was full of tadpoles, some very late frog's spawn, and loads of newts. She was looking forward to having numerous baby frogs which, come summer, would be hopping all around her garden.

Alan and I are on opposite sides of the same coin. Whereas, I have been a barrister, specialising in criminal prosecutions, for most of my working life, and instinctively think of being on the right side of the law, Alan has tended to be a bit of a naughty boy at times. He has never been deeply in trouble with the law, but he often mixes with the wrong sort and gets within a whisker of being dangerously near to being arrested for a criminal offence.

The second love of Alan's life, after Jane, is his hobby, football. Always football, and I, half-heartedly, share his enthusiasm, but I don't follow a particular team. He is a very keen Spurs fan, and with his yearly season ticket he goes to see every match that he can, both home and away. This time, while I was staying with Alan, he asked me to join him when he went to Leicester, to see Leicester City versus Tottenham Hotspur. As I have said, I know very little about football, but I was happy to accompany him.

For some time I had been quite eager to visit the Cathedral in Leicester to see the new tombstone of Richard III. After the discovery of his body under a carpark in Leicester in 2012, his bones were transferred to Leicester Cathedral.

And then, after some dispute between the Leicester Cathedral and York Minster, it was eventually decided that he should remain in Leicester, and a modern tomb was built over his bones which were reinterred in the Cathedral in 2015. So, Alan and I agreed to go on the early train so that I could become the typical tourist, while he was having a few pre-match beers with his pals.

It was a beautiful May morning, sunny and warm with that lovely fresh springtime smell in the air. The early train arrived in Leicester just after 10 a.m. Alan went off to meet up with his mates, and I said that I would join them later. It was, supposedly, just a fifteen-minute walk to the Cathedral, but because of painful arthritis in my left hip it took forty minutes for me to get there. I expected the Cathedral to be busy because it was match day, but I found it relatively quiet. On arrival, I had a quiet sit down to rest my sore hip, before joining a few visitors who were gathered around the new tomb of Richard III.

I contemplated it, and I couldn't quite decide whether I loved it or hated it. It didn't look at all royal to me, but it is grand. In a very modernistic style, it is a huge block of highly polished Swaledale rock, shaped in the form of a shortened coffin. It has a simple cross about 1 cm wide and 15 cm deep cut in it from side to side and top to bottom. This pale block is sits on top of a squat dark marble plinth, which has along with Richard's name, his dates, and his badge, has his sad moto – 'loyalté me lie', meaning loyalty binds me, written around the base. I say a sad motto because before Richard became King, I remember reading that he had been a steadfast and loyal supporter of his older brother, King Edward IV. He had been ten years younger than King Edward and having trained hard, he had become a brilliant soldier and commander, at only twenty years old, enabling him to keep safe for his brother, all the Scottish borderlands and Northern England.

After taking another quick sit-down, I walked away from the group of the visitors at the tomb, and headed down the side aisle towards the east window where I saw more tourists gathered. I was curious to see what was catching their attention and found that it was an unusual free-standing stained-glass window, which caught the light from a plain glass window above. I was surprised to see that it had very recognisable depictions of Richard III and his wife, Anne Neville. It was quite beautiful, and I thought very appropriate to have it there. Underneath, it was an information board saying that it was a copy of a window in Cardiff Castle in Wales. Next to the window, there was also a copy of the portrait of Richard III which I have seen hanging in the National Portrait Gallery in London.

The two of them together, the portrait and the stained glass window, gave me a real feeling that the tomb did after all belong here, and King Richard III had been given royal status, at last. I looked at the portrait which showed Richard putting on or taking off a gold ring on the little finger of his right hand. Immersed in deep thought, I tried to analyse the face. A strangely sad face. Perhaps, the face of a man who had lost both his wife and his only son within months of his becoming King? Perhaps, the ring was the wedding band from his dead wife, Anne?

Suddenly, I felt the presence of someone or something standing beside me. Thinking that it was one of the people who had stood with me at the gravestone, I started to say, "What do you think…?" Then, I turned to see who it was, and oh my goodness, it was he himself, King Richard III looking just like his portrait, standing right there, next to me! I nearly jumped out of my skin. I didn't realise at first that the man at my elbow was not real. He was a ghost! A royal ghost! I looked around and it was quite clear that no one else could see him, although a young woman in a pretty pink summer dress, shivered and moved away.

After, I had pulled myself together I spoke to him in a whisper, because I didn't want the people in the vicinity to think that I was talking to myself. I asked this vision, "Are you really King Richard?"

"Of course, I am," he replied, quite brusquely. "Otherwise, I wouldn't be wearing this fur-lined and gold-slashed gown, would I? And how do you like my gold and jewelled chain of office, my badge of Kingship?" He gave me a long, knowing look to make sure that I was listening to him.

"I'm so glad," he continued, "that you can see and hear me, because for the most part, I walk around the Cathedral when it is busy and when it is quiet at night, and no one can see me. Occasionally, people feel my presence but they're not quite sure why they feel odd or cold. They, then, shiver and walk away, just like that pretty girl did a moment ago.

But, you're the first being I've been able to have contact with since my bones were discovered under that car park. A car park of all the undignified places!" He sounded very offended. "One which was covering the remains of the Greyfriars church where my body was buried after the battle of Bosworth Field, in 1485."

"Oh gosh!" I said, astonished at what was happening to me. I could see this stranger who looked just like the King in the portrait. An apparition? But I couldn't touch him, or even smell him. Why, I asked myself, am I seeing a ghost?

What is it about me that is attracting the attention a ghost? I shrugged my shoulders, and then thinking that I might be able to have a chat with him, I sat down on a pew that seemed to be out of earshot of the tourists. If he were to join me then, then he might consent to being asked a few questions about his life.

As someone interested in history, I knew that I would never get a chance like this, again. I beckoned to him, and he came and sat down beside me. I was hoping that I might be able to find out more about the life of King Richard III. But, I didn't have a chance to ask him a question because he jumped in first. Not with a question of his own, but with a protestation!

"I didn't do it, you know. I didn't do it." He said in a sharp, almost waspish voice.

I was startled. "What?" I asked. "What didn't you do?"

"You know!" he exclaimed. "The children. I didn't do it."

I was flustered. "What children? What didn't you do?" I asked again.

It was his turn to be flustered. "Haven't you read any of your English history books? Surely you must know that I have been accused of, no saddled with, the murder of the 'Princes in the Tower.'"

Then, the penny dropped. Of course, the most heinous crime in English history. Richard III killed his brother's two children; twelve-year-old Prince Edward, who was due to be crowned King Edward V, and his younger brother, nine-year-old Prince Richard, Duke of York. He had them killed so that he, himself, could claim the throne and become King. Wicked King Richard! Evil King Richard! Monstrous King Richard!

It was almost as if I were back in the crown court where the arrested suspect usually protested loud and long that *it wasn't me wot done it!* How many of those court sessions have I sat in on over the years? How many of those arrested had crumbled at the end of my cross-examination and admitted their guilt. Was this interview with my royal ghost going to be the same?

"I remember! You did do it!" I protested. "You wanted to become King, so you had those two little boys killed. Yes, I remember all about it! You kept well out of the way, fighting invaders in the Scottish border lands, and you had one of your followers, was it a man called Tyrrell I seem to remember, or someone else, smother them as they slept in their beds?"

"You see, everyone does accuse me, even down to the details of how it was done." said my ghost of King Richard, in a profoundly weary voice.

"Well," I was instantly alert. Could I get the inside story of a notorious bit of English history? "If you didn't do it, then who did? And why does everyone say that it was you? And why were the two boys in the Tower of London in the first place. I thought it was a fortress in which they held traitors and other criminals?" I was getting a few strange looks from tourists passing by, so I got out my mobile and pretended that I was having a conversation on the phone. Richard took no notice and carried on talking.

"The Tower did hold traitors, but it was also a royal stronghold with royal accommodation, and the boys were there to protect them from their uncle Rivers, who was the Queen's brother. He wanted to usurp the role that had been appointed to me in their father's will. That I was to become the protector of the young King. In other words, to have the full powers of a King while Edward was still a minor. It was with his mother's agreement that I had them put the young King in the royal apartments at the Tower, to protect him. His mother who, afraid that there would be trouble between me and her rapacious relatives, had claimed sanctuary in Westminster Cathedral. Do you really think that if she had had any idea that I might harm her child, that she would not only have agreed to having the new King Edward V being kept safely in the Tower, but also have given me her younger son, Richard, who was named for me by the way, to be company for his brother?"

"Well, if you put them in the Tower for their safety, how come they were never seen again, and everyone thought that you killed them there?" I asked once more. I was being very brutal in my questioning. Almost like sitting in front of a high court judge.

"I did not," he protested, again. "This false accusation is all the fault of your Shakespeare! Your world famous, wonderful, bloody William Shakespeare." He said, sarcastically.

"How can that be?" I spluttered. I knew then that this wasn't going to be an easy ride like some of the criminals who just gave in under determined questioning. This was a killer defending himself. To be fair, I should say a suspected killer. Was it ever definitely proved that Richard III had killed his nephews? I thought that maybe I should take a less accusatory tone.

"It was hearsay what Shakespeare wrote about me. How he described me," said Richard.

"Remind me. How did he describe you?" I asked.

"Haven't you read or seen his play? How wicked, how twisted and evil he made me. Unable to walk properly upright, with a humped back and a withered arm. I was a soldier, for goodness sake! For years, I had been a soldier, and a very successful soldier too. Always fighting to control the North of England for my brother the King. How could I ever have done so with a body as described by Mr Shakespeare? Plus, all the evil plots and killings that he invented and put down to me. The killing of our brother George, as well as the murder of my brother's sons. My name became a synonym for villainy!" He sounded quite shocked as well as angry. "I thought everyone here was familiar with his works."

"Not really," I admitted. "I haven't studied Shakespeare since I was a schoolboy about forty years ago. His plays were written in old English, which I always found difficult to understand."

"Old English to you!" Richard exclaimed. "At the time, the play was written the language was too modern for me. It's taken me four hundred years to learn how to speak English as you all do today."

"What do you mean?" I asked. "It was written in your time, wasn't it?"

"You have no idea, have you?" Richard sighed. He was sounding very weary again. "Do you know when I was alive? And do you know when Shakespeare was alive?"

"What do you mean?" I asked again. I had never really thought about the dates of when Richard III was alive and when Shakespeare wrote his plays.

"I was born in 1452, and I was killed in 1485 – I was only thirty-two years old," said Richard, and again he sighed deeply.

"And Shakespeare?" I was forgetting to act as a barrister questioning a suspect, and I was becoming genuinely interested and very curious again.

"Shakespeare was born in 1564…"

"Oh!" I interrupted. "Over one hundred years after you!" I whistled through my teeth. "So! He didn't know you at all."

"No!"

It took me a few minutes to take in the implications of those dates. "So where did Shakespeare get the information from to write his play?" I asked quite tentatively.

"He got it, almost word for word, from one of England's recognised and beloved saints." I could sense that he was stringing me out, almost teasing me.

"A saint?" I didn't know that England had many saints. "Who was it?" I was now getting desperate to know.

"Sir Thomas More."

"Sir Thomas More!" I repeated. I dug deeply into my memory banks. "I remember him!" I said at last. "He was at one time the best friend of Henry VIII, who later had him executed for obeying the Pope and not agreeing to the annulment Henry's marriage to Katherine of Aragon, or to recognise their divorce."

"That's the one," laughed Richard. "Thomas More who born in 1478, and was made a saint over four hundred years later, in 1956. It was in your own lifetime, or just before you were born! St Thomas More who never told a lie, and who died for the truth in 1535!"

"I can't believe it!" I gasped. And I had another little calculation. "He must have been only seven years old when you died! So! How was it that Shakespeare got it 'word for word' from Thomas More, as you said?"

"Sir Thomas More wrote a history of Richard III. Me!" said Richard, emphatically. "And in it, he wrote that I had the Princes in the Tower killed in order to claim the throne of England."

"So, let me get this straight in my head," I had a good think. "You became King after the sudden death of your older brother, Edward IV, in 1483…"

"Yes." This time, it was Richard who interrupted. "And I was legitimately crowned King after my brothers' two sons, the so-called Princes in the Tower, were disqualified because my brother, Edward, had been contracted to another woman, whose name was Lady Eleanor Butler, before he married Elizabeth Woodville. Consequently, all his children were declared illegitimate. So, you see, I had no need to kill them. My elder brother George was dead, and his son was excluded from any succession to the throne by his father's 'Attainder.' Hence, the throne was rightfully mine!"

"How did that happen?" I asked. "It was very convenient for you, wasn't it?" I was once more the suspicious barrister.

Richard pulled a face and looked as if I had insulted him. "There was a man of God, a certain Bishop Stillington of Bath, who came forward just after my brother died, and swore that he, himself, had conducted this earlier marriage of my brother Edward to Eleanor Butler. And that he had documents to prove it."

Richard was then sounding weary again, as if he had told this story again and again. "Anyway, it was all brought up before Parliament and the members agreed. A Bill called Titulus Regius was drawn up, and Edward's children were proclaimed illegitimate and officially barred from any claim to the throne."

I was puzzled. "So, how was it that the sainted Thomas More, who was only seven years old when you and your army lost the Battle of Bosworth Field to Henry Tudor, knew all this and was able to write your history? It could only have been from hearsay."

"You've got it! That is the crux of the matter. Hearsay!" said Richard, rather triumphantly. "Do you take hearsay as truthful evidence at court?" He asked.

While he carried on talking, I wondered how he knew that I was a barrister.

"It was one of my bitter enemies, one John Moreton, Bishop of Ely, who told his version of my life to Thomas More. This was when Thomas, who was twelve years old at that time, served for two years as a page-boy in the Bishop's house."

"I take it," I said, dryly, "that Bishop Morton soon wormed his way into Henry Tudor's favour when he became King!"

"Yes, and he was well rewarded too," said Richard. "Surprise, surprise. Who do think became Archbishop of Canterbury soon after Henry Tudor became King Henry VII?"

"And what was in it for the new King Henry?" I asked.

"Justification!" Richard cried out loud, although, luckily, no one but I could hear him. "Justification!" he repeated. "Proof that I was such a wicked and vile King, a murderer and a usurper, and that I deserved to be killed. That I had had no right to have taken the throne from Edward's son." He paused, and then said flatly. "And the people believed him. Believed him, and took him to their hearts, especially when he married Elizabeth, the sister of the two missing Princes."

"Joining the Yorkists and Lancastrians together." I remarked. I was softening my attitude towards him as I recalled the image of the Tudor rose. Red outer petals and white on the inner ring symbolising the union of York and Lancaster. "So, he married the now bastardised daughter of Edward IV. How did that go down?"

"She was no longer called illegitimate because he revoked the Titulus Regius Bill and ordered that all copies of it were to be destroyed." Richard almost spat out.

"But, at least one copy must have survived for us to know today what was included in the Bill," I mused.

Richard was triumphant again, he almost giggled. I could see that in spite of the long passage of time, King Richard was still highly emotional and changed his mood from minute to minute. So, unlike the dark angry character painted by Shakespeare. "Yes," he said, with a laugh in his voice. "A copy was eventually found in the Tower, of all places. But it was too late to salvage my reputation," he ended, sadly.

I had another little think. I was digging deep into what little knowledge I had of Henry VII. "So," I puzzled "By revoking the Titulus Regius Bill, he made his bride to be, Elizabeth, legitimate once more." Then, another penny dropped. "That means that he also made her two brothers legitimate, too!"

"Splendid!" crowed Richard. "Now you realise that in doing so, Young Edward was made the rightful King, again. He couldn't have that. Therefore, it must have been Henry Tudor who made the two boys disappear, not me…! QED! Quod Erat Demonstrandum. That which needed to be demonstrated. Proof!"

I wasn't quite so sure that destroying the Titulus Regius absolved Richard of the murder, but I didn't say so. Instead, I asked, "did no one who had been on your side, on the side of the Yorkists, rise up against him? Or ask about the brothers then?"

"They didn't dare." Richard actually shuddered. "Did you know that after Henry Tudor became King Henry VII he had his lawyers make a law that found everyone who had supported me, guilty of treason, and therefore punishable by death?"

"Did he?" I knew nothing of what happened immediately after Henry Tudor became King.

"Yes!" Richard hissed at me. "And this is where his evilness shows. He declared that he was rightful King by 'right of conquest', and he dated this declaration from the day *before* the Battle of Bosworth Fields."

"What!" I exclaimed. "That meant that everyone who had fought for their rightful King at Bosworth Fields became guilty of treason!"

"So!" Richard was now exasperated. "Now, you must begin to ask yourself, just which one of us was evil and twisted? Was it me who had loyally, all my life dedicated myself to my older brother, the King and his family? Or was it the new King Henry, who had only the smallest legitimate claim to the throne, and who wanted all potential claimants from Edward IV's family, to disappear or die?"

I was curious. It was beginning to look like Richard was innocent after all. But I still felt inclined to play my role of prosecution council. "What hereditary claim did Henry Tudor have to the throne of England?"

Richard snorted. "His mother, Margaret Beaufort, was the bastard great granddaughter of the third son of Edward III, John of Gaunt, Duke of Lancaster. After his second wife died, John of Gaunt eventually married his long-time mistress, Katherine Swynford, by whom he had had four children. Whereas, my family line, all legitimate births by the way, came from the second son of Edward III, the Duke of York. Henry's father was a Welsh no-body called Jasper Tudor. John of Gaunt's bastard children were made legitimate by King Richard II, my ancestor and namesake, but in making them legitimate it was also ruled that they could never claim the throne of England. So, none of the Beaufort family were ever entitled to claim the throne."

I know that I was moving away from Richard's story, but I felt that I had to defend our greatest writer and poet. I said "you were damning Shakespeare a while ago, but he was really a very good writer! And yes, when he wrote his History Plays, he did distort so many of the facts, so many details were not true, but because they skirted around a basic truth, people believed in everything he wrote."

Richard pulled a long face as I paused and once more dug into my memory banks. I stopped being a barrister for a moment, and went into memory mode. "Do you know the speech of John of Gaunt in the history play of Richard II?" Richard shook his head.

It goes something like this, I said: "This royal throne of kings, this sceptred island. This earth of majesty, this seat of Mars." And he goes on about England being a demi-paradise, "This precious stone set in a silver sea…This blessed plot, this earth, this realm, this England!" I paused. "And an England worth fighting for," I mused. "I remember having to learn that speech when I was at school, and it made me proud to be English. To my shame, that is all I remember of it right now."

"Yes. We did, and you do now, live in an England worth fighting for. That Shakespeare of yours could write a good rousing speech," agreed Richard, "but what he wrote about me was so untrue it would have been laughed at by anyone who knew me, had he written it during my lifetime."

"I do know that John of Gaunt eventually married his mistress Katherine Swynford after all their children were born, but that didn't make them legitimate." I reflected. "Bye the way, talking of famous English writers, did you know that Katherine was also the sister of Phillipa, who was the wife of the medieval writer, Geoffrey Chaucer?"

Richard looked a little bored. "No, I didn't know that. But what's that got to do with anything? Let's get back to those lies which Morton, More and Shakespeare told or wrote about me."

I was getting the picture now. "OK." I agreed. Back to the courtroom! "So, it was in the interest of Henry Tudor, a Lancastrian, to get rid of all members of the York family who had a much better claim to the throne than he did – starting with the young King Edward V, and his brother Richard who were still in the Tower of London."

"Yes," sighed Richard. "And what better way explain the disappearance of the young King and his brother than to say that I murdered them both. He gets rid of the true claimants to the throne, he justifies his own claim, and at the same time he blackens my name for all time!"

Richard stood up and walked over, once more, to see the stained glass window showing himself and his wife Anne. He looked at her long and hard, and I could see the sadness and love in his eyes. He turned back to me and asked, "Do you know anything about my brother George, the Duke of Clarence? Shakespeare accused me of his murder too!"

Were we going off-track again? I accepted the challenge. "Wasn't he the one who was drowned in a barrel of wine?" I asked.

"Yes, he was found guilty of treason and condemned to death by our brother, King Edward," he said. "Not me!"

"How did that come about?" I asked. "I thought that the Yorkist in the Wars of the Roses had such a close and very strong family that it was the envy of the Lancastrians."

"Well," said Richard. "That was so, until Edward unexpectedly married Elizabeth Woodville. You see, we had strong entitlement to the throne of England, but Edward did not have the power and strength to hold the position. It was Richard, Earl of Warwick, who supported him and put him on the throne. He was the power behind the throne."

"Do you mean, Warwick, the Kingmaker?" I asked. "I had heard of him in my school history lessons, but I was never quite sure how or what he did to make Kings!"

Richard was getting into his stride now. He came back to the pew and once again sat down beside me. "The Earl of Warwick," he said, "was an extremely powerful man. He was one of the wealthiest men in the kingdom, and he owned vast estates in the north of England. He had not quite a standing army, but he controlled a huge and far-flung network of retainers. But he had no sons, only daughters and he wished to keep control of the King by using his daughters. Initially, he wanted his elder daughter, Isobel, to marry Edward. But as you know, Edward surprised everyone with his rushed and secret marriage to Elizabeth Woodville, which turned the powerful Earl against him."

"So, who did he marry her to?" I knew the answer, but I wanted to hear his explanation of these events that happened so long ago.

"He married her to our brother, George, who at that time was second in line to the throne."

"And didn't you marry her sister, Anne? That's her in the stained glass window, isn't it?" I was running almost as fast as he was in this recounting of his family story.

"Yes," sighed Richard. "Anne. My lovely Anne. We were all brought up together at Middleham Castle, you know."

"Where is that, and who do you mean by all?" I asked.

"Middleham Castle, my favourite castle, is in Yorkshire. It was the family home of the Earl of Warwick. Anne inherited it after the Earl died. George, my elder brother, and I grew up there with the Earl's daughters, Isobel and Anne. We all knew each other really well, and I had loved Anne since I was a child of ten." Richard had a dreamy look on his face, but suddenly became full of purpose again.

"So, why did George turn to treason against his brother?" Things were hotting up now. I didn't want to go too deeply into the complicated Wars of the Roses, and while I was genuinely curious, I wanted to get back to the 'evil Richard' of Shakespeare. But, Richard was getting carried away with his family history, so I just sat back and listened.

"This was a part of what was later called the Wars of the Roses."

I did know of the Wars of the Roses, but it had always been too complicated for me to take in. "Richard," I asked, "can you tell me a very basic, shortened version of those times? And, by the way, do you want me to call you Richard or Your Majesty?"

"Richard will do," he said grudgingly, and then he carried on. "You must know of the wars with France and the Battle of Agincourt won by Henry V. He had 5,000 men, most of them armed with longbows, and the French had 20,000 men. It turned out to be a disaster for the French. Henry V came home victorious, he married the daughter of the French King and was due to inherit the French crown too, but before the French king died, Henry died of dysentery. He was only thirty-five.

His son, Henry VI, was only nine months old, and grew up to be more interested in religion than in his country. During his reign, Joan of Arc became the leader in France and England lost all our lands there except for Calais. Then my uncle Richard, the Duke of York, launched a civil war and Henry VI fled to Scotland. Then his son, my brother Edward became King. Edward IV. He was supported by Richard Neville…"

"Oh! The Kingmaker!" I interjected.

"…Yes, but after Edward married Elizabeth Woodville, the Kingmaker, as you call him, changed sides and brought Henry VI back. That's when Edward and I left for France, but our brother George, who was married to the Kingmaker's daughter Isobel, remember, betrayed us and stayed behind to support the return of Henry VI. But after only a few months, we had gathered enough troops and support from the Burgundians, and we returned to England. We defeated Henry at the Battle of Tewskesbury, killed his son and imprisoned Henry in the Tower.

This time it was the Kingmaker that fled abroad, and he did what we had done, gathered support from France and came back to defeat us once more. He released Henry from the Tower and brought him back and reinstated him as Henry VI once more."

I remembered the confusing Shakespeare's plays, all individual plays in their own rights: Henry IV part one, Henry IV part two, Henry VI part one, Henry VI part two, and Henry VI part three! I hoped that he wasn't going to explain all of those changes of Kingship.

Richard didn't notice anything changing in my demeanour and carried on. "I'll spare you all the details only to say that my brother and I came back once more and fought the battle at Barnet where we won and Richard, (the Kingmaker) Duke of Warwick was killed.

Now, Edward was strong enough, with my support to be King on his own without Warwick, and without having to answer to anyone else."

"Wow!" was all I could say.

"It was all a bit complicated, even for those of us who lived through it. So, going back to George. After their first defeat at Tewkesbury, George was all sorry and submissive and declaring that he never really wanted to do anything to harm his brother, but goaded by the Earl of Warwick, it wasn't long before he started again with treasonable suggestions. At last, Edward had enough and had him charged with treason. He was put into the Tower, and then, he was tried and found guilty as charged.

My own problems with George had started with my wanting to marry Anne, who had already been married off at the age of fourteen to the son of Henry VI. He was killed a year later at the Battle of Tewkesbury, leaving Anne a very rich widow. Then, after the Earl of Warwick was killed, George expected that the whole of Warwick's fortune and lands, including Middleham Castle, would to come to him. But with my marriage to Anne, he had to accept that he would only inherit half. And that didn't go down well with George!"

To break the flow of words coming from Richard, I interjected. "Was that when George was drowned in the butt of malmsey?" I asked.

"That's right," said Richard. "He had been found guilty of treason, and he was due to be executed. But Edward was very reluctant to kill his own brother and eventually it was done secretly. The story is that an unknown person, carrying out the proclaimed death sentence, forced George into the butt of malmsey and held his head under until he drowned."

"What exactly is malmsey?" I asked. "Was it a drink that he was familiar with? Was it a common drink?"

"It's a sort of fortified wine made in the island of Madeira. Very expensive, very strong, very sweet, and very intoxicating. Anyway, George had been tried and found guilty of treason. And as usual with people found guilty of treason, the Act of Attainder specifies that his family and children were not allowed to inherit his land and monies, and more importantly, his children were barred from any future claim to the throne."

"Ah!" I exclaimed. "That is why the next in line for Kingship after your brother Edward IV died was you and not George's son, the Earl of Warwick."

"Yes, his surviving children, son Edward, Earl of Warwick and daughter Margaret, Countess of Salisbury, lost all rights to claim the throne.

Now here is the interesting thing. When Henry Tudor became King, George's son Edward was put into the Tower of London, and he was beheaded fourteen years later, on a spurious charge of treason and trying to escape. And his sister Margaret was kept close at court, even after she married John de la Pole and had two sons.

This shows how the Tudors were full of deceit and ambition. Margaret was a close attendant to Katherine of Aragon, and helped to raise baby Mary, later to become Queen Mary. Now, I want to show you how wicked the Tudors were.

Margaret, the Countess of Shrewsbury and a very wealthy woman, in her own right, had her son and grandson executed for treason, but Henry was unable to capture her elder son, Reginald who escaped to Rome and became a powerful member of the Catholic Church. He wielded considerable influence on the Pope's decision not to allow Henry to divorce Katherine. Henry VIII took viciously against any Catholics who stood by the rule of the Pope saying that his marriage to Catherine was sound, and therefore, could not be granted an annulment or divorce. Consequently Margaret, who supported her son Reginald, was imprisoned in the Tower of London on a trumped up charge.

She was held there for two years, and eventually, Henry decided that he had had enough of obstinate Catholics who would not accept his marriage to Anne Boleyn, and ordered her execution. Do you know how old Margaret, Countess of Salisbury when she was killed?"

I thought that Richard had almost forgotten that I was there, his unbroken talk on the Plantagenets had gone so long. "No," I said. "She must have been alive for some time to live through your reign, and the reigns of Henry VII and Henry VIII. So, how old was she?"

"She was sixty-eight!" he exclaimed. "That woman was sixty-eight! A very old lady for those days."

"That's awful!" I was quite shocked. But Richard hadn't finished.

"It gets worse," said Richard. "It took an inexperienced executioner eleven swings of his axe to kill her. That poor old lady! What she must have suffered."

I was horrified. "How disgusting," I said. "I have often wondered how the men and occasional women summoned up enough courage to kneel down and put their heads on the block knowing that they were about to undergo terrible pain in their dying. I can see now that it was some sort of mercy that Henry VIII allowed Anne Boleyn to be despatched by a highly skilled French swordsman."

"And finally," said King Richard, "maybe there is a puzzle for you to solve. Perhaps you could do some research to find out what happened to every member of our family, the York family after I lost my battle to remain King? I think that you will find that there were not many who survived the Tudor Kings!"

It was as if he had sensed for himself that my career as a barrister has kept me in touch with police detection. I got up to stretch my legs and ease my aching hip, and together we walked back to the stained glass window and his portrait, and I asked him why the painter caught him in a look that looked so sad.

He heaved a great sigh, and said, "This painting was done soon after my wife, Anne had died, and this was only a few months after our only son had died too. And contrary to the rumour that has been printed in your history books, I really loved my wife. I did not marry her purely for her inheritance, which is what my brother George accused me of. The ring you see in the painting which I am putting on my finger, is her wedding ring."

"So," I said. "Being King Richard III had brought you no happiness at all?"

"Just duty." He sighed again. "I had promised my brother Edward years ago that if he ever needed me to secure his kingdom, that I would do so. In fact, I spent most of the time of his reign securing the Scottish borderlands. I kept well away from all the intrigues of court and the Queen's ever pervasive family!"

"OK," I said, "you've convinced me that you were the rightful King and you did not kill your nephews Edward and Richard. Your sister-in-law the Dowager Queen Elizabeth allowed her daughter Elizabeth, who in due course was to marry Henry Tudor, and her sisters to come out of sanctuary in Westminster Abbey and join you and Anne in your court. Which she surely wouldn't have done if she believed that you had murdered her sons.

The children of your brother, George of Clarence, were also alive and were living at court alongside your wife Anne, your son John, and your illegitimate son. You seem to have been one big happy united family." I returned to my position as cross-examiner of the main suspect. "But now, the main question remains, that is: why were the two boys never seen in public again?"

I turned round to face Richard with that big question hanging in the air between us, but he was gone. His ghost had disappeared, and my question was never answered!

And what did I hear faintly echoing around the Cathedral? "Why not look for Edward in Devon. Coldridge, Devon."

I was stunned and could hardly believe what had happened in the last half hour or so. I wandered around the Cathedral once more to steady myself, and to see if there were any vestiges of the ghost remaining. Did I hear something about Devon? I wasn't quite sure. There was nothing, nothing. He was gone. So, I staggered out into the sunshine and made my way slowly to the café where I was to meet my brother, still pondering over the question of the guilt or innocence of King Richard III.

Alan, soon, came in with his pals who were all laughing and singing and waving their Spurs scarfs. As one of their number had been unable to go to the match, I was persuaded to use his ticket and take his place at the game.

I had never been to a first division football match before, and I must admit that it was quite exciting. All the good-natured shouting and singing was quite stirring. And when Spurs scored, the roar from the fans was deafening. Everyone was so excited, especially when Spurs were the winners, 3 goals to 2, and I too, was caught up in the heady atmosphere of the stadium.

It wasn't, until we were on the train going back to London that I had a chance to recapture the strange discussion that I had had with Richard III in the Cathedral, but I decided not to say anything until we got home. But even then, after all the excitement of Alan reliving every moment of the match with Jane, I felt that it wasn't the right moment to tell my story.

After a short pause when no one spoke, Jane turned to Alan and said, "What a pity that your brother died of that awful heart attack last month. It sounds as though he would have enjoyed the game. Were you able to find anyone to use the ticket you bought for him?"

"No," replied Alan. "But I'm sure that he joined us in spirit. And he had been so looking forward to visiting Leicester Cathedral, and the new tomb for Richard III." Alan sighed. You two might have enjoyed an exchange of views about Richard III. What do you, as a senior school history teacher, think of him?"

My ghostly spirit hung around just long enough to hear her reply.

"Oh!" she said. "That's easy to answer. He was an evil, murdering bastard, and he deserved everything he got!"

June 2020, Hastings Old Town

The old fisherman is sitting quietly supping his beer outside the Dolphin pub, which is near the bottom of All Saint's Street. He is ignoring the 'ooing' and 'ahing' of the crowds of tourists as they walk through the Old Town munching their fish and chips out of paper bags. He spots his pal, Alfred Peterson, opening one of the famous tall, black net huts, on the beach just across the street. The net huts are, as always, the subject of awe and speculation, and a small crowd is gathering around to peer into Alfred's hut to see what it looks like inside.

He calls out to his friend. "Hey! Freddie! Do yer fancy a pint?"

Alfred calls back. "Just a mo. I'll come and join yer." He locks up his hut, crosses the road and sits down on the pub bench alongside his mate Mick. He asks, in an irritated voice, "How many times have I asked yer not to call me Freddie? Yer knows damn well that I's called Alfred. And that's what I want to be called. Alfred."

"Sorry!" says Mick, with a chuckle. "You wait here *Alfred,* and I'll fetch yer a pint."

As Mick goes off to fetch beer for the both of them, he mutters under his breath, "Bloody tourists! I'll be glad when the season is over, and life can get back to normal."

On his return, it's Alfred who replies "There ain't no normal these days," he says. "But I suppose that we should be grateful that they come 'ere and spend their cash. Did you sell all yer catch today?"

"Yer," grumbles Mick. "There weren't much out there last night. But I did pull up some nice crabs." He waits until a small crowd of tourists has pushed past them to go inside the pub. Then, he lowers his voice. "I saw it again last night," he says.

"Did yer?" asks Alfred, sounding alarmed. "Where? Was it out off Pevensey Bay, like when I saw it?"

"No. She were bobbing in calm water just off Rock-a-Nore. Fairlight side. Looked like she were at anchor. Looked like she were waiting for sommat to happen or someone to join her," says Mick.

"Did yer go close, or see her number?" asks Alfred.

"Nah," says Mick. "She didn't have no lights on. Not even low down. She were just sitting there quietly in the dark. Old Joe said, he saw a fishing boat just like that, with no lights on, last week. He didn't go close neither."

"P'raps, I'll go and take a look tonight," says Alfred. "I've got some cuttle fish pots that way that are due for liftin'."

"Trouble is," says Mick, "she's always in a different place when she's spotted. Joe saw her off Dungeness. Do yer think that she's a real boat? Maybe, she's a ghostly apparition."

"Apparition!" exclaims Alfred, recovering his humour. "Well! There's a fancy word for this time of day."

Two ghosts, dressed in eighteenth century common sailor's gear, are sitting on the steps next to the Dolphin, which lead to the top of the East Hill. They are listening to Mick and Alfred's conversation. One of them giggles. The fat one. He says, "They must think that the boat is the bloody Marie Celeste, or sommat like that."

Alfred sits up sharply. He pokes a startled Mick. "Did yer hear that laugh?" he asks, as a look of fear comes back into his eyes. "A weird laugh. It give me the shivers, and it come from just over me shoulder."

"Nah," says Mick. "There ain't no-one there. All them grockles have gone inside now. Yer just got the jim-jams what with me talking about the boat, and apparitions." He laughs. "Come on, let's take a gander at yer boat. P'raps, I'll come along with yer tonight."

It's now ten o'clock on a bright starlit night. Midsummer, and it is not quite dark, but it is getting shadowy on the beach where there is no lighting. There is no wind and the sea is as still as a millpond.

"Cor!" says Alfred, as they drag his boat over the rollers to the water's edge, "It don't get no easier to launch these bloody boats, do it?"

"Nah," says Mick. "But we's getting on now. Lost all our youthful strength. Thank Gawd that we got them winches to pull 'em up accrost the shingle when we come back."

They don't say much as they sail beyond Rock-a-Nore, hugging the coastline and heading for Camber and Rye, with Alfred pulling up a nice catch of mackerel and a couple of cuttle fish on the way.

Suddenly, standing out against the lights lining the Dungeness Bay, Alfred spots the unreal elusive fishing boat. "Look Mick!" he exclaims. "There she is!"

"What's she doing there off Rye Harbour?" questions Mick. "And why ain't she got no lights on? I told yer so, Alfred, didn't I? It's got to be the same one as I seen yesterday. This is too creepy!"

Suddenly, they have to blink their eyes, as for a couple of seconds or so the small fishing boat changes to become an eighteenth-century, three masted galleon. A Dutch East India Company trading ship, with full sails and bristling with cannons bursting through every porthole. Then, before they can really take in what they are seeing, it turns back to a simple fishing boat again.

"Wow!" says a stunned Alfred. "Did yer see that?"

"Yea," says an equally stunned Mick. "It ain't possible. An old times galleon ship from history. But we both seen it, didn't we? I know it can't be, but it were real. What's happening here?"

"Did yer see all them cannon guns pointing right towards us? Do yer think it's smugglers?" asks Alfred. "Are they doing things to frighten us or to hide their boat? Like them modern laser light things or sommat clever like that? I knows that smuggling still goes on, but I don't wanna have nothing to do with it. What yer don't knows about yer can't tells about, is what I says."

Suddenly, impossibly, the two ghosts who had overheard their conversation at the Dolphin pub, are casually sitting on some empty cuttle fish pots on Alfred's boat deck.

Alfred and Mick are truly stunned now. "What's going on?" asks Mick.

"Who are yer? And how did yer get on me boat?" asks Alfred. Both of them questioning at the same time.

"Are yer real, or are yer ghosts?" added Mick.

The short, rather fat ghost spoke up in a voice that sounded foreign to Mick's ears. "We are ghosts. Or spooks is how we say in Dutch." (Sounding like 'sporks'.)

"Dutch? Sporks?" askes a surprised Alfred. "Have yer come from 'olland, then? What's yer doin' here?"

"Yar," says the first ghost, pointing to himself and his companion. "I am Wilhelm and he is Pieter. And we come from that Dutch ship you just seen. It is called *the Amsterdam,* and it sank in the mud on the eighth of January in 1749. Yar, we are spooks."

Then, the tall black bearded ghost speaks out, in the same strange accent. "Yar, I am Pieter. And we have come to give you warning. You are right about smugglers. There are many out there, especially near the sand banks in the Channel. Most of them are on large sailing yachts. They are dangerous and vicious drug smugglers. You should keep away from any strange boats that try to get your attention while you are out in the water doing your fishing.

Many also are looking like immigrants trying to get to England on rubber boats. With tricks and guns they want to trap innocent fishermen like you into smuggling their drugs into England. They will make it look like their boat is sinking and call to you to rescue them. Then, they will pull out their guns and pass to you the drugs in packages and threaten to kill you or your families back on shore if you don't deliver the packages to the men who will be awaiting your return to the beach in Hastings.

If it ever happens to you don't you try to call anyone. No police, no border control boats, no lifeboats. Do nothing or they will kill."

A dazed Alfred looks hard at his uninvited guests. "So, I've got ghosts on me boat warning us about smugglers. Why? What's smugglers to do with you. Two bloody foreigners what's got nothing to do with us? Why don't yer go back to do yer 'aunting in 'olland?"

"It's because since January 1749, we have been stranded in England, mostly we are in Hastings, near to where our ship went down," says Wilhelm in a soft, saddened voice.

Alfred seems to accept that he is talking to a ghost. The penny drops. "Do yer means that yer come off that shipwreck down at Bulverhythe, down St Leonards?"

Wilhelm nodded.

Mick joins in. "Yeah. I knows the one. The skeleton of the wreck shows itself two or three times a year when the tide is real low." He turns to his pal Alfred. "I were down there only last week with me grandson, Johnny. He complained about walking the three miles to Bulverhythe. Blooming kids moan about doing any walking these days, what with their parents taking them everywhere by car. They don't know what their legs are for! Anyway, when we got there he were so excited to walk around a real shipwreck, and to walk inside it, too. I promised to take him to the Shipwreck Museum in the Old Town, come Monday."

Alfred turns to the *spook* Pieter. "So, what happened to the Amsterdam? I heard somewhere that she were a real fine ship"

"It was," says the ghost. "It was the first sail of a new ship of the Dutch East India Company, and it had very valuable cargo to take to the Dutch islands in Indonesia for the trading. Three times we are sailing from Holland. Two times we go in November 1748, and we come back into port because of bad weather.

Then we go again in the next January. Very cold. Very bad storms. On board there is much chests, twenty-seven chests, of Dutch silver guilders for the trading. Very much barrels of wine, and luxury things for the trade. There was more than three hundred mens on the ship, and about half of these peoples were soldiers to protect this cargo. After only one week in the storms there is many peoples sick and dying. We think we have the plague on the ship. All the mens are frightened."

"January is bad time to set sail if the weather is stormy," says Mick. "Even we don't go out in our small boats if the seas are high in January. Dangerous."

"Silly, I calls it," mutters Alfred.

"Well," continued Pieter, "that decision was made, and we common sailors have no say in the matter, so, we set sail for the third time. Again, violent storms hit us as we come into the English Channel. By then about fifty mens, soldiers and sailors, have died of the plague, and as many more are dying. The storm is so fierce that our rudder is broken away off Pevensey. The Captain, who also has name Wilhelm, Wilhelm Klump, wants to sail on to Portsmouth for the mending the rudder, but the crew and soldiers want to go home. There is much mutiny, rioting, much drinking of the wine barrels, much fighting and many more killed."

"And," added Wilhelm, "they kill also the young cabin boy. He name is Adrian Wegevren, and he is the nephew of my wife. He is killed on his sixteenth birthday. Poor boy. Sad!"

By this time, Alfred is really interested, and he has almost forgotten that he is the Captain of his own ship, which itself is in danger of running aground. "How come if you lost your rudder at Pevensey," he asks, "that the ship went down at Bulverhythe, which is just outside Hastings?"

Wilhelm takes up the story. "The mutiny peoples, they turn the ship, but without the rudder they cannot control it. When it is nearly safe at Hastings, it gets stuck in the muddy sands at the mouth of a small river. It never moved more, and almost at once it begins to sink into the muds. Some mens like me and Pieter got away before the English pirates come to kill and take the treasure in the cargo hold."

Mick suddenly shouts out, "Alfred, for Christ's sake, get ahold of yerself and turn this bloody boat around before we get stuck in the mud of the Rother river. We are nearly at Rye Harbour!"

While Alfred turns his boat out to sea, Mick comments, "I'm surprised that local pirates from Hastings didn't kill all the survivors. Especially with all them chests of silver spilling out and everyone grabbing handsfull."

"Well, they did," says Pieter. "But in January 1748, all the pirates in Kent and Sussex were keeping their heads down, and we managed to escape."

"Oh yea, I read all about that," says Alfred, "1748. That's when the Revenue Men was rounding up and hanging the remainder of the hated Hawkhurst gang of pirates. They had terrorised the locals for fifteen years. The Revenue Men and the militia had already hanged the leaders. I remember the name of one of them cos it's the same as my uncle, Arthur Gray. Funny that! And the soldiers was catching all the pirates that they could.

Our local pirates were not so wild and wicked as the men in the Hawkhurst gang. Them gang members was ruthless. Wicked, violent killers. There were 'undreds of 'em. They had their base hidden inland in Hawkhurst, and they had gang members working out of the Hastings Caves on the West Hill, and the Mermaid Inn in Rye. And even in towns and villages down the coast to 'Ampshire and Dorset.

They didn't just kill their victims, they tortured 'em too. If them people didn't do what they was told they was beaten to death, stuck with knives, bones broken, and finger nails pulled out. Some were even buried alive. Just to teach everyone to respect them and do whatever they were told to do. Everyone from local churchmen, publicans, landowners and even local magistrates. And of course, all the common people. So, the small time smugglers in Hastings kept their 'eads down. Didn't wanna get noticed by the big boys."

"Well," says Mick. "So, 'ow did you two ghosts meet yer end, then? You are ghosts now in Hastings, but I expect that after yer escaped from the Amsterdam, yer wanted to get back 'ome to 'olland? Didn't yer?"

Pieter, in spite of his rough sailor clothing, his tall and strong and manly body, his beard and his long tangled dark hair, looks as though he is about to cry. "When we climb down from the ship, we hide. We don't want the Hastings pirates to see us. We only take a few silver guilders to buy food and old clothes.

We don't want to look foreign. We both want to get back to our families in Holland. But I never see my wife and little girl no more." And ghostly tears fill his eyes.

"What happened?" asked Alfred.

Wilhelm takes up the story. "We live rough for three, four weeks, sleeping in hedges and old barns in the daytime, catching rabbits to eat and buying little bits of bread if we could. And walking at night. We try to get to Dover to find work on boats that go to France. And then we get to a country farm near Rye.

The woman, she has no husband. We make the farm work. You know. We work to keep fed the pigs and the sheep, and the dig for turnips. The woman she looks after us well. She likes us and she keeps us there long time, she want to make us two husbands. Two husbands for one woman! She likes us to be in bed with her. Both of us mens at the same time."

Pieter continues their story. "She pretty woman name Mary and I begin to feel for her, but then I remember that I have wife at home. Wife, Marjia. Almost the same name in Dutch. I love my Marjia and I feel bad that we are still in England.

Then one day, the Mary, she says that she is to have baby. She don't know which of us mens is father, and she wants to marry me for baby to have father. I tell her that she is good woman, but I have already wife in Holland. And Wilhelm does as well have wife, and we want to go home. Back home to our wifes. Mary, she is angry. She is jealous that we have wifes that we love. She tries to make us stay but as she is getting fatter with the baby, we still says 'no'. Then she tells the militia that we are escaped pirates of Hawkhurst gang.

We are taken away and we are put in goal. Mary is sorry. She cries and says that what she said is not true. We say always that we are only sailors, not pirates. No one believe us that we are sailors from the Amsterdam. The jailor tells us that Mary has a baby boy. And we get hanged in Rye."

"Aah!" says Alfred and Mick together. "So that's why you is ghosts," adds Mick.

"Yar," says Pieter. "We never get home. I never see my Marjia and my daughter again. I never see new baby, but jailor says Mary calls him Johnny Peterson. For me as father. But now we are spooks, ghosts, and we always at sea, and we warn sailors of danger."

"Peterson! Pieter's son!" exclaims Alfred. "My family name is Peterson, and I know that my father's family, the Petersons, goes back hundreds of years.

Always fishermen out of Hastings. Could it possibly be true that you are my ancestor? Wow! I can't believe it!"

This time it is the ghosts that are surprised. Pieter looks hard at Alfred and says, "Is it possible? I did feel a connection to you when I first saw you at the Dolphin pub this morning."

"Yes," says Alfred. "I knew that something was up this morning when I heard laughing, and there was no-one there. My Gawd! I can't believe that I could be talking to me ancestor. You could be me great, great, great, great, and even more greats, great grandfather!"

Mick laughs. "So! You got Dutch blood in yer!"

Alfred laughs too. "It's better than having Froggy blood in me!"

They are now about fifteen nautical miles from shore. "Well, thank you," says Alfred. "I'm happy to have you looking out for us, even though you are only ghosts. Sorry! Sporks! We will be very happy for any help and advice you can give us. Watching out for smugglers, or even telling us where the best fish are running!

I think that we had better go back now." He turns to his wheelhouse to set the boat about, and when he turns around again his ghostly guests have vanished. "Whoa!" he exclaims. "Where did they go?"

Mick is looking bewildered. "I dunno," he says. "One moment they's here on yer boat, and the next – they's gone. Let's go home. We'll talk about all this tomorra."

"I wander what danger them two were warning us of?" asks a bewildered Alfred. "Surely not drug smugglers?"

Just then, they hear voices calling. And they spot a rubber dingy full of men who look cold and frightened. "Help us, we are sinking!" they are calling…

July 2022, M 40 Motorway, Oxfordshire

It had been twenty years since they had last met, but they recognised each other instantly. She, who had always melted at his touch. He, who had had a lover with whom he would share his body, share his thoughts, and share his longings for the future.

"Michael," she gasped. "It's you! What's happened? Where are we? Oh! My dearest, I thought that we would never meet again." She reached out for him, instantly wanting him once more, and found that she could not touch him. "What!" She exclaimed. She was utterly dazed.

"Emma! I was going to Oxford," said Michael, still in a state of shock.

"So was I. What's happened?" She asked again.

"There was a lorry ahead of us. It jack-knifed. It hit me full on," he said. "It must have hit your car too. I was just overtaking a red BMW."

"That *was* my car!" exclaimed Emma. "Oh my god! Are we dead? Are we ghosts?"

"I don't know what we are. Or where we are," he said. "Perhaps, we are in some sort of halfway place between Heaven and Earth."

They looked at each other and took in what they were seeing, and what their condition was. Their ghost bodies were whole, unlike the remains of their earthly bodies which were being carefully looked after in two ambulances on the M40 motorway below.

"I wonder where my violin is," said Michael, still dazed by the crash and his death.

"And where is mine?" asked Emma. "It's the most valuable thing that I own. That I owned," she corrected.

They were quiet for a while, taking in what had happened to them both. "I suppose that the others in the crash have survived," said Michael, "otherwise I think that they would probably be here with us. Were you travelling alone?"

"Yes, I've been living alone, with my dog, for six years now. Ever since my husband died. Thank goodness that I left my dog at home, with my friend. And you?" She asked, miserably, wishing that she had been able to find him six years ago, and reconnect. If only that had been possible. And now, if this was it. The end of life. How she wished bitterly that she had not been able to spend those last years of her life with him. He had always been the one she missed most. The real love of her life.

"I was also on my own in the car, but I live with…"

Emma held her breath. Was he going to say that he had a new wife? Her ghostly heart was beating fast.

"…with my old mother."

His mother! Why was she so relieved? Silly. Especially, since they were both dead now! She tried to sound nonchalant. "Perhaps the lorry driver, and anyone else fatally injured went straight to Heaven. Perhaps, they are waiting for us there," she mused.

"Then why didn't we go straight there too?" asked Michael.

"I don't know. Maybe, because for our past sins. Maybe, Heaven's doors are closed to sinners. Maybe, it could be because of what we were doing twenty years ago!" suggested Emma. "I was cheating on my husband, and you were cheating on your wife!"

"I know, but both of them knew and accepted that we were lovers, as well as the members of our quartet. So how can that be sin enough to exclude us from Heaven? Do you remember David? My cousin David who played the viola? He used to talk about us all the time," said Michael. "I know how we all laughed when he called the pair of us 'the demonic duo.'" He paused in an awkward silence, not knowing what to say. "Do you still play the violin?" he asked. "Or perhaps I should ask 'were you still playing the violin until now?'"

"Yes, I was. And I was playing even better than I did in the old days. Do you remember the rubbishy old violin I used to play?"

"Yep! The one with the A string that broke all the time!" he giggled. "Sometimes right in the middle of your solo part."

Emma laughed too. "Well," she said. "My father had a beautiful, two-hundred-year-old violin which he left to me when he passed away nearly sixteen years ago. It has a beautiful mellow sound. And I am sure, it was because I am, was, playing his instrument that my own playing improved. I do hope that it wasn't smashed up in our car wreck." She sighed. "I wanted to leave it to my son. He plays music all the time, although, it is mainly on acoustic guitars. Never a violin!" She smiled to herself. "Perhaps, if it wasn't smashed in the crash, he will play it someday. His grandfather would love that."

"Were you going to be playing in Oxford, then?" asked Michael.

"Yes. I was heading for the annual Summer Music Festival. For the month of July, they use the Colleges and the dorms as part of the general Oxford Festival while the undergrads are on holiday. I was due to be playing with the Maidenhead Quartet at Magdalen College."

"Oh my God!" exclaimed Michael. "I was going to be playing there too! With my band called The Canadian Jazzers. Bloody hell Emma! Magdalen College. We would have met up together again in real life. That might have been embarrassing!"

"No. I don't think so. Not after all this time. You're not embarrassed to see me now, are you?" Emma smiled at him. "Do you remember how I used to pick you up to go to gigs. You had had your driving licence confiscated, the consequences of getting all those speeding tickets."

"Yes, and I also remember what we used to get up to on the drive home after the gigs!"

Emma's ghostly cheeks reddened. "It's amazing how much space there used to be in that Mini when we needed it," she laughed. "Oh! How I longed to make love with you in a proper bed. How I longed to spend a whole night with you. How I longed to lay naked with you under the blankets." She stopped talking any further about their illicit relationship, quenching the unstoppable desire that she had for him every time she saw him. "So! Where have you been these last twenty, is it twenty? Yes, it must be, twenty years?"

"I was in Canada for eighteen of those years."

"Canada!" Emma was taken aback with surprise.

"Yes," said Michael. "You know that I had ambitions to expand and change my style of playing. Well, I did what we talked about so often. I went to Canada. Vancouver." He looked at her yearning face, her still beautiful body, and he realised just how much he had missed her, too. How much he had wanted her when he was in Canada. "I was invited there by a member of a Canadian folk/rock group called The Wild Totems, who I met in London. Do you remember that gig in the crypt of St Martin in the Fields?"

Emma shook her head. "That must have been soon after our quartet broke up."

Michael thought for a moment. "Yes, it probably was. It was also about then that Anna left me."

Oh! My darling. Why didn't you try to find me then? thought Emma.

Michael met her thought for thought. You were still married to Andy then. He nodded to himself, and without realising that they were able to read each other's thoughts, he continued, uninterrupted. "Well, this chap I met in London, Jean-Paul Le Brun, was a native Canadian, who played music adapted from both the Native North Americans and the French Canadians. He made the prospect of a wildly different future sound so exciting that I was persuaded. I was off to Canada within weeks. I lived in Vancouver for nearly eighteen years."

"So that's why I haven't heard of you for years. Did you get married again after Anna left you?" asked Emma, while trying to stop the waves of jealousy that were sweeping over her.

"No. But I did have a partner in Vancouver for a few years." He looked saddened. "But she didn't want to leave Canada. And I was so desperately needed by my sister to come home. For my mother." He stopped any further explanation. "So, what shall we do now?" Michael looked around. "We seem to be floating above the accident scene. Let's see if we can move around."

They sort of held hands without touching, and with a strange force of will they were able to get themselves down to ground level. The crash site on the motorway had been almost cleared and most of the police and ambulances were gone.

"Well," said Michael. "I don't know why the spirits have not allowed us through those famous *pearly gates*, so I suppose that we had better find some useful way to pass our ghostly days!"

"Ok!" sighed Emma. "Perhaps, this is what they mean when they say *no rest for the wicked*. But, since we are almost in Oxford, let's see if we can solve the mystery of the disappearance of David. Do you remember the last time we saw him? It must have been when we were playing at Joanna's wedding reception. In the great hall of Balliol College."

"Yes," said Michael. "That was in July 2000. Twenty-two years ago. How on earth, pardon the pun, do you think that we could possibly solve that mystery after all these years? I know that the police looked into his disappearance at the time we reported him missing. They found nothing sinister."

"Shall we have a look around Oxford?" suggested Emma. "I'm sure that, as ghosts, we will be able to sneak into corners and listen into conversations completely un-noticed."

"I'm not sure. But first, I had better check on my mother to see that someone, perhaps my sister, is looking after her. She is still quite fit, but she's not really able to live on her own. Shall we go together, and then think of what we need to do to relinquish these ghostly bodies, and return fully to the spirit world."

By using their thoughts, they found that they were able to reach Michael's mother at her home in Sussex. They were shimmering, and holding hands as they showed themselves to her in her sunny garden room.

"Is that you, Michael?" demanded his mother in a forceful and overpowering voice. "And who is that you have with you?" She peered hard. A piercing look that could have cut through toughened steel like a laser. "Is it that Emma? I thought that you had finished with that creature, Michael."

Michael and Emma looked at each other. "Is this what you have been putting yourself through since your return from Canada? For nearly three years?" she asked Michael through thought projection.

He nodded, and gave his mother a withering look. Without noticing anything that was going on between her son and *the creature*, his mother continued to hold an almost one-sided conversation. "I always wanted you to give up that stupid music group. It took you away too much from your real job, as head of the music department of that private school you taught at. The John Magnus school, wasn't it? You could have become the headmaster if you had concentrated on your proper job, and not gone running all about the country with that silly quartet, playing for peanuts." She was replaying the old script that she had repeated and ranted at him for yeas.

"Then you ran off to Canada, leaving me on my own. Despite having made a promise to your father, on his deathbed, that you would always look after me."

She took a deep breath, and carried on without giving him a chance to say anything. "You ruined your marriage by consorting with that creature, and your job prospects, too." She paused again for breath. "So, why have you gone back to that creature? And why have you brought her here? To *my* house."

"Mrs Stevenson," stepped in Emma. "I am not a creature, as you call me. I am, in fact, a ghost. And so is your son!"

"Pff! Don't be so silly," she snapped back. "There are no such things as ghosts. They do not exist! Pure fantasy! So, get out of my house! Michael had enough of you before. It was your fault that he went off to Canada. He left his wife and his own mother, and his profession to off to play jazz in Canada."

"It wasn't jazz, Mother, it was folk/rock," said Michael, in a weakened voice. He took on the look of a beaten schoolboy.

Emma could hardly believe her eyes and ears. Why had Michael never told her about his overpowering mother? Was he ashamed that he was always browbeaten by her? Was this really the reason why Michael hadn't contacted her when his wife left him? Was this hard-skinned woman behind all the sadness in their lives?

All those questions remained to be asked, but Mrs. Stevenson hadn't yet finished her tirade. "After all, I did to get rid of that useless David who used to come round here all the time. Always a sob story. Always wanting cash to bail him out of some scrape or other. I know that he was your cousin and your best friend, Michael, but he really was a waste of time."

Michael stood transfixed "What? What did you do to him mother?" he asked, eventually.

"I didn't *do* anything to him. I just told him that his mother was a prostitute, and the man he thought was his father was also his grandfather. My own brother! Clifford. And on top of all that, David wanted to marry your sister, Mary. I felt that it was my duty to warn him off. No more incest in this family. Thank you very much!" She was actually puffing out her chest to show off her bravery.

Michael and Emma stood as if turned to stone. It surely wasn't real what they were seeing and hearing. She must be going mad in her old age!

"What!" cried Michael. "I don't believe it! Are you saying that Uncle Clifford had sex with his own daughter, and they produced David?" He was so astonished that his ghostly form blotted out for several seconds. Emma was so shocked that she was speechless.

Michael's form slowly re-appeared. "Let me get this straight, mother," he said, his voice trembling with shock. "If this is all true, David never knew that his grandfather, your brother, who lived with him and his mother, was also his father. You were the only other person who knew, and you just blurted it out to him? I know that he had been told by his mother since he was a small boy that his father had run off, and his mother was bringing him up on her own, with the help of his grandfather. Are you sure of all this, about his grandfather being his father?" He looked at his mother in continued disbelief.

Mrs Stevenson bridled. "Of course, I'm sure of it. It had been a family secret for years, and it was time to tell him the truth," she snapped at her son. "It was time to tell him, time to get rid of the bastard boy. Get him out of our lives."

"Mother, he is your only nephew," said Michael. "The only cousin that I have!"

"Oh my God!" exclaimed Emma, out loud this time. "No wonder he disappeared from our music circle. And disappeared out of your family life, too. Poor David. What a state of mind he must have been in. I wonder what happened to him. Will we be able to trace him, do you think, Michael?"

Before he could reply to Emma, his mother jumped in. "Michael is not going anywhere. Certainly not with you!" She almost spat at Emma. "He is needed here with me. It is his duty to look after his mother."

"Mother," said Michael quietly. "Didn't you hear what we said when we arrived? When we suddenly appeared in this garden room of yours? Emma and I have just died. We both died in our cars in a motorway accident this morning. We are ghosts. I can't do anything for you anymore."

"I don't believe anything you say," spluttered Mrs Stevenson. "You are just making up a story because you want to go running off with *that creature* again. You want to desert your mother once more, like you did when you ran away to Canada. Well, your sister's not going to cover for you again. It is your *duty* to care for me! Your promise to your dying father."

Emma sent a mental message to Michael. "Your mother is a nightmare."

Michael messaged back. "Yes, I've had this all my life. Well, especially since my father died. I was only twelve, and she took total control of me from then on, continually reminding me of the promise that I had made to my father as a child. Her possessiveness was overpowering. It wasn't because of you that Anna left me. It was because of my mother. She was so jealous and hateful to Anna. Anna tried to ignore it at first, but in the end it was too much for her to put up with. That's why we parted. That's why we never had children. We knew that mother would butt in continually, and end up by taking over. Our divorce was never about you. Anna was never jealous of you. It was always about mother.

That's also why I had to escape to Canada. I enjoyed eighteen years of sheer heaven without my mother interfering in every moment of my life. My sister, Mary lived quite close to mother then, and it fell on her to be at mother's beck and call. Then, poor Mary had a nervous breakdown. She's still under psychiatric care. Our mother drove her mad. That's why I came back from Canada."

"Whyever did you never tell me about your mother's possessiveness before? And why didn't you seek me out after Anna left?"

"Nothing would have changed. Mother would have hated you, too. Probably even more than she hated Anna. Besides, you were still married and raising a family. We couldn't change anything. Mother would have been just as back biting and spiteful. Maybe, even more so. And when I came back, I had my sister to worry about as well as this spiteful woman who I am ashamed to call my mother. I didn't know that you had been widowed. I didn't seek you out because, although I still thought about you every single day, I didn't want to rock the boat in your corner of the world."

They broke off their thought conversation. "Mother," said Michael. "You may or may not believe that I am a ghost, but I am. I cannot stay here on earth any longer. I hope for your sake that you live a less resentful life, and that you learn to live in comfortable peace with your future carers. Goodbye and may God bless you."

As he and Emma were fading out of her life, they could hear her... "However did I give birth such an ungrateful...?"

Emma and Michael looked at each other. "Oh, Michael," she said, with tears in her eyes. "However did *you* manage to live with that?"

Michael shrugged his shoulders. "I would never have guessed that story about poor David. I wonder what we can do about seeking him out."

Suddenly, they were aware of another presence. "Hello Michael. Hello Emma." It was David. "I'm so glad that you stood up to your mother at last. I'm sorry to say this to you, but she is a really horrible and spiteful woman. It was she who drove me to kill myself. Soon, after she told me the truth about my parentage. I took to painkillers and booze.

I had gone back to my own mother and demanded the truth from her. She wept bitterly crying out, "He raped me, you know. I was only fourteen and he raped me, his own daughter. My mother had already left him because of his sexual demands. His horrible, perverted demands. Why? Oh! Why didn't she take me with her?

I could hardly take in what I had been told by both your mother and mine. I guess I went out of my mind. I bought three boxes of painkillers and a bottle of Vodka. Then I went away and rented a room in Brighton in the name of Robin Smith. I did it there. And the police didn't seem to care. 'Just another drug-taking drunk,' they said. No investigation was ever made."

As much as ghosts can, they all hugged. Michael and Emma seemed to merge into each other, looking forward to spending eternity together, and they welcomed David to join them into their new spiritual world.

Then gradually, they faded out from this world, travelling onwards towards their new future…

August 2018, Hever Castle

It was summertime, and the family was back at Hever. Tommy and Joanna were excited at the thought that they might see their ghost again. Although, their mother had told them over and over that there were no ghosts, they still believed in their visions.

It was a lovely summer's day, a typical English summer's day with plenty of warm sunshine and a cool breeze to prevent it from getting blistering hot. They had found out in advance from the Hever Castle website that it was a day when the guides were dressed up in period costume and Tommy and Joanna were looking forward to that too, but first of all, they wanted to explore and play in the water maze.

They had come prepared, dressed in shorts and T-shirts, and their mother had spare tops in her bag to change into if they got too wet. The water maze area was full to bursting with whole families and kids following various pathways to the central mini fort, whilst trying to dodge the water spouts that shot up when a sprung stone was stepped on, releasing a fountain of water onto any unsuspecting child. It was great fun, and everyone was laughing and happy, including Joanna and Tommy. He quickly worked out which were the water release stones and was trying to give an unsuspecting Joanna a right royal soaking!

After they had had their fun in the water maze, and changed their tops, their mum suggested that they investigate the hedge maze.

"Are we going to get lost in it, Mum? Asked Tommy. "Will there be nothing but our whitened bones to be found eventually?"

Joanna wasn't going to be drawn in such a silly game. Having reached her fourteenth birthday in May, she had suddenly become a proper teenager. She was alternately a happy girl and a part of the family, and then a grumpy 'why should I?' moody and 'leave me alone' young lady. And these moods came on and went away without warning. Poor Tommy, who was still only twelve, was puzzled by this treatment from his sister. Their mother was always saying to Tommy, "Just leave her alone. She'll be back to normal in a short while!"

"Actually," said their mother, "The maze is not very big, and not very old. But it is a proper maze from the olden days, but only one hundred odd years old. It wasn't there in the time of Anne Boleyn. So, you won't be seeing her there this time! It is supposed to be relatively easy to find your way to the centre and back again."

When they reached the maze, they found King Henry VIII was standing at the entrance. The clothes he was wearing were heavy and very warm, especially on that hot summer's day. After chatting with the crowds of people who were gathered in the forecourt in front of the castle, and posing for many a picture, he had decided to walk in the maze which was always shaded and cool.

Tommy went right up to him. "Hello, your Majesty!" he said laughing. "And where are all your wives today?" Then, he ran around the King. "I can't see any of them here. Perhaps you have been busy chopping off heads again!"

The guide dressed as Henry VIII laughed too. "Well," he said. "I did have one or two of them here just now, but they were quarrelling so much that I had my guards march them off to the Tower of London. That's the best place for quarrelling women!"

"Hang on a minute," said Joanna, dropping her grumpiness, and joining in with the silliness of the situation. "That's not fair. It's all your fault that they are quarrelling. They just want to prove that you loved them best, even if you did chop off their heads."

"But I only chopped the heads off two of them, you know," said the King.

"Only two!" exclaimed Joanna. "You shouldn't have killed any of them! They were only doing their best to please you, and you went around looking for other women. I bet that behind your back, people called you a 'dirty old man!'"

"If I had heard that, I would have chopped off their heads, too." The guide pretended to scowl. "And if you are not careful young man and young lady, I'll have you marched off to the Tower right now."

The children's mother joined in the fun. She got down on her knees in front of the King and pleaded with him. "Please, Your Majesty," she said in a suitable cringing voice, "Please, spare my children. They are usually such good children. And I have always taught them to speak politely when they are talking to the King and Queen. I really don't know what's got into them today!"

The guide pointed to the two children. "Be gone!" he hissed at them. "Be gone. Go into that maze, and if you come out alive, I may let you live."

Tommy and Joanna laughed and ran off into the maze. "We'll be back sooooon," they called out to their mother.

She and King Henry laughed. "Thanks for making their visit fun," she said. "I think that I'll sit here in the sunshine and let them explore the maze together."

"That's good," said the guide. "It's an easy maze to follow. It will only take them about fifteen minutes to get to the centre and back. Cheerio! I've got my duties to do inside the castle now." And off he went, chuckling to himself.

Tommy and Joanna found their way to the centre with no problem at all, and they were disappointed in how easy it had been. They met no one on the way, and sat on the stone bench for a few minutes. "Neat!" exclaimed Tommy, "We're good at this. I thought that we would have taken at least one wrong turn."

"Yes," said Joanna. "But I do wish that I had a cooling ice cream to eat right now."

"Perhaps," said Tommy, with a laugh, "we could suggest that there could be an ice cream seller here in the middle of the maze. I'm sure that they would sell lots."

After a while, they started to make their way back. Suddenly, Joanna caught a glimpse of a lady, also in period costume, in front of them, but she disappeared almost immediately around the next corner.

"Did you see that lady?" she asked her brother. "Perhaps, she is another volunteer, dressed up as Anne."

"Do you think that it could be our ghost?" asked Tommy. "Let's run and see if we can catch her up". They ran and turned the next corner getting ready to call her, but all they saw again was another glimpse of a red skirt disappearing around the next corner of the maze.

"Hi!" Joanna called out. "Is that you Anne? Hang on a bit so that we can find our way out together." Now they could see her clearly and she waited for them to catch up.

"Hi!" said Joanna again, as she tapped her on her shoulder, thinking that the lady was another guide dressed up as Anne. And to her surprise her hand went right through her. Then, both Joanna and Tommy gasped with horror when the lady turned around and they saw a grinning skull beneath her medieval headdress. Joanna screamed, and Tommy gave a very nervous laugh, then suddenly her face reappeared. It wasn't one of the guides – it was the ghost of Anne Boleyn, once more.

"Hello Joanna. Hello Tommy," she said. As if this were a usual meeting, and they had last seen each other only a few days before. "Are you here again? I thought that we were not going to meet up anymore. It's been a long time since I saw you in the long gallery. Let's walk back to the bench at the centre of our maze."

"It *is* you!" Joanna gasped in surprise, as she followed her. "I had begun to think that somehow I had fallen asleep that last time we talked together, and that our meeting was all a dream. But Tommy saw you, too."

"Yes," said Tommy. "And it was me who saw you first, not my sister."

"And," said Joanna, "I've still got the little pearl button that you gave me. I think that if I handed it in, I would have been called a thief. So, I kept it! I also thought that if it were true, and I hadn't dreamed you up, it would only be in the long gallery that we would see you again. But here you are! This maze is new to you, isn't it? Only just over a hundred years old, mum said."

Tommy joined in. "Have you been scaring other people like you scared us just now? It was quite a long time ago since we last saw you."

"Oh! Yes, it was in the winter, wasn't it?" she exclaimed. "But I don't spend all my time revealing myself to strangers in the long gallery. In fact, you two are the only live humans that I have ever revealed myself to."

"Oh," said Joanna. "So, why in particular have you revealed yourself to us?"

"I don't really know," said Anne with a puzzled look on her face. "I suppose that I had been feeling a little bad tempered. You know. The smashed portraits and display case. Then, I saw Tommy come into the long gallery where the tourists weren't supposed to go, and I just felt like talking to someone, again."

"You went away so quickly last time," said Tommy, "And I saw you walk off with that little boy you told us about. I would have liked to be able to, at least, say 'Hi' to him."

"I am happy to see you both again," said Anne, "but I don't think that I will be able to get Jules to show himself to you."

"Poor little Jules," said Joanna. "You know with the hospitals and medicine of today, I'm sure that they could have repaired his split tongue. In fact, some silly young people think that it looks good to have their tongues pierced with a stud, and when it goes wrong, or gets infected, which it does sometimes, they have to go to a hospital to get the doctors to make it better."

"And you must be one of the silly ones with that stupid ring you have in your nose. You look just like Peppa Pig!" said Tommy in a mumbled voice so that Joanna could barely hear him.

Joanna perked up. "Talking about accidents and illnesses I have been saving this question just in case we saw you here today. So, here it is: what can you tell us about life and times under the reign of Henry VIII? Especially, I would like to know what people did when they became ill, and what they did to relieve pain and suffering in the 1500s?"

"Well, the plain fact is that there were very few cures," said Anne. "And if people became really ill, then most of them died. Adults, children, and babies. The commoners had the simples and cures, made from wild plants, that could give some relief. They got what help they could from their local priests and wise women.

And how they suffered when my dearest husband closed, and then, destroyed all the monasteries and abbeys. Those places were as valuable to the common folk as your hospitals are to you today." She sighed. "We knew nothing about infections and how they were caught and transmitted from one person to another. We also knew nothing about anaesthetics so everyone, including mighty kings, with their own personal doctors, had to suffer when they were ill or needed to be cut."

"Needed to be cut," repeated Tommy. "Why would anyone need to be cut? They didn't do operations like they do in hospitals now, did they?"

"Sometimes, if a person had a fever, the doctors would cut an arm and let the blood flow out. They thought that the fever would be reduced by bloodletting. And sometimes, if a part of the body was infected, the doctors cut them open to get all the pus out," said Anne, with a grim look at Tommy.

"Awesome! Did they have to scrape the pus or squeeze it out?" asked Tommy who was beginning to enjoy this conversation. "That's real gross!"

Joanna tried to divert Tommy to stop him being disgusting. "And your poor Henry," she asked Anne, "what happened to cause that awful ulcer on his leg?"

"Well, I often cautioned him about taking part in tournaments, when he was in his forties. But, he would not listen to me. He didn't want anyone of his friends and rivals to think of him as a coward, or that he was getting old. He shouted at me every time I made the slightest suggestion that he should ease up on dangerous sports."

"So, how did his leg ulcers start?" Joanna asked.

"It was after another of our blazing rows," she said. "He insisted on taking part in a tournament at Greenwich Palace in the New Year of 1536. I could say that it served him right!" she said with a hard look upon her face. "All the bad things started to happen in 1536. That was the year that he murdered me. And soon afterwards, his illegitimate son, the Duke of Richmond, died.

Henry had had leg problems before, mostly resulting from injuries he received during his sporting days. Mainly jousting and hunting. These injuries to his body and legs when he was thrown from his horses, were soon healed with rest, although it was always hard to get Henry to take any sort of rest. He thought that it made him look like a weakling. Then, there were salves and simples to put on wounds.

But in January of that year, when there had been a hard frost and the ground was frozen, there was a joust held at Greenwich. Henry was wearing heavy armour, and he was unseated from his horse by his challenger's lance, and fell on the hardened ground. His horse was also wearing heavy armour and he fell on top of Henry, who was crushed beneath the animal.

Henry was knocked unconscious and was carried to a nearby tent where his doctors and surgeons tried to revive him. I had been so angry with him that I had refused to watch him in the tournament, and because I was heavily pregnant I chose to remain at the palace. I was eventually told of what had happened and that Henry might not wake up. I wanted to rush to his side, but the shock caused me to miscarry, as I told you last time we talked. I lost the boy child that could have saved my life.

Henry woke up after two hours to find firstly, that all his ministers thought that he was dead, and that they were quarrelling about who was heir to the throne. Then, he was told that our son, who would have been his heir, had died before he was born. He knew that I had begged him to give up jousting, and so he was doubly angry with me for aborting his son and for being justified regarding the danger of his jousts.

It was all horrible, and Henry was almost accusing me of deliberately miscarrying the child. It was madness, but I suppose that it could also be the result of him having been unconscious for two hours."

"Did he suffer with those leg injuries as a result that fall?" Joanna asked.

"Yes," she said, "he broke a leg, crushed beneath the weight of his horse, and when the bone mended it was the real start of the ulceration on his skin. He was so angry with me that he would not let me touch it, and, of course, Lady Milk-

Sop Seymour was all too ready to wipe his fevered brow and hold his hand to take away the pain."

"Wicked!" said Tommy. "Was it all smelly and oozing with thick yellow pus?" he had to ask.

"Are you feeling sorry for him now?" Anne was somewhat annoyed.

"But the ulcer did develop into an awful, debilitating mess, didn't it?" Joanna asked.

"While I was still alive," said Anne, "it did not trouble him too much. It was only after he killed me that it developed into what became that dreadful, stinking, suppurating wound that would never heal." And she added, almost under her breath, "and it served him right, too!"

Joanna could see that she was vindictive, and probably, understandably so. She thought for a couple of seconds, and then asked tentatively, "Did you have something to do with that from your ghostly position above?"

"What do you mean? Do you think that I took positive action to prevent him from recovering?" She looked at Joanna accusingly, then she dropped her gaze. "Well," she hesitated, "I did wish him evil, and I did do my best to let him pay for what he had done to me, my brother, and our friends."

"Wicked! What did you do?" Tommy asked. "Did you make it worse for him because he had chopped your head off?"

"There were several doctors treating him, and I was able to make sure that the medical cure books that they referred to were always open at the pages of cures that would make him suffer the most," she said, without any sense of shame.

"What did those books say had to be done to make him better?" Tommy wanted to know.

"The main thing was that they did not let the wound heal properly. As the gash in his leg was closing naturally, they were instructed by those medical books to remove any sign of pus collecting under the renewing skin, so they cut it open again and again in order to drain off the pus, and it never did close properly again."

"Yuk! That's gross!" said Tommy. "I knew that there would be lots of dripping, smelly pus."

"Oh! Stop it, Tommy," scolded Joanna. "Don't keep going on about smelly pus."

She turned to Anne's ghost. "Oh! Anne!" she said. "How could you have been satisfied when you saw what pain and suffering this treatment caused the King? He might have become a monster, but he was still very brave to submit to and suffer what was done to him." She stopped and thought for a moment. "Maybe it was that very suffering that he underwent daily that caused him to become a monster!"

"I did think that I was justified at the time," Anne sighed. Was she really ashamed of what she had done? "I used to think of all the people he had killed. I thought that it was justification for them that he was suffering the most. And serve him right!"

"After all the years that have gone past, do you still feel that way?" Joanna asked. But just as Anne was about to reply, a young couple had found their way into the centre of the maze. She turned to Anne. And found that she was gone. The spell had been broken.

"Hello, you two," said the young man. "Did you find it easy to find the centre?" They both laughed.

"And did you see King Henry and his wife, Anne Boleyn?" his girlfriend asked. "I'm sure that we saw them going into the maze, and we followed them, but they must have disappeared!"

Joanna laughed and Tommy started to say, "But we did see…"

"Shush!" said Joanna. But the young couple hadn't heard Tommy.

The girl looked around. "No! No, Queen Anne here," she said. "I think that I saw her by the drawbridge, and I was sure that she and King Henry were going into the maze."

"Oh! Well! We had better go and find her, before she disappears. Again!" said Joanna.

And the two went off to find their way out of the maze. "What shall we tell mum this time?" asked Tommy.

"I really don't know. I think that she will say that we have been making it all up again." Joanna was left undecided.

September 1996, Bodiam Castle

September thirteenth. The birthdays of my two grandsons, Richard and Charles. They were twins, but, due to the miracle of IVF, their birthdays were two years apart. Richard was ten years old that day, and Charles was eight. Their mother, my daughter Sarah, who had struggled to get pregnant with her husband, had chosen to have her babies that way. So, we now had two almost identical boys, the younger one sort of copying his older brother step by step.

Like most siblings they were, at times, great pals, and at other times they were at each other's throats. How I hated it when they were quarrelling. Richard saw himself as top-dog, and wanted always to be in charge, and poor little Charles was made to feel that he was second best. Their family lived in Robertsbridge, in East Sussex, and for that birthday, when I was on a visit from my home in the New Forest, I had collected them from school with a large picnic basket, and I took them to their favourite playground – Bodiam Castle, which was only about four miles from their home.

The first funny thing that happened was when we were crossing the bridge/walkway to the entrance of the Castle. We stopped to watch the fish which were collecting near and under the bridge, waiting to be fed by visitors who were tossing bread and biscuits to them. There was one small child in a pushchair who threw her dummy into the water. Then, an amazing thing happened. The head of a huge old carp came to the surface and took the dummy in his mouth! If only I had had a camera! What a brilliant photo it would have made. Two seconds later, after the fish had dived down, the dummy came floating to the surface.

When we had finished laughing, we entered the Castle, crossed the central green lawn, and the three of us climbed the central, south facing tower. After pausing for breath at the top, I looked at the fabulous views far down below. There directly below us was the moat with ducks and more huge fishes swimming so near the surface of the water. There was a young mother with two little girls who were busy throwing pieces of bread to the ducks, which were competing with the fish. It was a competition as to which creature could grab the food first. Beyond the moat, there was the beautiful green Sussex countryside with a few of the surviving fabulous Bodiam hop fields. The hops all ready for picking.

And here, on the top of the tower, was a lovely flat roof for us to sit on to have our picnic. Nothing special, just ham sandwiches, packets of their favourite cheese and onion crisps and fizzy drinks. A flask of sweet tea for me, and, of course, at nice birthday cake filled with strawberries and fresh cream.

While the boys were gobbling their food down quickly, I asked them what they liked best about Bodiam Castle.

"It's all the towers, Nan," said Richard. "There are loads of them, and they've all got lots of skinny winding stairs to get up, and some of them have walkways to connect them, and some have had the floors rebuilt so you can go into the old rooms, and look out of the tiny slit windows. And there aren't massive signs everywhere saying you can't do this, and you can't do that."

"It's the climbing of those narrow and steep stairways that does for me. Afterwards, when I get down it makes my legs ache!" I laughed.

"And," said Charles, "they've also got these cool rooms at the bottom where they show videos of what the castle used to look like. And they show what the lives of the soldiers and families who lived in the castle would have been like."

"And, Nan," added Richard, "did you know that there's a kitchen down there which has a well, a very deep well. The water looks disgusting, but I suppose in the days when it was used it would have been a lot cleaner. They must have had to boil all the water that they used for drinking."

"I don't know what hygiene was like in those days," I said, with a grimace of disgust. "But I don't think that they drank much water. I think everyone, including the children, drank weak beer."

"Coo!" said Charles. "What even little kids like me?"

"Yes, even little kids like you. It wasn't very strong beer, and you wouldn't have got drunk, but it was boiled in the making, it was safer than drinking dirty water." I turned to Richard. "Do you know who built the castle?" I asked.

"Yes," he said. "We learned about it in school. It was a man with a very funny name. I think it was Edward Darling something." He stopped to think. "Yes! It was Dalyngrigge!"

Little Charles chimed in. "Dalyngrigge. Dalyngrigge. Smelling like a dirty pig!"

"Stop it!" I said, laughing. "And Richard do you know why they built this little castle right in the middle of the flat countryside with no enemies in sight? It looks like it was made for defence, but there doesn't seem to be much room to house a lot of soldiers."

"Oh! Nan," he said, "just look over the top of this tower. Can you see a river down there? It is the river Rother and when this castle was built in thirteen hundred and something, invading boats from France could sail right up to here. They could cross the English Channel and sail right up this river from Rye."

His brother piped up. "And did they have Knights on horses? And did they have fighting and tournaments here?"

"Yes," said Richard. "Look down there at the car park. That's where there used to be fields, and where they held the tournaments."

"I suppose that must have been the time when England and France were always at war. It was called the 'Hundred Years War.' Can you imagine the country being at war all that time?" I asked. "Although it wasn't really fighting all the time, and a lot of the fights were small skirmishes."

"What's 'skirmishes'?" asked Charles.

"It's sort of little fights, but not real battles," I said. "A bit like when you and Richard fight. Short quarrels, and you make up again." Richard was frowning, ready to argue, but I got in first and asked him, "So what happened to the castle. Why is it now a wreck? Did they teach you that at school?"

"I think that happened during the Civil War," said Richard, scratching his head as he tried to remember more. "The Cavaliers owned the castle then after the Roundheads won the war they took it away from the losers somehow." He scratched his head again and continued, "The Roundheads deliberately destroyed it to stop other Cavaliers from using it as a base to fight from. I think that they set it on fire, and all the wooden doors and then the floors fell in. Whew!" He stopped for a moment, and said, "I can't remember any more!"

"Wow!" I said. "You're ever so good at remembering your history, Richard. But did you know the both of you have the names of the most unlucky Kings of England?"

"But," protested Richard, "Richard, the First was famous. He was called the Lionheart. Cos he was so brave at fighting."

"Yes," I said, "he was very brave, but he wasn't a very good king of England. Do you know that out of the ten years that he was King of England, he only spent six months here in England? All the rest of the time he lived in France, and he went off to fight in the Crusades."

"Wow!" said Richard. "So, was nobody left in charge?"

"Well," I said. "He left his brother John in charge, but he wasn't a very good King either." I looked at Charles, and I could see that he was getting a little bored. "Do you two know the stories of Robin Hood?"

"Yer," said Charles, and he started singing.

"Robin Hood, Robin Hood riding through the Glen.

Robin Hood, Robin Hood with his band of men.

Feared by the Bad, loved by the Good.

Robin Hood, Robin Hood, Robin Hood."

I was astonished. "How did you know that song? I remember it as a TV programme when I was quite young. That must have been in the late 1950s. I remember the actor. He was called Richard Greene. Another Richard. I don't suppose that those programmes are on TV anymore."

"I don't know," said Charles. "I haven't watched any Robin Hood stories on the telly, I just know the song."

I looked at him hard. *Surely* I thought, *there can't be another time-traveller in the family!* I was thinking of my grandmother and the 'gift' she had passed on to me. Then, I let go that thought, and I carried on talking about the English Kings called Richard.

"So," I said, "Richard the First, although he was brave Lionheart, was not much of a king for England. Richard II was such a bad king that he was captured, locked up in a castle somewhere, and starved to death. And Richard III was also a bad King. They said that he killed his two little nephews so that he could make himself King, and then he was chopped to pieces in a battle with Henry VII."

"Ha! Ha!" said Charles, laughing and pointing to his brother and making chopping movements. "Ha! Ha! Richard's not a good name. Bad kings all of them!"

"Hold on, young Charles," I said. "Do you know what happened to the first King Charles? Do either of you know?"

"No!" they said together.

"Well," I said. "King Charles I was on the losing side between the Cavaliers and the Roundheads that you were just talking about, and he had his head chopped off!"

"Wow!" said Charles. And "Wow!" said Richard. "I wonder why our mum gave us the names of such losers."

"I don't know that," I said. "Come on. Let's clear up remains of this picnic, and I'll climb down and have a little rest in the sunshine on that lawn in the middle of the castle. Those steep steps in the towers don't half make my legs ache! But you two can carry on playing, or watching the videos and stuff while I enjoy a rest in the sunshine for a while!"

No sooner then I was settled comfortably on the bench in the sunshine when another lady, a middle-aged woman, came and sat at the other end of the bench. She was strangely dressed all in black, with white linen deep cuffs and matching collar. She also had a white linen head covering. She looked a little bit like a nun.

"It wasn't true what the boys said up there about the castle being destroyed deliberately to stop it being used in the Civil War," she said flatly.

"What?" I cried. I was so surprised. "What? How do you know what we said up there on top of the tower? Me and my grandchildren were all alone!"

"My name is Martha," she said. And…

And suddenly I was in a time-slip again. I became a ghost. I was…Martha!

Martha was proud of her bed above anything else she possessed. The big, strong four-poster had come all the way with her from Newport, on the Isle of Wight, when they had sailed to America in 1630, eight years previously. Her preacher husband, Oberon, was a tall, strong, dominant and imposing man. He had enthused Martha and his followers, getting them to agree to start a new life, in the New World, where he would be their unrestricted leader. They had all sailed on the Merribelle, one of the ships accompanying the Arabella, the ship taking Governor John Winthrop, to New England.

John Winthrop held very strong Puritan beliefs and was seeking to re-establish English Protestantism in the New World. He was determined to clear away all 'popish' idolatry, 'popish' prayers and forms of worship, and even enforced the abandonment of all celebrations of Holy days, even Christmas and birthdays.

To begin with Oberon and his followers were in full agreement with Governor Winthrop, but after years of obediently following the regime of long, long daily prayers and endless readings from the Holy Bible, they were beginning, once more to turn back to some of the Old Ways, especially the celebration of birthdays, Holy days and Christmas. Oberon was changing too. It was almost as if his ways of praying were making him and his followers feel closer to God. And now, Martha believed that Oberon was beginning to think of himself as a new Messiah. Did he think that he *was* God?

She looked down on her bed which had stood proud in her Boston home as a reminder that not everything coming from the Old Country was sinful and wicked. (Although, what she and her stony-faced Puritan husband did in the bed could be considered as wickedness. But, she told herself, it was her duty to submit to his dominant fumbling and possession of her body on Friday nights, after prayers. Every Friday as regularly as the four phases of the moon.)

But eventually, when Oberon would no longer agree with, or submit to the new laws that were being made daily by Governor Winthrop and his Council, he and all his followers had been forced to leave Boston. Exiled into the wilderness like Moses leading the true followers of God out of Egypt!

Martha's bed had once more been disassembled and had been transported, with the exiles in a small fleet of fishing boats. Cast adrift in the ocean in the depths of winter. But God had saved them and had shown them the way to a sheltered bay about halfway between Boston and Cape Cod. There they found a group of eighteen houses, which for the most part were no more than hovels, which Oberon declared had been provided for them by God. In truth, the homes had been abandoned when the small English community that had lived there had been attacked the previous summer by Pequot Indians.

Martha accepted the teaching of her husband who said that the Native Americans of the Pequot tribe were no longer to be addressed as 'Indians.' That was a false term used by the original settlers from the Old World when the first adventurers thought that they had discovered another, shorter way of reaching the continent of India by crossing the Atlantic Ocean, now called Ocean One by the Puritans, instead of journeying around the African Cape.

As soon as Martha's bed was once more re-assembled in the most imposing and solid of the houses, Oberon called a meeting of his band of followers.

"All the while, we were making this difficult journey to this now sacred place," he said in a new and deep imposing voice, quite unlike his usual talking tone, "I have felt the calling of God. We are to settle here and start to build a City of God's Children."

It was not long before his followers understood just what he meant. They had become mesmerised by his teachings and his new self-belief that he had now become the new Messiah.

"It is required by God that all the children who will be born in this new City of God to be indeed God's Children. And it is I, who God has decided, who will be the father of them all. From now on, it is forbidden for any of you men to have sexual congress with your wives. And all you women and girls from the start of menstruation will only have sexual congress with me."

All of Oberon's followers, who he now called his disciples, were astonished but neither protested nor exclaimed against this outrageous announcement. It was as if they had all been entranced by a magic spell. Only Martha, being the one woman thus far to be initiated into the sexual perversions of her husband, was not convinced and not totally subjugated. She did not believe that Oberon was a new Messiah, and she looked around at the adoring faces of their exiled group hoping to see some protest. But both the men and the women seemed to have accepted Oberon's abusive demands. The young girls looked puzzled but, as they turned to their parents for explanation, the same blank look of adoration crept over their faces too.

Martha was about to protest…

…I was back to being Nan again, and I looked around to see where Richard and Charles were. There they were, looking down from the gatehouse tower and waving. I waved back, but I was totally disorientated. Martha was still there, sharing the same bench with me in the sunshine of Bodiam Castle.

"Who are you? And what are you doing here? If you were a Puritan settler in the Americas, then what are you doing here back in England?" I was puzzled. "Am I you? Am I talking to a ghost? I have time travelled before, but this is different!"

"I am a ghost. The ghost of Martha Goodman. And I live here now," she replied simply.

I seemed to accept everything that was happening around me. I was no longer Martha, but I was talking to Martha. "What's happening? I am here in Bodiam Castle, aren't I?"

"Yes, you're back in Bodiam, as am I," said Martha.

"How come?" I asked. "A few minutes ago you and I, as one person, were in Massachusetts, America. What happened to make you come home?"

"Well!" sighed Martha. "We didn't have much time in the new found settlement before the long arm of John Winthrop and his armed cohorts reached out and were threatening Oberon with imprisonment, and scattering our tight band of followers. They were becoming more and more submissive and subservient and were indeed treating my husband like God. They were his disciples. Just like the followers of Jesus!

Finally, to escape the regime and rules of Boston, we all elected to return to England. John Winthrop was only too please to get rid of his troublemakers. He arranged that we should return to England on one of their supply ships. It was in June of 1644 when we sailed up the English Channel and passed the Isle of Wight from where we had set out fifteen years previously. And when we reached Rye, we sailed up the River Rother. And there it was. Bodiam Castle sitting splendidly on top of this low hill.

We all disembarked and approached the Castle cautiously. The building had been abandoned and the entrance bridges across the moat had been disassembled leaving access very difficult. However, all those years in the wilderness in America had taught everyone how to build and make shelters for themselves. Access to the Castle was achieved, and we all settled in to make Bodiam Castle our new home. Once more my lovely four poster bed was reassembled in the fine room in the very tower that you climbed up this afternoon."

"Do you mean," I asked, "that you all settled in here without any of the Parliamentarians, the Roundheads, forcing you out?"

"No," said Martha. "It seemed that as we were Puritans, they accepted that we were no threat, not Cavaliers in disguise, and we were left unchallenged. Oberon was happy. With his charismatic voice, eyes and leadership qualities, he had all his disciples, which included nineteen families, enclosed within the walls of this castle, and virtually falling on their knees to worship him.

But what he wanted most of all was his continued access to all the females in our group. We were beginning to have children born in the group who were all half-brothers and sisters. But what made me draw up the courage to leave him, 'deserting the Christ group', as it was called, was that he started to have sexual relations with his own daughters, my daughters and his, as soon as they were old enough. In fact, in some cases, before they were old enough. Just ten years old!"

I gasped. "Could this really be true? Why had I never heard of such awfulness before?" I asked that very question of Martha.

"Because I did manage to escape," she said. He tried to catch me, and I'm sure that he wanted to kill me before I told others what was happening in the castle. I managed to dodge the guards at the castle entrance. And I didn't use the causeway, I jumped into the moat and I swam."

"Didn't anyone come after you when they realised that you had got away?"

"No." She was very firm in her reply. "I didn't swim straight across the moat. I swam to the side and I hid in the reeds. I hid there for hours until I was sure that they had given up the search. I was wet, dirty and shivering with cold when I eventually climbed out of the water. I crawled most of the way to the church in Bodiam village, and I called to the village Father to help me."

"And did he?" I had to ask. "I would have thought that your Puritan sect would have been hated by the locals."

"They did hate us! But when I told the Father the truth about Oberon's real reason to keep his *flock* separate from the world, he would not believe it at first." Martha sighed. "But I was able to convince him, and the villagers banded together to rescue the children. Some of the men had been soldiers on the side of the Roundheads during the fighting. I was glad when they sacked the castle.

All I really wanted was my children and my old four-poster bed. But somehow fires were started. I don't know whether it was Oberon's disciples or the village folk who started it."

"Oh my God!" I exclaimed. "Are you telling me that everyone in the castle died in a huge conflagration. Everyone including the children?"

Martha was crying now. "Even my own children. My own babies."

...All of a sudden, I was Martha again!

I was staring at the building. Flames were leaping through every door and widow. Suddenly, there was a huge crash as the floors fell in. I knew that everyone and everything was lost. I knew that I would never again, in life or in death, find peace. I knew that my soul would ever range the world seeking some kind of solace or forgiveness...

"Nan! Nan!" Charles was shaking my shoulders. "Are you sleeping, Nan? It must be time to go home now."

I came to with a start. It seemed like I had been living in another world, another time, for hours. But it had only been about five minutes since I had waved to the boys. I looked at the bench. My companion, Martha, the real ghost of Martha, had disappeared.

"It's been a smashing birthday," said Richard. "We've had a super time, haven't we Charlie?"

"Oh! Yes, we have. Thanks Nan." He turned to his brother. "And don't call me Charlie!"

October 2016, Battle Abbey

The two soldiers are sitting on the grass, with their backs resting against King Harold's memorial stone. "Look at them school kids," says Egbert. "Hundreds of 'em with their teachers today. Yer wouldn't think that there was so much to see, would yer?"

"Well. My friend, Egbert. You know zat zere is also much to tell les enfants, especially on this date," says Henri.

"Of course," Egbert whistles through his teeth. "It's the fourteenth today, ain't it?"

"Oui. Le quatorze Octobre 2016. It was in 1066 the day zat we squash-ed ze les Anglais forever," gloats Henri.

"Alright Henri. Yer don't need to lay on the accent for 'ze tourists,' they can't see us anyway," says Egbert. "We've been dead for nearly 1,000 years, so don't keep going on about it. Every time we meet up, it's the same story." Egbert frowns. "You's always crowing about 'ow yer had the best team, and you was the winners. Always the same conversation between us." He frowns again. "And don't call me Egbert! Yer knows that I want to be called Bert! My old pals always called me Bert or Bertie. In fact they used to call me Buck-toothed Bertie."

"Zat is OK. I call you Bert. But what is zis Bucked-toothed?" asks Henri.

Egbert was sad to think of his lost pals. "They called me Buck-tooth cos my front teeth, before they was knocked out in an old battle, used to stick out like a rabbit's teeth. A buck is what we call a male rabbit."

"Oui. Bertie. And that battle was exactly neuf cent cinquant (950) years ago, to calculate it exactement," says Henri, being his usual pedantic self.

"Oh! Here we go again. Blooming picky with the details. You Froggies! Yer always know best," laughs Egbert.

"I am not ze Froggie, as you are saying. I am ze Norman. You call me Froggie – I call you Egbert!" says Henri. "And ze best soldiers are ze Norman soldiers!"

"Yer might have been better soldiers," says Egbert. "But you were still killed that day. Like me."

"You Anglais," sneers Henri. "Zat battle, you could 'ave won, n'est pas? But zere was too much of ze running down ze hill. Too much of the blood running down ze hill as well. Zere is a lake at the bottom. We Normans called it le 'lac de sang', or Senlac as zey call it now. And then zere was 'Arold, he was dead wiz ze arrow in his eye!"

Egbert sighs. "You blooming Froggies," he says again. "1000 years hasn't made you easier to get on with, you know that Henri? Every day we sit on this same hill looking over the site where you Normans stole the land from us Saxons. And every day I've had to listen to your Norman nonsense about how it was your crown anyway, and how you won this amazing victory of talent and might over us, and how we are better off because of it. Well listen up.

Number 1, It weren't your crown. It were 'Arold's.

And, number 2, you was damned lucky to have won. 'Cos our men were exhausted," sighed Egbert. "Don't you forget that in the middle of September 'Arold and our army had marched 200 miles from London to fight and win a battle against invading Vikings, at Stamford Bridge, near York.

I 'ad me mates there with me then. There was Big Stefan, Short-legged John, Wonky-eyed Will, and MeadyMike. We had all got our bows an' 'arrars, swords an' shields, and joined the march up north. Sicknote Simon tried to get out of it, claiming he had the plague and a note from his mum. But a quick burning of his hut left him with nowhere to hide. So, he joined us too, though he did lag behind a bit.

Before the battle at Stamford Bridge our Sicknote Simon would do anything to get out of things and be sent home. Trip into the fire, eat a few dodgy berries, that sort of thing. One evening he even feigned a witch's curse and claim that he was being possessed. Big Stefan was good at bashing out those demons!

Meady Mike brought along some good drinking, and we passed a few good nights watching Wonky-eyed Will trying to chuck stones at squirrels to cook over the flames for supper. He always missed and if anyone from a nearby campfire got hit and complained, then Big Stefan would always step up and say 'What?'… That would shut 'em up.

We all survived Stamford, and were in good 'ealth and strong voice ready for the march home, when Arold heard that your William had landed at

Pevensey. So, we 'ad to march another 200 odd miles to get back 'ere to fight William. Your lot 'ad only marched about 25 miles from Pevensey to get 'ere!"

"But ze victory it was for us, oui?" sneers Henri. "And our Guillaume le Conquerant, he is ze new King of les Anglais. Hein?"

"Yer, and all me pals got killed 'ere. Then your 'orrible William the Conqueror, did make hisself King," says Egbert bitterly. "And he even got hisself crowned in our Westminster Abbey, on Christmas Day, 1066. Bloody Cheek!"

"And then ze Normans are ze masters of les Anglais!" Henri states as a triumphal fact.

Just then a group of ten-year-old school boys, all clutching their work sheets, come running towards us, and right through the two soldiers, to climb onto Harold's memorial stone. "Here it is!" one of them cries. "We can tick it off the list."

"Ooligans!" grumbles Egbert, as he pulls his ghostly self back together again. "They ain't got no manners or respect these days."

"Shall we show ourselves to zees bad enfants and give zem ze big fright?" suggests Henri.

"Nah," says Egbert. "We should try to ignore them, and hope that they go 'ome soon."

They move away from the memorial stone, and go inside the ruined abbey, where they sit together on a windowsill watching the madness of school children rushing about outside.

Egbert muses for a while before voicing his thoughts, then he says, "I remember early on in the battle, before your lot got to us, our silly Sicknote Simon suddenly developed a migraine and claimed that he had left his spare mix of fox-dung-badger-spit-raspberry-flavoured-migraine-cream at the top of the hill. Mike cured 'im quick, bangin' 'im on the 'ead with 'is mead mug. That sorted him out till one of your lot charged up on yer 'orses and got the both of them with one blow of yer axes."

Again he fell silent as he recollected his lost pals. All hacked to pieces by Norman knights. They didn't stand a chance against the Norman heavy horses and axes. He, too, was cut down, while he was fighting alongside Meady Mike. Mike, covering his eyes and turning his face to the woods, hoping that none of the Norman knights would see him.

"Oui, we are the winners that day," says Henri smugly. "And I am sure zat it was your silly friend, Wonky-eyed Will, who gave us the victory. By ze way, what is this Wonky-eye meaning?"

"Old Wonky-eyed Will? It means that he couldn't see straight with one of his eyes. He always looked kind of sideways!" says a puzzled Bert. "How do you mean that old Wonky gave you the victory?"

"Well," says Henri. "Just before I have ze arrow to kill me, it hit me in ze neck, oui, I saw your Wonky-eyed Will. He pick up ze bow and ze arrows from ze floor, and he shoots ze arrow. And he shoots it at your 'Arold. Who ends up wiz ze arrow in ze eye!"

Bert is immediately on the defensive. "That can't be. Wonky couldn't shoot arrows. He had only a sword to fight with." He ponders for a moment. Then. "Bloody Hell!" he shouts. "An own goal! I don't believe it!"

"You see ze Normans, zey did not have ze bows and ze arrows," says Henri. "Ze Normans, zey 'ave ze horses and ze swords and ze axes. I am sure zat your 'Arold vas killed by his own soldier. And I am sure that it was your Wonky, he did it. Just you look at ze Bayeux Tapestry. You will see ze 'Arold viz ze arrow in ze eye, and ze Normans, zey 'ave no arrows."

"That Bayeux Tapestry, just a Norman comic!" laughs Egbert. "It just shows a soldier about to be hit by an arrow. It's not certain that it was 'Arold. And it doesn't show who fired the arrow. But if it was 'Arold, it was a Norman what killed him.

Anyway the Bayeux Tapestry wasn't made in Bayeux, it was made by Saxon nuns in Canterbury Cathedral, in Kent. It should be called the Canterbury Tapestry."

"How do you tell me zis, Bertie?" protests Henri. "It is in Bayeux and it stays in Bayeux. It is the history of this famous story. Guillaume le Conquerant killing ze English King, and he makes 'imself ze King of England. Now do you say it was made by Saxon nuns?"

"Bert, not Bertie. Surely yer knows yer own history mate," protests an exasperated Egbert. "Your Guillaume had a brother, or a half-brother, called Odo. He were the Bishop of Bayeux in yer Normandy. When Guillaume pinched our crown, he made his brother Archbishop of Canterbury, which were the top job in the church 'ere in England. Anyway, the new Archbishop got the nuns to sort of write a story of William the Conqueror. But only the priests and educated churchmen could do writing, so the nuns got to tell the story in pictures. That was so that everybody could learn the story of their wonderful conquerors, they didn't need to be able to read."

"Zen the Bishop of Bayeux, he steals the tapestry when he went home to Bayeux?"

"Yers got it in one!" says Egbert. "It's funny. As yer said in yer silly French way…"

"I beg your pardon! In my silly Norman-French way," stipulates Henri precisely.

"OK. In your silly Norman way, 'ze Normans are ze masters of les Anglais,' and yer has the tapestry to prove it to the common folk like me what can't read," says Egbert with an expert French shrug of the shoulders. "By the way, when are you going to stop talking with that silly accent. I know that after all these centuries you have learned to speak proper English?"

Without waiting for an answer he carries on talking. "But although the Normans became the masters, and they were horrible, cruel masters, they never quite dominated the Anglais."

"OK," sighs Henri, "I can do it for you." He sighs again and changes the way he is speaking. "What are you meaning?" he asks. "The Normans they took everysing away from the people. They were the Conquerants."

"That's better!" says Egbert. "Yes, they were the conquerors all right, and they did take everything away from the people," he agrees. "But, you see, they didn't take away the English language. I think that it is the language that makes a people."

"What are you meaning?" asks a puzzled Henri.

"Listen to everyone, the kids and the teachers, talking around us! What language do you hear?" asks Egbert.

"English?"

"That's it! English! Not French!" says Egbert. "You Normans conquered les Anglais, but you didn't manage to force them to speak French, or Norman-French, if you prefer. You didn't make it illegal to speak English, and punish those who did. To be properly conquered the people lose their own language and are forced to use the language of the conqueror. You know, like the people of South America. They all speak either Spanish or Portuguese."

"Then what happened to le Francais 'ere?" asks Henri.

"You actually made English richer."

"How did le Francais make this?" Henri is puzzled.

"Well, let's see," said Egbert, with a scratching of his head. "Now here's a way to explain it. What's your Norman-French word for 'pig'?" he asked.

"It is 'le porc'," says Henri.

"OK. What are the words for 'bull' and 'sheep'?"

"These words in French are 'le boeuf' and 'le mouton'," says Henri. "Why do you ask me this silly question?"

"This is what I mean about making the English language richer," explains Egbert. "Our language didn't die away after William the Conqueror made hisself King of England, instead Norman-French words were added to the English language. For example, I think that when the new Norman barons took over the lands and castles that they had pinched from the Saxon lords, naturally used Saxon peasants for servants. And when the new masters demanded 'porc,' 'boeuf' or 'mouton' for their food, Saxon peasant cooks scratched their heads and when they understood what their masters wanted, they now had new words to use. So, the live animal was still called 'pig,' 'bull' and 'sheep,' and then the dead animal, served as meat was named 'pork,' 'beef' and 'mutton.'"

"Ah! Ha!" exclaims Henri. "And now les Anglais are speaking le Francais without knowing that they do it." He thought for a moment and then asked, "And what about the word 'swine'? That is also the word for pig/porc. N'est pas?"

"Yea," says Egbert. "Now that was a word of old Saxon, weren't it? Proper Saxon!"

"And ze Saxon came from where?"

"You're trying to goad me now, Henri," says Egbert.

"Ah oui," laughs Henri. "I know that the Saxon, he comes from Germany, eh? So ze English has been conquered before, hein?"

"Yer. Yer. Yer. I've 'eard it all before," says Bert with a wry smile. "You ain't gonna pick no more quarrels with me today.

Anyway, as I saying before yer rudely started in on me again…it wern't just words for animals and food that were added to the language. Over the years following what is now called the Battle of Hastings, 'undreds of French words were added. Especially in administration, justice, parliament, and laws.

But only the lords and barons spoke French. And eventually, because they married good old Saxon girls, the French died away. Yer knows what them women can be like. They always gets their ways. 'No sex tonight, monsieur, unless you speak to me prettily en anglaise.' And the babies – they spoke Anglais like their mothers. So, Voila, how you are les conquerants?"

Henri has his own jibes. "It is very funny you English. You think that you are special peoples, n'est ce pas? But you are all the bastards. Yes?"

"We ain't bastards," protests Egbert, getting a bit annoyed. "We were all proper English after 1066!"

Henri laughs. "You are very funny. But before 1066 you were and are still the bastards."

"Why do you keep saying that!" Egbert stands up and raises his fists as if to strike.

Henri laughs at him. "You can't kill me, I am already dead. And so are you. So, you call yourself English. But the England it 'as been conquered many times before we, the Normans came 'ere. Let me tell, n'est ce pas?"

Egbert sits down again and grumbles, saying nothing.

"Well, let us see. OK?" says Henri. "There was the Celts, the Vikings, the Franks, we Normans are also Franks you know? Then there was the Romans, the Angles, the Saxons…"

"Yer, I know," says Egbert shamefaced. Then he suddenly perks up. "But it's like what I says before, we always came out the winners. All those people either left and went 'ome, or mixed in with us English. Leaving behind words of their languages that, in time, became part of the English that is spoken today!" If it possible for a ghost to puff out his chest, then that's what Egbert does. Then he adds, "Even with all the foreigners who now come to live here. They become what is now called British, and lots of their words are added to our language too!"

He ends is little speech with a triumphant waving of his arms.

Then all the schoolboys come running into the old church ruin. And Egbert and Henri decide to 'give up the ghost' and just disappear!

November 2002, Caldwell Manor

It was a beautiful day, 1st November, and the day after Halloween, when I went for a walk in the beech woods near my home in the Ashdown Forest. The sun was shining on the fallen leaves which made a golden, rustling carpet for me and my Jack Russell dog, Champion, to enjoy. I was limping quite badly that day due to a permanent back pain I had as a result of a fall off a ladder a couple of years previously. Some days it was better than others, but today it was particularly bad.

But, in spite of the pain, I was determined to enjoy as much as I could of the fabulous autumn that we were having that year. And I knew that the path I was taking through the woods had a few fallen trees that I could perch upon to rest when I needed to.

This beautiful beechwood was at the back of Caldwell Hall, a splendid old manor house which had been owned for generations by the Caldwell family. The ownership of the beech wood had been for several years in dispute between the current owners of the Hall and the local council because Johnathan, the deceased husband of Marion Caldwell, the forceful matriarch of the family, had made a gift of part of the woodland to the people of the Ashdown Forest for them to enjoy. And to enjoy without being attacked as trespassers by the Caldwell sons, who would walk in the woods carrying loaded shotguns! I knew them to be pompous and aggressive to anyone who they considered to be lower class and common. They hated it that we local village *idiots* were allowed free access to their upper class and aristocratic world! And since their father's death they spent years and spent a fortune on lawyers, who even took the case to the High Court, to contest and overturn the terms of his will. It took many years to resolve but eventually the gift was backed by the courts.

That day, I was not bothered about the brothers, I was remembering the games my friends and I played in these woods when we were children. We used to make bets and dares on who would be brave enough to climb over the walls into the grounds and get nearest the Caldwell house. I was the baby of the group and I was never brave enough to do more than climb the wall and perch there.

So, there I was sitting rather awkwardly on a beech log with Champion nearby happily running about through the dry, fallen leaves, and thinking about the past, when suddenly I saw a handsome young woman wearing tweeds and a bright red hat who strolling along the path in my direction. To my surprise she came right up to me. "Hello Ben," she said, in a very sweet and ladylike tone of voice. I was startled. "You *are* Ben Roberts, aren't you? Don't you remember me? In the old days I used to be your sister Mary's best friend."

I looked at her again, and now some teenage memories slowly came back to me. I could see in my mind's eye, a pretty teenage girl with flowing blonde hair walking down the road with my sister Mary. They have their arms about each other, and they were making their way to the bus stop. Their usual destination was the cinema or the coffee shops in Tunbridge Wells. "Are you Emily. Emily Robinson?" I asked hesitantly. "Didn't you get married to Edward Caldwell?"

"Yes. Indeed I did," she said quite flatly without any expression.

She was leaving all the work of the conversation to me. "Did you divorce him then?"

"No. He murdered me!" she said bluntly.

"Murdered!" I was flabbergasted. I had never heard about any murder in this part of the world, let alone the murder of my sister's best friend. "I thought that we hadn't heard from you in such a long time because my sister died. That was now thirty years ago and you were well ensconced in the Caldwell family. I know that they don't like to mix with us, the local yokels!"

Emily scoffed. "Ha!" she exclaimed. "Ain't that the truth!"

"So! You were murdered," I could hardly believe what I was seeing. "Are you a ghost now?" Am I really speaking to a ghost? I know that it's Halloween, but ghosts? Are you tricking me?"

"No tricks. No wailing spooks or phantoms in white sheets. Just me, and I am a real ghost. And, yes, I was murdered," she repeated. And I have been unable to communicate with anyone since it happened, but now I've got you to help me." She said it flatly without any hint of a 'please will you help me?'

Because of the date, I still couldn't believe that this was not a hoax. But I played along. "Help you?" I queried. "Help you with what?"

"Get the buggers who did it caught and sent to prison, of course." She sounded exasperated, as though it was my duty to help her.

This was a ghost demanding some action on my part to right a dreadful wrong which had happened in the past.

I pinched myself to check that I was not dreaming, and I sighed. "I suppose that you had better tell me your story then."

"Oh! Don't sound so enthusiastic," she said, sarcastically. "I have been waiting years, as a ghost, to reveal myself, and it does gets easier on and around Halloween. And now, when at last I find someone with whom I can make contact, you can't be bothered!" She paused and looked me straight in the eyes. "Whatever happened to the man of God who spent his working life trying to bring calm and peace into people's lives? I know that I am dead, but I still want justice!"

I wasn't quite sure whether we committed Christians believed in ghosts. I had never seen one before. But I felt mean. She made me feel mean and selfish. I heaved yet another sigh. "Oh! Go on," I said. "Tell me your story."

"Ok!" she said, "I think that I will start with my schooldays. I loved your sister Mary. She was my best friend at school. Do you remember the girls Grammar School in Tunbridge Wells that we both went to?"

I nodded, and she carried on. "During term time, we both used to get on the bus together each morning in Forest Row, then it was a forty-minute ride to school. And then we took the same bus ride back home again at the end of the school day. We did that every school term for six years. So, we got to know each other really well. I don't suppose that you remember those days because you were so much younger than us?"

"No, I don't remember anything much of Mary's schooldays, apart from the school she went to, because she was six years older than me." I tried to think back. "One thing I do remember was that when I was about ten or eleven that she had fallen in love with a boy who didn't love her. She wouldn't say who it was, and she was always crying. It made me sad too."

"That's right," said Emily. "It was my brother John that she was in love with. Every time she came round to our house, she would moon around after him! Do you remember that my father was the local doctor? I'm sure that your family was on his books."

"So that's who she was in love with!" I exclaimed. "She never said. And yes! I remember Dr Robinson. Of course! He was your father. He retired years ago, and we were transferred to Dr Hobbs who took over your dad's practice." I thought about the old days when I would sit in the doctor's dull yellow-painted waiting room holding my mother's hand and wondering just what the doctor was going to do to me this time!

"My brother, John, was a couple of years older than the two of us, and I suppose that, at the time, he didn't want a girlfriend because it wasn't long before he was due to go off to University to train and study to become a doctor, just like our dad. It was through him, you know, that I came to know the Caldwells." She paused. "That was my undoing.

They were a good-looking family. The older brother, Charles, was what we used to call *rugged.* He was very tall, well over six foot, strong and sort of good looking with a hard square jaw, and dark brown eyes under heavy eyebrows. His brother Edward was totally different. So different that they didn't look like brothers at all! He was of medium height, and he had a nice, comfortable face with lovely blue eyes and pale brown hair. I was immediately attracted to him as soon as we were introduced.

The whole family were always very snobbish and we, my brother and I, were just about acceptable to their mother as friends for Edward and Charles because we were the doctor's children. There was an older brother called Michael, but I never met him as he had already left home, so I didn't know him. No one talked about him, and I wasn't curious. Then, I don't know why or by whom, it was decided that Edward should marry me."

I was puzzled. "What do you mean by 'it was decided'? Didn't you fall in love with him?"

"All I know was that an heir was needed for the Caldwell family, and I think that I was chosen by their mother as a suitable, healthy breeder. For my part, I was young, only eighteen, and I fell in love with a handsome young man, a fabulous manor house, stables full of lovely horses, gardens, grounds and woodlands, and yes, the prestige of marrying one of the Caldwells." She paused. "I was a fool!" she said bitterly, "and it wasn't long before I began to pay for my mistake."

"Tell me about the mother, Marion Caldwell was it? Your new mother-in-law, and how she influenced your married life?" I asked. I suppose that I should have been excited to hear of the struggles which led to her murder, but I was resigned to it ending in me having to go to the police and tell them that I had been talking to a ghost. I didn't want to be thought of as a fool.

"My mother-in-law. What can I say about her?" She stood quietly for a moment, trying to choose the right words to describe her. "Physically, she was what one would call handsome. She was dark blond, like Edward, not at all pretty, but of striking presence. And like her son Charles she was tall, thin and powerful. She was gifted in speech and could say things in either a very pleasant or deeply unpleasant way.

To begin with, it was what I realised later, a totally insincere manner. She oozed charm and expressed delight in my company. And having been assured of my acceptable parentage, my healthy young body, fit to breed, as it were, I think that she selected me as the saviour of the Caldwell line. I am sure that it was she who pushed her son Edward into proposing marriage to me."

"But, what was she *really* like," I asked again.

"I can tell you about that in two words. Bullying and controlling!" Emily was angry now.

"It started the moment we came back from our honeymoon." And then a dreamy look took over her face. "Once away from his family, Ed was lovely. We had a wonderful two weeks in Venice. He was loving and he was gentle. I was a shy virgin, and he coaxed me into lovemaking. It was wonderful. He was wonderful. If I hadn't been absolutely in love with him before our marriage, I fell head over heels in love with him during our honeymoon. In Venice, we saw all the famous sights: St Mark's square, the Cathedral, the Accademia and Rialto bridges and the wonderful churches which were like art galleries.

After our evening meals, several times we took romantic Gondola rides in the moonlight. In the daytime, we discovered all the back streets too, with their little bridges criss-crossing the canals. He bought me a beautiful leather handbag, and a real silk shawl. I had never owned anything made of real silk before, and I really treasured them. He also bought me two lovely dresses and a silk parasol to protect me from the fierce midday sunshine. I came home on a rosy cloud of expectation of living in comfort in a fabulous home, with a loving husband at my side. That he would continue to be my own true love, my knight in shining armour." The dreamy look vanished.

"But he was horrid! Once back with his family, especially his domineering mother and his elder brother Charles, he changed completely. All three of them bullied me and gave me no space to be just me. I was not allowed to go into town by myself. When I did any shopping, I was always accompanied by my husband or my mother-in-law. I couldn't even go to visit my mother and father. I wasn't quite a Cinderella, but they made sure that I was occupied with household duties almost all the time.

We did have a housekeeper, a parlour maid, a cook, and a gardener who did all the main work, and I was made to feel that my position was only just little bit above them. Not quite a servant and not quite part of the family. The only pleasure I had was when I made sneaky visits to the stables." Now she took on the dreamy look again. "The horses. Just the smell of them filled me with an inside warmth. How I loved to caress their soft noses and have them snuffle me for an apple or a carrot, if I was able to persuade the cook to find a stale one in the kitchen larder.

As I said, the only time I managed to go outside I had to sneak out without anyone seeing me. It was the ultimate control that they all had over me. I had thought that my husband would at least be kinder and soften his family's attitude towards me. But even in the bedroom Edward changed towards me. There was no longer any gentle loving, only hard demands and quick satisfaction for him.

The only person in the household who had any time for me was his father, Johnathan, who was a semi-invalid. Sometimes in my spare moments I would go to him. Perhaps to take in his morning coffee, or his lunch. He liked to have his daily routines, and his eleven o'clock coffee was one of them. He didn't join the family much, not even for the evening meals because he liked to go to bed early. During the daytime, he was often to be found in the heated conservatory. He loved his flowers, and he had a fine collection of orchids. 'Hello, pet,' he would say to me. 'Would you be kind enough to fill that little watering can for me?' And when I passed it to him, he would thank me very nicely and explain again and again just how much sunlight and water the plants needed. Not too much of either so that they would produce their flowers. These were of such magnificent colouring that the conservatory was ablaze with colour, and each stem lasted for weeks and weeks."

I jumped in to stop the flow of words for a moment. I asked, "Didn't your father-in law try to stop the bullying. He must have seen and heard what was going on?"

"No," she replied. "He was quite a sweetheart, but he lived in a world of his own. In those days people would have said that 'he was away with the fairies' but, of course, nowadays his condition would be recognised as dementia. Unfortunately, he died only a year after I joined the family. Then all the brakes were off."

"What do you mean by saying that the brakes were off?" I asked.

"You know." She sort of struggled to explain exactly what difference the death of her father-in-law made to her life. "I suppose that it was that there was no longer anyone or anywhere that I could run to, to be treated with kindness, and they knew it. Nowhere in that huge house did I feel safe. Nowhere I could be without feeling that there were several pairs of eyes checking on what I was doing."

I was a bit exasperated with her apparent feebleness. "Then why the hell didn't you run away?" I asked.

"I couldn't. I just couldn't," she replied. "I was virtually locked in. The immediate gardens around the house had high walls."

(Those walls were the very ones that I had just been thinking about before my ghost had appeared.)

She continued, "Far too high for me to climb. And the driveway had eight-foot-high wrought iron gates which were also impossible for me to climb.

These main gates had an entry phone and anyone who wanted to come into the grounds or go to the main house had to phone through and someone, usually Mrs Hughes, the housekeeper, would press a button which would open the gates if that caller or delivery man was accepted.

Even the stables were shut off to me now, and another locked gate was put in place between the main gardens and the stables and paddock."

I was somewhat bemused, somewhat disbelieving in what she had said. "What was the reason, do you think, that the Caldwell family watched over you and kept you so close?" I asked.

She sighed. "I think it was because they, more specifically my mother-in-law, were determined that I should produce an heir, and that there should be no doubt of the child's parentage. There were no DNA tests in those days to prove a child's paternity. I did hear whispers from the parlour maid and the cook that several years ago the oldest son Michael, who was just as horrible as his mother and brothers, had been married once, and that his wife had runaway when she found out that she was to have a baby. Then, he ran off too. Perhaps he wanted to find his wife. I don't know. I just supposed that he did because I never heard anyone speak about him. But, an heir to the estate was lost. And there were no family photos which included him. I think that they wanted to make sure that I didn't run off too!"

"Did your mother-in-law ever actually hurt you?" I asked her. "In what way was she nasty to you, and why?"

"I vividly remember at least two occasions when she hit me. The first time was when she crept up behind me while we were all having afternoon tea. She poked me hard in the back for something or other, or for something that I had failed to do, or not done to her standards. I yelped, more in surprise than in pain, and I dropped my teacup, and it broke. 'You stupid bitch,' she almost spat in my face, and then she slapped me hard, hard enough to make a bruise, saying that the tea service was an extremely valuable, and irreplaceable antique left to her by her great grandmother."

"Did no-one in the room speak up for you or say anything in your defence?" I asked.

"No one," she said, "not even my so-called beloved husband. You must understand that none of her sons ever opposed their mother in any way. She was the supreme powerful matriarch of the family, and ever since their births, she had crushed her sons into obedience, almost as much as she crushed me. I am sure that as children she had never cuddled them, but she had beaten them regularly for showing any sign of spirit. As adults they never, ever, dared to speak against her or go against her wishes."

"Phew!" I exclaimed, almost to myself. "I really don't understand why you didn't run for the hills the very first time you met her."

"Ah! But, as I told you, this monster could turn on the charm and I was trapped in her sticky web before I realised the danger that I was in."

"Not a nice lady then!" I was sympathising. "How did she treat you on a day-to-day basis?"

"Mostly, she would put me down saying nasty things about me. For example, knowing that I was nearby she would say something like, 'where is that useless creature? She's never here when you need her.' And on seeing me she would say, 'I want you to go to my room and bring me my embroidery,' or something equally useless for which she had no immediate need. 'Right now!' Or perhaps, seeing me in a summer dress she would remark to someone else nearby how awfully common it was to wear cotton dresses with flowers all over them.

That sort of thing, little nibbly things which on their own would never have mattered. But the criticisms went on and on, hour after hour, day after day, always belittling me at every turn and making me feel that to the family I was worth less to them then the dirt on the soles of their shoes. I hated it. And because I was a virtual prisoner in the house, I could never escape it."

"So, how did she behave towards you when she found out that you were expecting?" I asked.

"Ah! Yes!" and this was first time I saw her smile. "It was eighteen months after my marriage when I did fall pregnant. At last, I was treated more tenderly by the family, especially by my husband Edward, and for a while I was lulled into the belief that he did care for me after all. Even Marion, my mother-in-law. I wouldn't say that she was kinder towards me, but she was less critical, less biting. But I was still watched over like a hawk by both brothers, and especially by her.

My pregnancy went well and in fact I was, at last, allowed to see my father who was summoned to the Hall to check my health and progress in the pregnancy. We had a lovely gossip about home and family while he was checking me over. He, then, pronounced to all that I was doing well, but that I needed plenty of rest and good food. Plus, a few treats to appease the cravings of pregnancy. And I was treated well. In fact, I was treated better that I had been since the day that Edward and I had returned from Venice."

I smiled at her. "That must have been so good to be treated with kindness after so long."

She smiled back at me and carried on with her story. "In due course, I gave birth to a lovely little baby boy. It was a home birth, of course, with a midwife employed to look after me and the baby. Such a sweet little baby. I loved him dearly from the moment that he was born. But he wasn't really mine, and I wasn't even allowed to name him. The family took over immediately, and they named him James. I would have preferred Johnathan, for his grandfather. I suppose that I was lucky that they allowed me to hold him at all. My mother-in-law tried to interfere, but he was still my baby. And because I fed him myself until he was weaned, for this time only she had no say in the matter.

He became the joy of the whole family. I adored my baby. He was the only one in the world who I truly loved, and who loved me too. For the first eighteen months after he was born, I was so happy. As happy as I had ever been in my life. How everyone laughed and joined in at his attempts to walk and then talk, but gradually my mother-in-law started taking control. At first, it was his clothing. Nothing I liked or bought was ever good enough, all too common like his mother. Marion had to choose everything that he wore. Then, it was his toys and baby reading books. I had no say in what he played with or the books that were read to him. Only his father and grandmother were allowed that privilege!"

"Are you saying that you had no choice, no control over your baby's basic needs?" I asked. "Were you never allowed to take him to visit his other grandparents? Surely, the doctor was a fit enough person to handle a baby?"

"Exactly nothing!" and two ghostly tears rolled down her face. "My son, who had been the joy of my life, was gradually taken away from me. Once he began to walk, my mother-in-law started treating him like a puppy in training. She always had a sweetie or a treat in her pocket and if she saw him with me she would call him away from me to be at her side, rewarding him with one of these treats.

"I overheard her several times talking me down, telling him what a useless mother I was, and how such a sweet and clever child deserved better. While he went out daily with his father and his uncle, when sometimes I was included, I was hardly ever allowed to be alone with him myself. On the few occasions when I did so I liked to walk with him all through the gardens and woodlands. When it was allowed, the walks and games we had in these very woods became like a treasure to me. I used to laugh and sing with him, and to teach him funny little songs. But if he ever repeated those things in the house he was told to 'stop that nonsense and behave himself.'"

I felt so sad for her. "Did you feel that your little boy, James was it, loved you and recognised you as his mummy?"

"Of course," she smiled at memories that were clearly showing on her face. "For the first five years of his life, I was absolutely his Mummy. Edward was Daddy, and my mother-in-law, Marion, was Grandmother. Never Granny, mind you," she laughed. "He was a healthy little boy. A proper little boy. I taught him to recognise the alphabet and he started to read some baby books. His favourite book was a simplified version of Hans Christian Andersen stories. He loved especially the Ugly Duckling story.

But most of all he used to love playing outside. We would play and laugh together, and I got the gardener to fix up a rope swing to a low branch of a beautiful elm tree on the edge of these woodlands. What fun we used to have."

Then she became serious, and a look of pain crossed her face. "When he was just five years old they enrolled him at a local private school. From then onwards, I lost most of my daily contact with him. His father or uncle drove him to school at 8:30 in the morning and collected him again at six o'clock in the evening. I hardly ever saw him from then on except during our evening meals, which we shared with the whole family, and it was always his grandmother who put him to bed. It was only at weekends, when he would be allowed to spend short periods alone with me. And how I treasured every minute I shared with him.

Eventually, when he was seven years old, he was sent to a boarding school where he mixed with the children of the upper class, or whose parents were so wealthy that they became a class apart. I hardly ever saw him. He was lost to me, and I was oh, so lonely. Although Ed and I tried, I didn't get pregnant again and James was my only child."

"How did you feel about Ed by then?" I was curious about this strange relationship: this young lady virtually a prisoner within her own home, and her child almost abducted. I wondered why she didn't call for help. If not the police, of whom she might be afraid, then why not her own family, especially her father. "And why didn't you try to escape? Or at least call for help?"

"Even now when I look back on my time on Earth I ask myself those same questions." She sighed. "In spite of everything, I still can't believe that I loved him, but I suppose that I did, and I thought that being loving towards him would bring our son back home. But that never happened.

Edward was part of the family conspiracy to have an heir to the Caldwell estate who was untarnished by people of the modern world. At most times, when we were alone, he was nice to me. But as soon as he was with his mother and his brother, he became just what his mother had made him – a control freak and a bully. I gradually I lost my faith in him, and then my love for him eventually faded away. Then I had nothing. Not even the courage to run when occasionally I could get beyond locked doors and gates."

"How often did you get beyond the locked gates?" I asked.

"While my mother-in-law was focusing on the separation of my baby from me, I was at least allowed to go the riding stables. I loved the horses, the smell of them and the touch of them. And their response to me. And I, gradually, began to replace the loss of my child with love of the horses. I loved particularly a gentle grey mare who would whinny, almost as if she were calling me, every time she saw me. Her name was Cinnabar, named by my late father-in-law for one of his beloved orchids. I was very shy, but slowly I began to get to know the stablemaster, young Henry Jones, who had been with the family since he was a boy.

I say *young* because that's what they all called him. His father had also been called Henry. He had been the boss of the stables until he died, and then young Henry took over. That was well before I married Edward. I think that although he was called young Henry, he was several years older than Edward, well into his thirties. Anyway, after the death of his father, Henry took over the stables and continued to live with his mother in a small cottage, where he had lived all his life, not far from here in these woods.

"When my son was taken away from me completely and sent to boarding school, the only joy left to me in my life was visiting the horses, especially Cinnabar. Slowly, slowly I began to put my trust in Henry, and he began to learn of my wretched life in the big house. And, of course, eventually we fell in love! It was a platonic love, but it was real, nothing was ever said between us about love, but I'm sure that we both felt it."

"And, I suppose, Edward eventually found out. So, what happened then?" This, I thought, would be the climax of her story. Her husband killing her. But no, there was still more to tell!

"It was very strange," she said, wistfully. "It happened one day when Henry and I were just talking in Cinnabar's stable. I had never learned to ride, and I thought that I might like to sit on her back, just to feel what it would be like. I stood on a mounting block and Henry tried to help me climb up on her back. But it was more difficult than I thought it would be, and I fell off. I landed on the other side of the horse, into a soft pile of straw. I didn't hurt myself at all, and I sat up and laughed and laughed. Then Henry joined in. He came round the back of the horse and pulled me to my feet, and still laughing, he put his arm around my waist.

Edward must have been outside the stables and hearing the laughter, he was curious. I don't think that he had heard me laugh for years. He walked in just as Henry was about to release me. He saw the look that we were giving each other and guessed at once that I was in love with Henry.

"What's going on here?" He didn't shout. It was a sort of low hiss, and I knew that I was in trouble. Henry and I were in love with each other, but nothing inappropriate had ever taken place between us. With me, because I was still unsure of myself, and with him, out of respect for his employers.

I tried to brave it out. "Nothing is going on here except that I have made a fool of myself trying to get onto Cinnabar's back. And I fell off!" I laughed again, hoping to dispel the tension in the stables.

"Get back to the house. I will deal with you later," Edward hissed at me. "And as for you, Jones," he said in a low, dark voice, "I think that we will have to think about you continuing to have a job here."

I shouldn't have interfered. "You can't dismiss him," I cried. "We haven't done anything wrong. And if you send him away, he and his mother will have nowhere to live. Their cottage is their home."

I ran back to the house in tears, and I went straight to my bedroom. When I tried to go back down again later, I found that my bedroom door was locked. I was trapped. When I was eventually let out it was only to face the family who were lined up against me in the morning room. It was almost like a courtroom scene, and I was the prisoner in the dock! They had obviously discussed my future together.

My mother-in-law came right up to my face and slapped it with full force. Then she snarled at me. "You are an absolute disgrace. An utter disgrace to this family, to whom you owe so much, and who you have deceived ever since you came here. I should have known better than to let a guttersnipe like you marry one of my wonderful sons…"

In spite of myself tears were gushing from my eyes, but I still attempted to defend myself… "I, I…"

"Don't you dare to say anything," she continued, still in my face. "You slut! You will stay in your room until we, no I, decide what to do with you. Of course, Edward will no longer share your bed or your bedroom…" I looked at Edward, but his face was like a granite statue… "And, of course, you will no longer visit the stables or any of the woods and gardens. Slut!" she spat at me again. "And they all left the room, locking me in once more."

"So, how did you end up being murdered?" I asked. I had been sitting on the log for quite a while by then, and I was ready to move on – both physically and in the story telling.

"I suppose that they didn't really want to kill me," she mused.

"But, what happened?" I persisted.

"Perhaps, it was my fault, after all." She looked down at her feet, still wearing the shoes she had bought forty years ago.

Now she was surely stringing me along. "Tell me what happened?" I said through gritted teeth.

"Remember, I was locked inside the morning room," she repeated. "Well, I was kept there for hours, and inevitably after a while I needed the loo. Not many toilets in the old manor house, and certainly not adjacent to the morning room. I banged on the door and called out, but no one took any notice of me. Not even the housekeeper, the cook, or the parlour maid, whose name was Lucy, and with whom I was on relatively pleasant terms.

Eventually, when I could hold myself no longer, I turned to the windows. The morning room was on the first floor, with the windows facing south, and there was a wide spreading, mature wisteria shrub growing up the wall, almost to the upper floors and cut away from the windows. I carefully climbed onto the nearest branch, but it wasn't as strong as I thought it was. The branch broke and I fell, catching onto twigs of branches as I did so. I hurt my arm as I hit the ground, and I yelled in pain. Edward and his mother came running. 'Ed. Get hold of that bitch,' she called. I stood up, and I was about to make a dash for freedom, but Edward caught hold of my skirt and stopped me from getting away. And then I could hold my bladder no longer, and I wet myself in front of them!

My mother-in-law slapped my face again and punched me in my stomach. 'Filthy bitch! Filthy slut!' she spat at me as she pushed me away from her with full force. I fell over and hit my head on a rock that bordered the flowerbed. I heard my husband say, 'Oh God, you've killed her,' and all went black. But I wasn't dead. Yet.

I must have been unconscious for a long time. As I slowly came to, I realised that I was the bottom of a pit. A deep pit with beech trees above which had the sunlight filtering through the branches. This pit turned out to be my grave. I opened my eyes long enough to see the trees and the grinning face of Charles just as hc threw a spadeful of earth on top of me. I tried to make a noise, but I couldn't.

I know that Charles saw my eyes open, but he said nothing to Edward, who was there but I could see that he was a very unwilling party to the whole incident. I found out later that he had been told that I had died when I hit my head on that rock. I am sure that if he had known that I was still alive, he would never have let Charles kill me. Deliberately suffocate me in that pit."

"Well," I gasped. In spite of her being a ghost and having told me that she had been murdered, I was still taken aback. "How soon did you become a ghost? And what do you think that I can do after all this time?" I asked. "It's now almost forty years ago since you died!"

"First of all, I'll take you to the place where they buried me, and perhaps you can think of a way to proceed." She started to walk towards the chain link fence that divided the beechwood between the Caldwell's private land and the area that had been donated to the public by Johnathan Caldwell. Then, as if it were no barrier, she just passed through the fence as if it were not there.

I called my dog, Champion, and I followed her to the fence. "Hang on a moment," I called out. "Firstly, you know that I am not allowed to go beyond this fence, and secondly, I couldn't do it anyway. There is no gate, and I am not fit enough to climb over."

She slowed down, and then she pointed at a hollow between two enormous beech trees. "Well, I think that you won't need to climb over. My grave, if you can call it a grave, is just over there."

The penny dropped. "So that is why the Caldwell brothers fought so hard, and at such great cost to overturn the provisions of their father's will. This part of the woods, which use to be in the heart of the Caldwell estate, was now just a few feet away from where they had buried you! Almost within the view of the general public!"

"Yes! Exactly!" was all she said.

"Ok!" I said. "Now we must think about the whole situation. If you have been buried there for thirty odd years, then how am I going to be able to *discover* your bones? I can't just go to the local police and say that there may a body buried in the Caldwell beech woods. I certainly won't be able to tell them that I have been told so by a ghost. Everyone will laugh at me and send me packing, calling me a crazy old man."

She stood and looked at me. Then, she looked at my dog. "Perhaps," she mused, "you can say that your Jack Russell got through that hole in the fence," she pointed to a small hole at the bottom of the fence a few feet from where I was standing, "and that he found a bone which he brought to you."

"Yuk!" I shivered. "That would mean that somehow I would have to dig up part of your skeleton. I can't do that. And, anyway, it would be horrible! Are you so positive that you want to be discovered, and have a police investigation and all that that entails?"

"Yes," she said in a very determined manner. "I want it to be all out in the open. Those precious Caldwells! It's still not too late for them to be sent to prison, and for the rest of their lives!"

"How old are they now? And how have they been living since you died?" Now I was getting curious once more. "And what happened to your son?"

"My son. My poor deluded son." She sighed. "He would have been forty-nine now. The family made sure that he lost all memory of me, and he was brought up to believe that I had run away with young Henry. He disappeared too, you know. Edward and Charles killed him. Soon after they had disposed of my body they captured faithful Henry, who should have got away after he realised that I was missing. They tied him up, put weights in his clothing, rowed him out to the middle of the lake and tossed him in. He drowned. I saw it all happen, and I couldn't do anything to prevent them from doing it. It was horrible. And he must have gone straight to heaven, because I have never seen him in the ghost world." Another strange ghostly tear ran down her face.

She controlled herself after a moment. "I'm sure that no-one will ever be able to produce his body. But if you suggest to the police that young Henry's disappearance might be connected with mine, they might get an investigation going into his story too, and put two and two together."

I was dumbfounded. Another murder! It was hard to take in. "I see your tears, but how can you talk about this all so calmly? I thought that you loved young Henry. And still you don't talk about your son. Does he still live in Caldwell Hall? No! You have just said that he would have been forty-nine. Did he die too?"

Again, she started to cry. Real sobs this time. I had almost got used to her ghost tears. They were very uncanny. Not at all like human tears that drip down on ones face, but more like cartoon tears. An impression of tears rather than an actuality. "My darling baby," she gulped. "He died when he was only twelve years old. And his death was indirectly caused by the Caldwells too."

"Oh, dear! What happened?" *Poor woman,* I thought. *Nothing but pain, death and disaster in her short life on earth.*

"It was the fault of that awful boarding school that they sent him to. The Social Development Master took him, with a group of the boys from his class, on an up-market trip to a skiing resort in Wyoming, America, called Jackson's Hole.

He wasn't an experienced skier and the stupid, no criminal, teachers encouraged him go down a very dangerous double-black run, called the Corbet's Couloir. The run is so steep that it is like falling off the edge of the mountain, and only expert skiers should try it. He lost his balance almost immediately. My darling James broke his back when he fell. Mountain Rescue got into full swing to reach him, and he was air-lifted by helicopter and taken to the nearest hospital. He died a few hours later."

"This must have happened after you had died, and I suppose that as a ghost you knew what had happened." Almost in tears myself, I wanted to hold her hand in sympathy. But, of course, I couldn't.

"Yes, and I know that a ghost can grieve." She stopped sobbing, and her face turned hard. "That's another reason why I want those Caldwells to be punished. If they had not sent him to that hateful boarding school, my darling James would probably still be alive today."

"I suppose that this was their punishment for that," I speculated. "Especially for your mother-in-law. After all she was the one who was hell bent on having an heir to the Caldwell estate."

"Yes." The tears stopped falling and now Emily was almost grinning. "The bitch had lost her heir, and her darling son Edward was not able to re-marry and provide a replacement heir because I was not officially dead. All my family had been told by them that I had run away with the stablemaster, young Henry!"

"What about Charles. Why did he never marry? And what happened to them both? If I ever get the police to believe me about your murder, we will have the murderers to find." Hearing so much of her story I had been drawn into it, and now I wanted them to be punished.

"My hateful mother-in-law is now in her nineties and she is an invalid. She spends her days in a wheelchair still bossing her sons and her staff, which now includes a live-in nurse."

"What happened to her?" I asked.

Emily was smiling now. "She fell down the main stairs to the hallway about four years ago." A real proper grin. "Poor thing! She is crippled." She added, sarcastically.

"How did that happen?" I asked. And then a suspicion came into my mind. "Did you have anything to do with it?"

"What me? I'm a ghost. I can't do anything in the living world." It was the sound of complete innocence, but she was saying this with the grin developing into a sneaky smile which spread all over her face. No real words were needed, she all but admitted that she had caused the *accident* with the defiant look she was now giving me.

"Are you sure?" I asked again. "I have read somewhere that some ghosts can do things like moving small objects around, or creating gusts of wind that can blow papers or open the pages of books. Did you do anything that *helped* your mother-in-law to fall down that flight of stairs?"

"Well." The look of innocence was back. "There might have been a slippery silk scarf dropped on the top step. How could I know how it came to be there or what happened to it after her fall." She mused, almost to herself, as if she were really questioning what had happened. "Although, I think that I did see something like that caught up in the corner of the hallway after she fell."

"So, you did arrange the *accident*." I didn't question. It was a statement. "I expect that you were annoyed that she didn't die. You could have welcomed her to your halfway world, between life and death."

"You know," she said. "At first I *was* somewhat disappointed. But actually, I think that the life she has left to her now is far worse than a quick death. She deserves all the pain and discomfort she gets. And what is more, if her two sons are sent to prison for murder, she will probably never see them again."

I could see that she was almost gloating, and I didn't want to encourage her to dwell on what she had done to her hated mother-in-law. I sort of changed the subject. "And what about your husband and his brother? How are they and what are they like these days?"

"My husband Ed is now seventy years old. He is still fit and well and spends most of his time organising the Caldwell estate. And his brother Charles is now seventy-two. He wanders around with his head in the clouds. He doesn't have dementia, but he doesn't seem to live in the real world either."

Emily had finally succeeded in convincing me to go to the police. "Ok," I agreed with a great sigh. "I will try to get the police to listen to my version of your story, and start an investigation."

"Wonderful! She exclaimed. "And now I have just had an idea that might help you."

"What?" I gasped. "Not some fancy thing that you have made up, is it? Lies won't help." I called Champion, and I started to walk away from her.

"Hold on!" She was suddenly in front of me again. "All I have been telling you is true, and I wanted to get you interested enough to believe me and go to the police."

I stopped walking. "So, what is it now? Do I need to sit down again to take in your next revelation?"

"I can see that walking is uncomfortable for you." She was almost showing sympathy for me! "Yes, let's go back to that fallen tree and I will tell you my idea."

I groaned. I was tired and I wanted to get back to my comfortable chair in my nice warm home. What cranky tale was she going to unfold now?

"The place where I was buried right is over there, the spot I pointed out to you. And after all these years the grave, if you want to call it a grave, has sunk a little. But what makes it different now is that a group of badgers have decided to dig a new set just beyond those trees, and they have made their pathway right across where my bones lie.

"I'm sure that it won't be long before my bones will be disturbed by them. Edward and Charles chose this part of the woodland to bury me because before the division of these woods no one came to this part of their land. Since seeing the activity of those badgers, I have been waiting around to see if I can communicate with anyone. And you are the first person that has been able to see and hear me. My force is much stronger at Halloween, and what a coincidence it is that you are someone sort of involved in my family history, and that I should know and recognise you after all these years."

"Well. Ok." I stuttered. "If there's nothing more you can tell me for the moment, I will have a good think about how I can go about setting up an investigation into your murder. It won't be easy without any real proof. I can talk to the police about my suspicions, but I can't say that I have been talking to a ghost. I will have to convince them that there is a puzzle to be solved here in the Caldwells' woodlands. They will need to be convinced because they won't be able to go onto the Caldwell lands without a search warrant."

"I know that it might be difficult," said Emily, "but this is the idea that I have.

"When I was a girl, my mum and dad bought me a little gold ring for my sixteenth birthday. It was like a signet ring, but with a tiny diamond rather than my initials engraved on it, and I wore it on the little finger of my right hand. It always stayed there, even after I was married, despite my new family calling it common. They wanted me to remove it because they said that it downgraded the Caldwell family ring, with the Caldwell crest on it, that had been worn by the Caldwell brides through the generations. A small triumph for me. My little signet ring stayed firmly on my little finger, and eventually I was not able to take it off. When Charles buried me, he removed my wedding ring, but he was unable to remove the one on my right hand."

She paused give herself time to let her big idea be revealed. "How about this: Your little dog, Champion, is he called, got through that hole in the fence, just like he did a few moments ago, and he began to dig around where the badgers have been scratching out a new trail. He came back to the fence with what looked like to you like a part of a human hand in his mouth, and before you could do anything he ran off again.

"You were naturally horrified and couldn't quite believe what you had seen, but you did remember seeing a flash of gold which looked like a ring on one of the fingers. You thought than you recognised the ring because when we were teenagers I lent it to your sister from time to time. And you saw her wearing it. You called your dog to come back to you, and he did eventually come back, but without anything in his mouth. That might help to get the police interested."

All I could say was, "Wow! I think that you have told me enough. I will have to think this through. You will be the first know if anything starts happening here in the woodlands!"

"Ok!" she said quietly and drifted away, back to where she had come from.

****

My old friend Ben Roberts came to see me at home last week. I don't live in Tunbridge Wells anymore. I live in Crowborough, where I have just retired as the senior partner in the Harrison Medical Centre. As a doctor, I was sad to see how much pain Ben was in due to an old back injury. Ben and I don't see each other very often, but we do meet up occasionally for a pint in one or other of the pubs in our area. Although, there was quite a difference in our ages when we were young, now that we are getting on, eight years seems like nothing at all. Ben and I have remained friends through the years. We have both suffered family loss with the death of our parents, the death of his sister Mary from breast cancer, and the disappearance of my sister, Emily, who was Mary's best friend.

I always felt guilty that it was I who introduced Emily to the Caldwell family. That was when I was a schoolboy and before I left home for university, to follow in my father's footsteps and become a doctor. At that time, I was a great pal of the two Caldwell brothers, Charles and Edward. They also had an older brother called Michael, but he was never around when I visited the family. I never realised until I met their parents just how much the boys were restricted in their friendships. No common working-class boys were good enough for Mrs Caldwell. Not to play with her sons! I was just about acceptable because my father was a doctor. Sometimes, Emily and I were invited to Sunday walks in the grounds followed by afternoon tea in the morning room.

Edward was OK when we were young, and I was quite pleased for Emily when he proposed to her. Emily was always a bit odd. She was what we in the family used to call *hifalutin* when she was young – always wanting the best servings of the family food, the best china plates to eat off, always she felt that she must buy clothes and shoes in the best shops. Nothing was good enough for her! I think that our parents indulged her too much, just because she was a girl.

Anyway, it was *she* who had pestered me to introduce her to the Caldwell family because she knew that they were *posh*, even grand. Just what she thought she deserved in life. I don't even think that she fell in love with Edward. I think that she fell in love with becoming Mrs Caldwell. But she didn't reckon with the other Mrs Caldwell, her mother-in-law, Marion Caldwell, who was to become her nightmare and her nemesis.

To be honest Marion Caldwell was a snob of the first order. A snob and a real bitch too. How she bullied those boys of hers! And she was obsessed with the Caldwell lineage continuing although, of course, she was not a Caldwell herself! I believe that her maiden name was Rossiter, and that she came from a wealthy old family of wool traders from Harwich.

Anyway, Emily married Edward and I didn't hear much about her after I left for medical training in Edinburgh. My father went to see her a couple of times when she was pregnant. He said that she was well, the pregnancy was going fine, but he found her a bit withdrawn, even a bit agoraphobic. I remember that Marion Caldwell refused to let her have her baby in hospital, and she employed a midwife who attended Emily while she was giving birth, and who stayed with the family for four weeks after baby James was born to help the new mother. After I completed my medical training at Edinburgh University, I stayed at the Edinburgh Hospital for four more years, first as a registrar, and then as a junior doctor.

I didn't return home until I opened up my own general practice in Crowborough. That was after Emily had disappeared. All I was told was that she had run off with the Caldwells' stable manager, which seemed very unlike her. But that was the end of that, and we, my parents and myself, just stopped talking about her.

I hadn't thought about her for years when a strange thing happened. I had that visit at home from Ben. Ben is the little brother of Mary, who was Emily's best friend. So, as I just said Ben came to see me yesterday with a very strange story, which he said he wanted to discuss with me before he went to the police.

I was at once intrigued, and then I was truly *gobsmacked.* This is the basis of his story. He told me that when he was walking in the Caldwell woodlands with his dog, Champion, the dog managed to wriggle his way through a small hole in the fence dividing the private and public parts of the beechwood. After a few minutes, Champion came running back carrying something in his mouth. He dropped it by the hole in the fence, but not near enough for Ben to reach through.

When Ben, who is not very agile because of his back, stooped down to see what his dog had found, he was both astonished and disgusted to see that it looked like part of a hand. The bones of a human hand, and on the little finger was something that he recognised. The ring that my parents had given Emily on her sixteenth birthday! He was just about to exclaim and tell his dog to bring his gruesome trophy to the hole in the fence when the dog picked it up again and ran off and drop it where Ben could see the markings and tracks of a recently scraped out badger's run. He called and called his dog, and he did eventually come back through the hole, but without the hand.

"What do you think of that?" Ben asked me. "Your sister who supposedly ran away with a stable manager thirty odd years ago, could have died and been buried in the Caldwell woodlands all this time. Do you think that we should do something about it? Should we go to the police?"

"Whoa! Whoa!" I exclaimed. "This is such a shock, I can hardly take it in. Let me gather myself together and think about this. Perhaps we both should go to the place in the Caldwell woods where you think you saw the hand."

"The trouble is," he said, "If we wait too long the badgers or any other wild animals might have dug out and destroyed the grave site. If you agree that it should be looked into we ought to go to the police straight away. I came to you first because you are her brother and they might take what you say more seriously, than if I were to go on my own."

So, Ben and I sat and talked over the incident in the woods with his dog Champion, and what might have happened to Emily all those years ago. I had always felt a bit guilty about accepting Edward's explanation of her disappearance without question. To tell the truth, I had been busily getting on with my life and the work I needed to do to build up my practice, to take time out to question the Caldwells more closely. Ben was convinced that Emily had come to grief at the hands of the family, but he had no evidence of murder other that what he thought he had seen in the woods. In the end, he convinced me that we should go to the police the next day.

"I wonder if a warrant to search the woodlands be given by the local magistrate on so little evidence," I said to Ben, laughingly. "I don't think that we have any real evidence at all."

"I know," he replied. "But I do think that there is something in that law which says that a search can be made without a warrant if there is any chance that the suspect could destroy the evidence while the police are waiting for a warrant to be issued."

"But," I argued, "the Caldwells don't yet know that the grave has been disturbed. I hardly think that they take a daily walk to the boundary of their land."

"No," Ben agreed. "But the badgers might do their work for them! Let's see what they say at the police station tomorrow."

****

So, that's how the police investigation started. It took some convincing to get the local police to take my statement seriously, but eventually, because I had Emily's brother with me, they agreed to give the woodlands the once over.

And as soon as they introduced themselves at the Caldwells' front door, they realised that there might be some truth in my suspicions. The two brothers were immediately full of bluster and protest, wanting to call the family solicitor right away.

Of course, I was not allowed to take any part in the proceedings, but I was able to direct them from the public side of the fence. It took them less than a week to disinter the remains of poor Emily, have those remains examined by the forensic pathologist who promptly identified her as Emily Caldwell, pronouncing that the wound on her skull, and the soil in her airways proved that she had been hit on the back of her head and then buried alive, and all this was definite proof of her murder. The two brothers, Charles and Edward were charged with her murder, and they were kept in custody while further investigations were being made into the disappearance of the stable manager, Henry Jones.

I took no part in the police investigation, but I did go back to the place where I had met and talked to the ghost of Emily after all the police activity in the woods had died down. I sat down on the same log and called out quietly, "Emily, are you still here?" I wasn't sure that she would still be around. I thought that she might have left her ghost world and returned to wherever spirits live in the afterlife. Maybe, even to have re-joined her Henry, and her son James?

But a few moments later, she was there at my side once more.

"Well! Well! Well!" she exclaimed. "So, you did manage it. I'm so grateful to you. And I hope that I will be around to see the two of them jailed for life. The old bitch is suffering already. And all thanks to you."

"What do you mean by saying that you hope to be around. Are you ending your ghostly time on earth?" I asked.

"Yes. I can already feel the spirit world pulling me." She said quietly. "I am wondering if I will be able to meet up with my parents, James and Henry there. Thank you so much, firstly, for believing in me, and then, making sure that the police followed your clues. Goodbye, Ben."

And her form just faded away before I could say any more. I must say that after all the excitement, I did feel deflated. *Oh well,* that's that I thought. Then I hobbled my way back home, settled down into my comfortable chair, and before I could drop off, my wife Sue confronted me.

"OK then, Ben. Give all. How did you manage to find out about Emily?" She paused long enough to take a deep breath, and then carried on. "And don't give me any of that guff about talking to ghosts!"

So!!! What could I say?

December 2018, Ightham Mote

It was a dark, cold evening and Joanna and Tommy, who were wrapped up in their warmest coats and hats, were being taken by their mother to Ightham Mote, a medieval moated manor house, which is just outside Sevenoaks in Kent. They started to pull faces at the thought of visiting yet another National Trust house, but they had been promised a fantastic evening with a wonderful Christmas light show on the outside of the building, and brightly coloured decorations and a sparkling decorated Christmas tree in every room inside.

"Besides," said their mother, "You both keep on insisting that you saw the ghost of Anne Boleyn at Hever Castle, where there is no record of anyone else seeing her there. Well, here at Ightham there is a recorded ghost. And I want to give you a chance of showing your ghost busting credentials. Then maybe I'll believe your Anne Boleyn story."

"Awesome," said Tommy. "Was there a gruesome murder here, and a ghost to tell the tale?"

"Sort of," said his mother. "It's a very old building, and there are vague stories that in the eighteen hundreds, during renovations in the house the builders discovered a skeleton walled up in a closet in the tower."

"Walled up?" questioned Joanna. "Do you mean that someone was bricked up alive in there, and left to die of starvation?"

"Awesome!" commented Tommy.

"This may be true," said their mother, "but there is nothing to substantiate the story. If there was a skeleton, or even a pile of human bones found, then nothing of this discovery was kept, and nothing written down and verified. So, strange stories have developed.

One is that a pretty, young serving girl at Ightham Mote manor house, in the Tudor period, was bricked up by her mistress for wickedness. It was suggested that the girl had fallen in love with the house priest, who was also young and handsome, and he was in love with her. This was a time when to be a Catholic was forbidden by law and many wealthy Catholic families kept a house priest to take Catholic services, and especially Holy Communion, within their private chapel. So many of these households created a hidden room or bolt hole for the priest to hide in if the priest hunters came to search the building.

Many of the well-known Catholic homes at that time were under suspicion and were raided every so often to catch a forbidden Catholic priest. It was said that the mistress of Ightham Mote, who was a rather unattractive, middle-aged woman, was also in love with her house-priest and that she caught the two of them cuddling and kissing in his room. This mistress was so angry and wildly jealous of her housemaid that she had the girl walled up alive."

"That's truly awesome," commented Tommy again.

"Joanna," said her mother, "I know that you like to read historical stories, so you might be interested in the novel 'Green Darkness', by an American author called Anya Seton, which sets out this story in a very believable way. I have the book at home. I suppose that the writing will seem quite old-fashioned to you, but you may find it interesting if you want to read it."

Unseen by her mother Joanna rolled her eyes. She just said, "Yes Mum. Maybe when I have nothing else to do!"

The lights outside the house and the laser light show in the gardens were amazing, and even Tommy enjoyed them, although it wouldn't have been 'cool' for him to say so.

Inside the house was just like many other National Trust properties that the children had been taken to in the last few months. Some of the volunteer guides were dressed in Victorian costumes. The men wore frock coats and top hats, and the women wore long, tight waisted skirts and tight jackets to match, with huge, puffed sleeves. They spent a long time, too long for Tommy, in each of the rooms, and while their mother was chatting to a rather tall gentleman in a top hat, Joanna and Tommy went off to discover the tower where, supposedly, the skeleton of the unidentified girl had been found. The two determined 'ghost busters' tried everything that they could to invite a ghost, if there was one, to connect with one or both of them.

But nothing! They had absolutely no response at all. Not even a sense of chill or coldness in the tower. Tommy, especially, had built himself up to expect a new visitation, and he was bitterly disappointed.

They retraced their steps to the entrance and sat down, very grumpily, on a brick garden wall to wait for their mother, when one of the top-hatted guides came to join them. Tommy wanted to tell him what a rotten, boring house this was, when the guide spoke first. "She's not here you know."

Joanna was taken by surprise. "I beg your pardon," she said, and turned to look at him. "What do you mean by saying that she's not here?"

"Do you mean our mother?" asked Tommy. "Well, thanks! We know that she's not here, but she will be joining us as soon as she has had enough of your rotten, boring old house."

"Don't be so rude, Tommy," admonished Joanna.

But the guide took no notice and carried on talking. "I was watching you two in the tower room for the last half hour," he said quite casually, "and I can tell you that she's not here!"

Joanna was beginning to feel a little uncomfortable and Tommy was getting impatient and a little annoyed. "Ok," he said. "Then who do you think we have been waiting to see?"

"The girl." He said.

"Which girl?" Joanna was really annoyed now.

"The one that was walled up in the old priest hole in the tower," the guide said, at last.

"Oh!" she exclaimed. "That one! What happened to her?"

He peered at the teenagers as though it were they who were the ghosts. "When the skeleton was at last discovered, the poor young woman released herself from this world and she went off to the spirit world to find her lover."

"Oh!" Joanna said flatly. "Then who are you? And what do you know about the spirit world? And what ever happened to her bones?"

"Never mind all that. I just want to tell you both a story," he said.

Tommy went to touch his arm to sort of agree with him, and to his surprise his hand went right through the man's arm and into his body. There was a ghost here after all! But not the one they were expecting. "Awesome!" said Joanna and Tommy both together. They were astonished. "You are another ghost. Aren't you? A different ghost. So, who are you?"

"Before I tell you that, I just want to tell you a story," the ghost repeated.

"Is it an exciting story full of blood and murder?" asked Tommy.

His sister sighed. "Don't start that again, Tommy," she said. And to the ghost she said. "Well, I hope that it is a short story, because our mother will be here in a couple of minutes. And she doesn't believe in ghosts!"

"OK," said to the ghost. "Then I'll try to keep it short, though if your mother doesn't believe in ghosts, she won't be able to see or hear me."

The ghost they were talking to looked to be about thirty-five years old, but the Victorian costume that he was wearing made it quite difficult to judge his age. To Joanna he looked very fit, closely resembling her history teacher at school. Only her best friend at school knew that she had a full-blown crush on Mr. Adams, who like this ghost, was slim, quite good looking, and had a mass a dark brown hair.

"OK," the ghost repeated, "this is my story: Once upon a time there were two brothers. The elder one was the first-born of a young woman and her builder architect husband. This boy was blond and beautiful just like his mother, and he was adored by both of his parents. Two years later a second son was born. This time the mother was not well. She never recovered from this second, and more difficult, pregnancy and birth. The new baby was another boy, but unlike his blond, smiling elder brother, he was dark and scowling. His mother loved him from the moment of his birth, and she did her best to look after him, but she died as a result of childbirth complications only three months after he was born."

"Poor baby," commented Joanna.

The ghost continued. "The father never fully recovered from the loss of his wife and he always, unfairly, blamed his second son for her death. The two little boys grew up motherless and their father, while giving his elder son every bit of love and attention that all children needed, neglected his younger son, and could hardly bear to pick him up, hold him, or even look at him.

A wetnurse was employed to feed and take care of the baby, and until he was weaned at the age of two, he had as much care and love than he would ever get in his life. And it wasn't long before the older child understood his father's attitude to his baby brother, and he also began to blame the new baby for the loss of his darling 'mumma'. In fact, he started to hate his brother, and he didn't want to have anything to do with him.

When the wetnurse left their home, the little boy found himself with an older brother and a father who both hated him. He grew up to be a very sad and unloved child. Somehow, although he saw that his father adored and petted his older brother and ignored him, he nevertheless loved his father and tried, as much as he could, to get noticed and to push himself between them. He would do anything that he thought would please his father, trying to get the light of love to shine on him for a little while."

Tommy was sad. He asked Joanna, "Do you think that our dad loved us before he went away? I don't even remember him much now."

"Of course he loved us," said Joanna. "I remember him and how he used to take us to the park to play games with both of us. I still miss him, and I know that mum does too. That's why she never talks about him."

Joanna wanted to change the subject to get her brother away from asking questions about their father. Questions that she couldn't answer. So, she turned back to the ghost saying, "So, Mr Ghost. You keep talking about these two brothers, can you tell us their names?"

The ghost, who had been silently listening to the two of them discussing their father, joined in again. "The two brothers' names were Thomas, like you Tommy, and Matthew. Thomas was the older, favourite one, and Mathew was the sad, unloved one.

Matthew knew that his father did not love him, but he still wanted his father to take notice of him, and to love him. However, the father took very little notice of Matthew, and Thomas, given every advantage and went through life without a care. Matthew always did his best to disregard the affection that his father bestowed on his elder brother and tried his hardest to fight for his share of their father's love.

At the age of fourteen, Matthew was learning the skills of cabinet making, and for his father's birthday that summer he spent weeks making him an exquisite miniature cabinet made of beechwood which he inlaid beautifully with bands of ash. It was quite stunning and the best thing that Matthew had ever made. On the morning of his father's birthday he presented the little cabinet to his father and at the same time as his brother gave their father his present. Thomas's gift was a little mongrel puppy that he had found wandering in the local woodlands. It was a lightly given gift, costing Thomas neither money nor effort. Their father examined the miniature cabinet and praised Matthew for his skills. Then he put it aside to pick up and hold the puppy He was delighted with it, and he instantly named it 'Franco'.

Whilst Matthew's precious birthday gift, the little cabinet, was placed on the sideboard to collect dust, Franco became the delight of the father, following him everywhere he went at home and at work. From that day on, the more Matthew did to win his father's love, the more love and attention his father seemed to give to his brother. Matthew came to hate Thomas.

Both sons grew up with building as a trade and worked alongside their father. One day, while renovating the old Ightham Mote manor house, they discovered a walled up skeleton in an ancient priest's hole. Their employer, the new owner the manor, was horrified. He told them to get rid of the bones, and to break out the wall completely, which they did.

By then the jealousy of Matthew towards Thomas had grown and grown to a point of wanting to murder him, and now he had an idea of how to make his hated brother disappear, without his father ever knowing what had happened."

"Cool!" exclaimed Tommy. "How did he do it?"

"I think that I know," said Joanna. "Did he create another space between walls and brick him up like the skeleton that they had found? Is there another bricked up body here?"

"Yes. You're nearly right," said the ghost.

"Awesome," commented Tommy.

"So! What did happen?" asked Joanna.

"It was a few weeks later in another house which the two young men were renovating while their father was at home at his drawing board designing a new house for which he had a commission to build. The house where the two young men were working on was a really old, and it had very thick walls. The brothers were pulling down a crumbling wall between the kitchen and hallway which they were to replace and replaster. To their surprise they found a huge gap behind the chimney breast."

"So, one of them did the other one in, hid his body in the gap and rebuilt the wall," said Tommy. "Was there a lot of blood which seeped out between the bricks?"

"You've guessed it!" exclaimed the ghost. "Matthew seized the opportunity to rid himself of his hated brother. When Thomas was concentrating on the mortar mix for rebuilding the wall, Matthew crept up behind him, and he knocked him unconscious with his hammer. He then quickly bricked him up in the same way as the skeleton discovered at Ightham Mote."

"What happened then?" Joanna asked.

"Did he tie Thomas up and gag him to stop him from calling out?" asked Tommy. "He could have been saved otherwise!"

"Yes he did that, and he told his father a whole made up story about his brother falling in love with a young lady from the circus that had passed through the town some weeks before, and that afternoon he suddenly made up his mind to go and try to find her. 'Why did he not say anything to me?' his father asked. And I told him that Thomas was afraid that his father would talk him out of leaving."

"So, this is your story then. Is that all there is to it?" asked Joanna.

"Did they ever find Thomas?" asked Tommy.

"And, who are you?" asked Joanna.

"I think that you are Matthew," said Tommy.

"And where is the house that you and Thomas were working on?" asked Joanna.

"Did they ever discover his skeleton?" asked Tommy. "And did you ever feel sorry for what you have done?"

"Woah! Woah! Woah!" exclaimed the ghost. "I can see that you have guessed at the truth. That is why I became a ghost when I died. I wanted to find my father and brother, and to beg their forgiveness, but I was not allowed to go into the spirit world. I wanted…"

Just then then children's mother came and found them sitting on the wall. "The lights everywhere are just smashing, aren't they? Are you glad I dragged you here? Did you find the ghost of the girl?"

"No, Mum," said Joanna. "We didn't find her ghost, but there is another one here." She looked about her, ready to show her mum the new ghost, but he was gone.

"There was one here. Honest," said Tommy.

"Oh! Yeah!" said Mum…

2084, Survival City No. 22, England

04.30 hours. Sancha looked down on the beautiful sleek body of her sleeping lover, Joshua X 492. She did not want to get out of the soft, warm bed, but she needed to be back in her own sleep-space before the spy cameras started their daily sweeping of their home block at 05.15 hours. Joshua's enticing body entwined in the fine cotton sheets was almost too tempting. She desperately wanted to stay for her last few magical hours on earth, but it was too dangerous to do so.

Those sheets and the soft mattress were almost all that remained of his mother's belongings after she had been compulsorily euthanized, with immediate cremation, only a few months ago at the age of fifty. When Joshua was a small child, some thirty years ago, he and his lovely young mother Eva, had been forced to leave their destroyed home town on the shores of the Northumbrian coast, and were part of the second wave of forced migration to this secret, survival city under experimental Dome no. 22, which was located somewhere on the South Coast.

His mother's death while still in full health and in the prime of her life, had left Joshua traumatised and feeling totally abandoned. He was already in love Sancha, but now, with his mother gone, he needed Sancha more than ever. So, it was vital that they were never caught together, and risk total separation by the dominant Overlord Police, when the morning camera sweeps re-started.

She didn't know how long it would take to dematerialise, to become a spectre. She thought that she might have 48 hours in this semi-world before she became a complete ghost. All she wanted right now was to have as many of the hours possible that were left to her in the real world. To spend as much time as she could touching, being touched, and being real for Joshua.

She bent forward and kissed Joshua's brow softly, being careful not to wake him or disturb his dark hair which curled down to his shoulders. In his own sleep-space he was allowed to let his hair hang loose, but once outside, like everyone else, male or female, who lived in Domed City no. 22, in the atmospherically secured city, he was obliged to keep his hair tied back and covered by a cap. His cap was orange, denoting that he was an Educator.

As Sancha made her way to her own sleep-space, two floors above that of Joshua, she looked out through the windows of the stairway at the dawning of the morning sky through the thermoplastic layers of the Dome's outer skins. As usual there was a darkened sun that tried to show through the radioactive clouds, only succeeding in producing an orangey-yellow glow.

She had been born in Dome no. 22 and had lived there all of her life. As a consequence, she had never seen a bright yellow sun shining in a vivid blue sky with white fluffy clouds, such as her mother, the most senior Educator of Dome no. 22, had often talked about in her saddened moods of reminiscence. Because she had been the most senior Educator, she had had access to secret books that remained in existence and hidden away. These included a few treasured pictures books that showed how the Earth and sky had once been, but these books were not in general circulation and were banned by the Overlords, as documents that could de-stabilise their Survival City and cause unrest.

All the experimental Domed Cites in the United Kingdom had lost their ancient names and become just a number. Each one was controlled by a local Overlord who was subservient to the Master Overlord living in what remained of London, which was now a walled off area, and enclosed centre of power not unlike the Kremlin in Moscow. He in turn, had to report to the Soviet Overlord of all Europe, who still resided in the Kremlin.

How could all of this have happened right under the eyes of the old British and European armies? They had won the Second World War after all. How had they allowed the Soviets, progressively to take over the whole of Europe? First it had been Eastern Europe: Hungary, Czechoslovakia, Poland, and Eastern Germany. Then in 1954 they had dropped a small nuclear warhead over Paris, and the rest of Europe had immediately capitulated and submitted to the Communist Red Army. It was now nearly 140 years since the end of World War II the whole of Europe was still dominated by the Russian Communists. The UK had capitulated along with the rest of the European states, and the young ex-Queen, Elizabeth Windsor and her family, had been banished to the far-flung island of St Kilda in the Outer Hebrides.

At first all teaching and communications had been enforced exclusively in Russian, but the learning and speaking of Russian was resisted by local populace in all the subjugated countries. Then it soon became obvious that the Americans, with their world dominance in electronic trading and use of computer systems, invented by the Anglo/Americans in the 1960s called World Interlink, that English would become a universal language. And indeed that is exactly what had happened. By the turn of the century all the western countries of the world used and spoke English as their first language, and local languages were dying out, and only being kept alive by local writers and artisans.

Everyone, except for those in the experimental Domed Cities, in the United Kingdom lived in a high and unassailable walled off city, with no direct communication or access to anywhere beyond, and as a result, they all thought that everyone lived just like themselves.

The centres of each of the Domed Cities were supported by a ring of six domestic tower blocks eighteen stories high, identical to each other both inside and out. These tower blocks were surrounded by poorly supplied government shops, and administration offices. And all electrical power required for each city was produced by solar panel fields and a ring of wind turbines which encircled each one.

Time and time again people virtually incarcerated in the twenty-eight Domed Cities, situated mostly in the south of England, were told that the Domes were the only safe places in which to live. Thus they were being sheltered from the effects of targeted nuclear detonations in Europe, both large and small, made by the Soviets and other super-powers all around the world as competing countries tried to dominate the globe.

Under the Domes the inhabitants were taught that everything had changed in the old natural world. In the whole of Europe gone were the four seasons. Gone: the blue and green oceans filled with a myriad of fishes and other sea creatures. Gone: the fabulous variety of creatures from microscopic insects to huge mammals. All were gone, their habitats ruined by radiation. Only a few species remained, and they, like the surviving humans in Europe, were also enclosed in Domed prisons, called ectozoos. From the old zoos they had rescued elephants and tigers, bears and crocodiles and numerous small mammals right down to the tiniest of insects. The lucky few of all the creatures that had lived in the wild breathing in the air of savannahs, forests, mountains and jungles. Rivers, lakes and blue skies, clouds, rain storms and yellow sunshine – all gone. Natural skies had been replaced by a yellow fog that all but blotted out the sun in the day and the moon at night. A perpetual hot winter prevailed with endless fog and temperatures varying little from a high of 34 degrees in the daytime and 26 degrees at night.

Those people who ventured out beyond the steel framed, honeycomb shaped, thermo-plastic Domes were told that they were risking their lives and their health. And, in order to prevent damage to their health and skin, they were forced to wear all over body suits with breathing apparatus. Of course, only those permitted by the Russian Overlords were allowed to do this.

For each Domed City there were separate, smaller, domes for the production of food, for education, entertainment and gymnasiums, all with tunnelled access from the centre of each city. Movement from one area to another was only accessible on foot, and on ground level moving walkways. There were no churches, mosques, synagogues, or any other buildings for worship, because all religions had been banned with the Russian takeover.

The essential bio-controlled domes for food production were the most important of all the outer domes and the black caped workers, deemed to be Essential Workers, were allowed freer access to any part of the city, including external access.

Medical centres, with machines which could instantly detect any malignant cancer or the future collapse of any vital organ in the human body, were also a major part of the inner circle of each Domed City. But there were no hospitals, as anyone who was diagnosed with anything beyond a superficial complaint was immediately euthanized without a chance to say goodbye to friends and family. Crematoria were attached to all medical centres.

Sancha didn't want to think of her own death and what had happened afterwards, she was now thinking about Joshua's proposal. He didn't know that she no longer existed. Within 24 hours her solid form would disappear. He didn't know that she had elected to become a phantom. She knew that after this choice had been made, she would never be able to live in the spirit world, but she desperately wanted to stay in the human world so that she could be connected to Joshua, which she could do only as a ghost.

Last night he had acted like one of the ancients on Earth, and he had gone down on one knee and asked her to marry him. In the new life system it was the only way that they would ever be allowed to live together. Marriage, as a ten year Contract in this Survival City no. 22, had been created in 1964. And the custom was now used in all the Domed Cities. The Marriage Contract was enforceable for the whole of the ten-year term, and, if both parties agreed, it was renewable at its end for a further ten years, or however many years remained to them under the euthanasia laws.

As her slowly dissolving body sat in her drab armchair in her own sleep-space Sancha was considering what would have been her options if she were still alive. She truly loved Joshua, but as an X 384 aged forty, she had been eleven years older than he was. She asked herself whether he really would have wanted to be tied to an old woman, maybe even nearing the end of her own useful time. Could he, sub-consciously maybe, possibly be thinking of her as a replacement of the mother that he truly loved and depended upon?

Euthanasia, to control the number of people living in all Domed Cities, was now enforced on everyone who became irrecoverably sick during their allotted fifty-year lifetime. Life could be extended for the over fifties if there were extenuating circumstances, which included being an Essential Worker (EW), who were mostly men, and some highly classified Government Workers (GW), who were mostly female. Sancha had been already classed as a GW, but as she had worked as a very close assistant to the Overlord of Dome no. 22 she had hoped that her status might very soon be changed to a black cap as an Essential Worker, which would have given her at least ten more years of life if she remained childless and healthy after the age of fifty, plus more power and access to Government papers.

But she could also have extended her life by becoming a mother. Every accepted mother had her time automatically extended by twenty years if she were to have a child before she reached the age of fifty, and if she remained healthy. Because the citizens of this new world order were mostly annihilated at the age of fifty, the single child restriction that had been enforced on all women in the overpopulated world of the last century had now been lifted and was now replaced by the choice of having up to three children. It was now relatively simple to apply and be granted a licence to reproduce if the applicant was deemed to be a suitable woman. This meant that she had to be either a GW or an EW.

What would she have wanted more? A baby or Joshua? She could have had both if he had agreed. Or, if he did not want to raise a child, she could have had a baby on her own without marriage, and her life period would still have been extended by twenty years, but only if she and the child remained healthy.

In the Dome Cities there were several ways to reproduce. She would have preferred the natural way, between lovers or husbands and wives. But the most popular method, recommended by all medics, was IVF, where in a laboratory, the woman's egg was fertilised by a male sperm, was examined for any disease that could develop during the child's lifetime. If the fertilised egg was found to be faultless it could then be planted in the mother's womb to grow naturally. The resulting baby would then be extracted by abdominal section at the end of a thirty-eight week gestation. If the embryo was not perfect, it was always rejected and destroyed.

There was also an IVF programme where the perfect foetus could developed and grow in an in-house surrogate. But it was difficult to control and regulate a surrogate host mother if she was living apart from the natural mother. And to have the surrogate living with the mother-to-be would be like having to watch over a prisoner who was also living in what was already an overcrowded sleep-space.

Working closely with the Overlord of Dome no. 22 Sancha knew that a new mother would soon be able to select the newest form of development for her baby, which was taking place secretly in the Overlord's Science Laboratories. This was where the perfect IVF foetus could be placed in an automatic mechanical womb which supplied all the nutrition required for a perfect child to develop and grow. Those machines would even have a covered glass window for the 'mother' and physicians to inspect the developing baby at regulated times.

Sancha knew that she would have rejected all options other than the normal way of conceiving, and she shivered at the thought of a baby developing in a machine! She loved Joshua and she would have wanted to have her baby the old-fashioned way, with a choice of alternative ways for a painless delivery. Although she would have had to accept that if the developing foetus was found to have any faults that would lead to a sick or disabled child, she would be forced to abort it.

In her last morning in human solid form she walked about in her own sleep-space trying to decide how to tell Joshua that she was no longer alive. She had been afraid to tell him that two days ago doctors at the nearby medical centre had found a malignant cancer lump in her right breast, during the yearly examination that she and everyone else living in Dome no. 22, had to have. As a result, she had been instantly euthanized. She had not even been able to tell Joshua, and say goodbye to him. Or to have a last few days to spend with her friends. In a state of shock she made the only choice that she was allowed to make, that was to reject the spirit world, and instead, choose to become a ghost.

Now she was in her own sleep-space where the rooms were identical to those of Joshua's, including all the same drab wall coverings, and the same drab furniture placed in identical positions. All six of the sleep blocks were built and furnished in identical ways so that the supervision cameras and Overlord Observers could concentrate on what the occupants were saying and doing, and not on how each individual sleep-space was kept and furnished.

She looked in the mirror that she had in the one camera free, private space in her sleep rooms, her bathroom. She saw the reflection of a calm and good-looking woman looking back at her. She was unchanged from her living self. The harsh lighting was unforgiving and all the wrinkles developing in her forty-year-old face showed quite clearly. Joshua was eleven years younger than she had been, but out of that harsh lighting, she still looked young, almost as young as he was, she had never told him her exact age. But her number X 384 should have told him that she was several years older than he was.

It was all irrelevant now. But she was still thinking of his proposal of marriage. Did he really love her so? Had he really meant it? Or could it be that he really wanted a replacement mother rather than a wife? Perhaps he did not even recognise the fact himself. Would he have recoiled when they filled in the marriage application forms and he saw her real age? What if they did marry and after the ten-year contract expired she wanted to renew it for another ten years and he did not? What if they had had a child and he did not want to renew their marriage contract? Would he have abandoned both of them like most unattached fathers did? She sighed. Anyway, it was all irrelevant now.

Suddenly she made up her mind. She would have to tell Joshua that she was no longer alive, and that within 24 hours she would become a phantom. She wanted to tell him that she would have been so happy to marry him, and perhaps even have a child with him. So, as soon as visiting was permitted after 07.00 hours she would go down and tell him. All at once she felt strong enough to tell him the truth, her fears and misgivings were banished. She could not go back to sleep, and for the next hour she sat dreaming of how their future life together could have been like.

By 07.00 hours the fading body of Sancha was washed, dressed, with her long blond hair tied back and folded under her red cap, and ready for the emotional drama that would result from telling Joshua the truth. She ran down the cold concrete stairway to Joshua's sleep-rooms and rang his bell. She was surprised that the camera did not activate, so that the robotic machines using eye-scan could recognise her and open the door. She was even more surprised, with that failure, that the robotic voice did not ask who she was or what she required. What had happened? Was she already a ghost that the eye-scan failed to recognise? It was impossible that Joshua had reprogrammed his doorway to exclude her. Then she remembered that months ago Joshua had given her a key just in case there was an emergency or a power failure. Where had she put it?

Sancha ran back up to her own sleep-space, let herself in, and went to her office desk. Yes! There it was! Right at the back of the top drawer tucked in her 'personal' envelope.

Back at Joshua's sleep-space once more she used the key and let herself in. She was very apprehensive, and she moved slowly and quietly through the rooms.

"Joshua," she called out quietly. "Joshua, where are you?"

No reply. She was not just curious; she was becoming alarmed. What had happened here, and where *was* Joshua? The sleep-space rooms were so small that there was nowhere to hide. She looked in the cooking alcove. There was a cup of coffee, or what pretended to be coffee in the year 2084, on the eating surface, together with a half-eaten piece of toast. The toast and the coffee were still warm. What had happened to Joshua? He must have been there only a minute or so ago. So, where was he?

She noticed an unopened letter that was tucked under Joshua's coffee cup on the eating surface that, in her panic, she hadn't noticed before, and without looking for his letter opener, she tore it open. The pink form! The dreaded pink form! Surely that didn't apply to Joshua? He was young, fit and healthy. No one could be more alive than he was. But here it was on the pink form, dated yesterday. 'Joshua X492. You have been diagnosed as carrying the CN 136 virus. You will not be allowed the opportunity to spread this disease. You will therefore make yourself available for termination. You will be collected from your sleep-space at 06.45 hours tomorrow. You are forbidden to make physical contact with any living being before then.'

Sancha was astonished. Joshua. Her beautiful Joshua was to be terminated today. It was happening right now. She could do nothing to save him. She cried as hard as any ghost could. But then she realised that she had to be afraid no more. Within 36 hours he could become one of the undead like her. How could she get him to make that choice? Could she get a message to him before he was exterminated? She knew, from experience of only two days ago, where he was and what was happening to him. She accelerated her metamorphosis into becoming a real ghost. Would she be in time to reach him and get him to refuse the spirit world? To become a phantom like her? Then they would meet up together as new ghosts, and never more need to be afraid of being separated again!

Thanks to my son, Steve, for giving me Wonky-Eyed Will and his pals, and also for designing the front cover.

Thanks to my mother and father, Tony and Peggy Schembri for surrounding my early life with classical music.

To Chris Barber and his Jazz Band who filled my teenage years with traditional jazz, and to the local folk/rock bands for all their musicality. All these types of music have influenced my life long love of music.

And finally, to authors of the past whose stories have found an echo in mine: John Steinbeck, Josephine Tey, Anya Seton, and George Orwell.

Evelyne Morris was born in England towards the end of WW2, in 1944, but she comes from an international cultural background. Her grandparents were French/Italian and Maltese/Greek, and she was brought up in a college with foreign students from all over the world – Europe, the Far East, the Middle East, Africa and South America. She has a brother and sisters-in-law from Spain, France, and Japan, and she has daughters-in-law from Brazil and South Korea. She started writing after retirement, and this is her third novel.

Milton Keynes UK
Ingram Content Group UK Ltd.
UKHW020234281123
433366UK00008B/187

9 781035 803521